DRINKERS OF DARKNESS

GERALD HANLEY

DRINKERS OF DARKNESS.

NEW YORK
THE MACMILLAN COMPANY
1955

Printed in the United States of America

For

MILTON WALDMAN

CHAPTER ONE

THEY had not been able to do much with Mambango until Tamlin came. He seemed to have the necessary combination of love and hatred in him which could conquer the stubbornness of that blackish soil, that poisonously green jungle, and that sense of impending evil which the sensitive always felt at Mambango. Tamlin's drive was like his big, reddish-brown clenched fist ; knotted, nervous, brutal, which frightened the massed Africans when they stood before him for prayers on Sunday mornings. This was the *Bwana* who would frighten the devil, make him as willing a servant as that small, thin wife of his who knitted socks without end on the veranda of Tamlin's sun-eaten, crumbling bungalow.

Tamlin was forty-eight. One morning he looked at his eyes in the shaving mirror. A network of fine wrinkles radiated to the firm jaws and towards the small ears which lay flat against his skull. This network had deepened, like patient clawmarks in stone. He looked old.

" It's over," he thought. " Over." No more youth. No more hungers quite so sharp, or pains so corrosive. He would work harder now, for, being young, a time of doubt, error, distraction, was over, he thought. He tried to tell Maisie about it, but she could not possibly understand a thing like that. If he went on, she would look thoughtfully at him and prepare a dose of salts, he knew.

He looked at the half-ploughed lands with a new eye that morning, a look almost of hatred and triumph, for he was

7

full of love, as some men look at a woman at a certain time. "I'll fix you," he told the country which seemed dead under the huge sun. He was one of those men who never went down with malaria, and Mambango droned and sang at night with the hungriest mosquitoes in Africa. Even O'Riordan could not quite understand Tamlin, and O'Riordan was as sensitive as a woman about the insides of men.

It was near Christmas when Maisie Tamlin said to her husband, "Tammy, what about that party we planned?"

"They're having one for everybody this year, at the club. We're invited."

"Why didn't you tell me?"

"Now don't start, for Christ's sake. Just let it happen. It'll happen all right. You'll have your Christmas."

She sighed. She was going to say "I'm not *starting*, Tammy——" but she knew she had been about to and instead she bit off the end of the grey wool in her hand.

"Have you heard about Mrs. Mooning's latest?" she said.

"What's it about?" He put down the Overseas edition of *The Times*. "Scandal, or something new?"

"Scandal, *and* new," she said.

"Then keep it." He went back to the paper. She sighed again and fanned herself with a magazine, watching her husband. There had been times when she had cursed him silently, wishing she had never known him. Was that all there was in life for a woman? To be tied hand and foot to a man who treated you as his other, and somehow lesser, half. To be told one morning "We're moving next week." "Where to, dear?" And you never knew where it might be. The other end of Australia, the South Seas, South America, and now this hole, *this dreary hole*, in Africa.

They had no children. Tamlin had had no time, people said. Maliciously, some women had said it was because Tamlin did not know what to do, had never heard—there was so much work to do in the plantations. Poor Mrs. Tamlin, so dowdy, so under his thumb. If ever there was a case of slavery to a man, this was it. It seemed so often as if he did not know she was there, was alive. He could be coarse, and foul-mouthed too, when he was drunk, which was seldom. But God knows, there were no saints at Mambango. As O'Riordan said, " Between us, we make up the queerest collection of bloody riff-raff and stiffs ever known in the history of that unreliable bastard, man." That was on a Saturday night in the club, and all who heard agreed, sad with whisky and O'Riordan's knowledge.

The club was a cockroach-infested building which resembled a furnished barn. The last manager had built it before he was fired by the directors. It was the only place of amusement within a hundred miles of Mambango, and although it had that soft, yet sharp, smell of cockroaches, it was after all somewhere to go when a chap was going off his nut in his bungalow. You could quarrel there, argue, lie, laugh, or just sit and drink, or play billiards on the tattered table which was another present from the last manager.

Mambango had been just a part of the thick jungle and bush which stretched across the country for hundreds of miles until you came up against the Sango mountain range. A Lord Bonfleet, tired of massacring antelope and lion on his shooting trip, had, in the way of hopeful lords in a lean time, bought the area of jungle called Mambango. He never saw it. He was killed by an enraged elephant one day, and his son, restless after four bloody years on the Western Front, came out with three friends from his battalion. At Mambango, appalled, they attacked the jungle with nearly one hundred Africans, in between bouts of drinking and whoring, and after Lord Bonfleet had died of black-water, the others went to the coast, where the drinking was more civilised, and there severed all connection with Mambango.

Then a syndicate of those nervous seedy men who have escaped from clerkdom, who plan in pubs in London, bought it, because at that time there was a " future in Africa." They called it Mambango Estates.

Manager after manager broke himself at Mambango, either by bottle, by mosquito, or because the directors grew tired of their continually gloomy reports.

Then came Tamlin. He had mixed with all kinds of men, he liked to say, but by God, he had never seen a crowd like the one at Mambango.

Places like Mambango, in Africa, seem to draw the half-broken, the unmanageable, the adventurous, the secretive who have " their own reasons " for being in such places. And there are generally one or two of those there, of whom people say " Can't understand why he's here. Brilliant in his way. Could have done well for himself."

At Mambango, Tamlin found all these people. He examined them, for he was going to get work out of them, and no nonsense either.

They saw a small stocky man with a hard, flat face, when he entered the club for the first time to meet them. He looked brutal at first, but the women, and O'Riordan, noticed a delicate touch in the facial structure, or the large steely eyes, the small good teeth, or the smile which came and went as though he had forgotten himself for a moment.

Sneering at the back of the group, Plume, a tractor manager, said to O'Riordan, " He's going to make a bloody speech, I can tell," and Tamlin did. It was familiar stuff to those who had been in the Army and had either been told by an N.C.O., or, as officers, had heard them say to the troops, " You work with me, and I'll work with you," sort of thing. No one could quite say, but there seemed to be a faint threat in it. " If you *don't* work with me, etc.," sort of thing. Plume did not like it one bit, as he said to O'Riordan. But there was something about Tamlin that they grew to like, yet he was no man to displease where work was concerned. He sacked three men who, as he put it, " don't *do* anything, not a bloody hand's turn." He did not mind drinking, or fornication, but he could not bear laziness, not on any account. He was fond of saying this.

He did a lot at Mambango, none of them could deny that. And as O'Riordan said, " He's a cute one, all right, but I wouldn't like to fall out with him over who's best. He wouldn't agree with me about that. And he frightens the living Jesus out of the nigs, even on Sundays at the praying match."

It was the Sunday prayers which had surprised Mambango. The whites never really got over it, nor those who passed as whites; the Africans were puzzled for a time but they never knew what a white man would do next. If the white men had ordered them to stand on their heads, they would have done it, for the day had not come when strange orders were questioned. The white man was so unpredictable, an unknown, a somewhat frightening being whose ungovernable temper would show itself on the first sign of something which displeased him. And of all the white men they had known, *Bwana* Tamlin was the most strange, and the one for whom a man moved fastest. It was noticed that even the white men looked shifty and ready to spring to whatever *Bwana* Tamlin might suggest, when he was among them. After he had been at Mambango three months they gave him a nickname; " Chavamba," they called him, " The God Caller." One Sunday morning during the strange new *n'goma* of the prayers, *Bwana* Tamlin shouted, " I will lift up mine eyes to the hills," and he threw his head back and fixed his eyes on the mountains shaking in the heat, like one mad, like one who had eaten too much of the *m'panza* herb. He was calling to the God and no white man had done that before at Mambango.

They shuddered with fear, watching him, but God did not come, and for this men were grateful, but it was possible that one Sunday He would come, for *Bwana* Tamlin was not one of those white men who would be long disobeyed.

They were thrilled with fright when he shouted at a stupid one, but he would then talk gently to another; white men were like that, they grew hot and cold in the same moment, striking a man and then giving him a present.

His little wife, pale and thin like a peeled stick, gave men drugs when they were sick. Always this small woman was looking for men who had worms in their bellies, and she would give them the thick black juice which turned a man into a purging elephant. Men without worms would take the medicine to please her, for she had a soft heart and voice as if sorrow for men had filled her.

One night Mrs. Tamlin said to her husband, "I've had words with Mrs. Mooning, Tammy." It was on her conscience, for her husband discouraged gossip, scandal, "words," and all involved contacts with the Mambango whites whom, in his house, he spoke of as "the dregs." They were nearly all dregs, he had told her, and those whom he did not include in this category, might qualify at any time for this group. A dreg was somebody who *had* to come to Mambango for work ; technicians did not automatically qualify as dregs, for they had something to sell other than that vague qualification "ex-officer, able handle natives." The time had not quite come when it was necessary to add "public school" after "ex-officer," but you could see it coming, as the broken gentlemen often said in the club. But a technician usually became a dreg after a year at Mambango.

Tamlin eyed Maisie in that affectionate ironic way she knew so well. "Words ? " he said. "Why ? "

"It was over the Christmas party. When I told her we were giving a party for everybody she was quite catty. She said 'Why bother? We're having a mass booze up at the club for everybody out of the entertainment fund. So why bother?' I was thinking of your position, Tammy, after all"; she began to gabble as she saw his eye rolling on her. "After all, you're the manager and it's your position and everything——" He cut in and she sighed, yet still in trepidation after all these years before that mocking look of love and contemptuous amused tolerance. "So you've been at it again, have you?" he said. "Trying to push your man on in the world." He could imagine how Mrs. Mooning had said that. Big varnished red lips, still very attractive, but soon to wither now after years of booze and beds; Mooning had been the last hope after her second divorce. He had snapped her up in Dar-es-Salaam after a hangover, when he was about to leave for Mambango. Tamlin knew Mooning had told O'Riordan one night over a bottle, "I'm sorry I've got her now, but I wanted it steady, and after all I've got it. It's there when I want it." But it was not true.

She hated Mrs. Tamlin, the drudge, the slave, and she had thought that Mrs. Tamlin was trying to remind her of her position as the manager's wife when she had mentioned the party. Tamlin told Maisie this, patiently, with his usual crushing words like "You see? You think every bloody woman you meet is like yourself. You think they're honest and kind, when what *are* they? What *are* they, eh? What *are* Mrs. Mooning and Mrs. Pryce?" He waited. She looked at him. He liked her to appear stupid, which she no longer was after fifteen years with him, but he liked it. "Well?" he said. "What *are* they?"

"Bitches, dear," she said.

"That's right, bitches. They're both no good except on their backs. That's what they're here for."

"Tammy dear," she said, shocked, though she was no longer shocked.

" All right," he said, " I'm sorry. What did you say to her after that ? "

" I dropped the subject."

" Good. Keep it dropped. I told you they're having a party at the club. I don't want to get on in the world. I don't want to give a party, and that's all about it."

" But dear, you *are* the manager and we've never given a party since we've been here."

" That's right," he said. " And we're not giving one either, now or any other time. It's difficult enough living here without giving a party. You can invite that chronic bloody talker, O'Riordan, and that other queer bloke, and they can drink here and behave as if they're having a bloody wonderful Christmas. Why not do that and have done with it ? "

" I don't really know Mr. Plume," she said.

" He's all right," said Tamlin. " He's a harmless bloke."

" No, he isn't," Mrs. Tamlin countered. " He's been in gaol."

Tamlin turned sharply on her and said, " Who told you that ? " She coloured and fumbled with her wool. " You've been talking with Mrs. Pryce, haven't you ? " He nagged her until she admitted it, ashamed.

" It's probably another of those bloody Mambango fairy stories," he said. " That's all these bitches have got to do is talk."

" The men are worse," she said. " I've heard them saying the most shocking things to each other."

" They're not worse," he said. " And you shouldn't listen anyway."

But what she had said made him think. In places like Mambango it was possible to find a man of Plume's education who had been in gaol. He would keep his ears and eyes open.

" Invite Plume and O'Riordan," he said. " They can come on Christmas Eve for a few drinks."

" All right, dear," she said. She got up and kissed him and he put his arms round her. " I still love you, Tammy," she said. " I wonder why."

" Because I'm the most wonderful bloody man you've ever met, that's why, isn't it ? " He said it with that seriousness which was often a deeper and more kindly irony and of which she could never be certain. But she said, " Yes. That's right."

He disengaged himself, saying, " Now that's enough lust for now. Tell Yingu to bring me some more soda water. I'm going to have another sundowner although the bloody sun has disappeared hours ago."

She went off to call Yingu, happy to be away from her knitting. She knitted dozens of pairs of socks in a year, for Tammy was hard on socks. She loved to knit them, but like many unselfish and unsatisfied women, she resented this labour, yet was constrained to do it, furiously, passionately sometimes, like a man who must count the railings as he walks, or strive against stepping on the cracks between the paving stones, or failing, must retrace his steps. Working for Tammy was a necessity, for there was little she could enjoy. She never read a book. She did not want a radio. She liked to moon among her cookery books and please Tammy, and herself, because she ate more than he did, and before dawn she was awake, hungry. After years in lonely places, she would worry about her health sometimes, and she thought her terrible hunger might be due to worms. She had a horror of worms, and she would read about them in her old *Pears' Cyclopedia* again and again, revolted, and fascinated. " It is the half-cooked meat," she would tell people if they allowed her to develop the subjcet; it was the half-cooked meat that was the curse of Africa. If an acquaintance said that he or she was not feeling well, she would suspect worms. She never spoke about the malady to her husband now, for he had forbidden mention of it some years ago in Samoa. Her conscience told her that she had spoken too often about it. For some reason the subject made Tammy sick, and angry.

She spoke sharply to Yingu about the soda water. Yingu was slow. He lived in a dream of his own. He was sixteen, the age at which African servants went to pieces. As Tammy told her, in his horrible cynical way, it was because they had discovered what it was for. Like bees full of pollen, they drowsed and bumbled half-wittedly about, until the door of manhood finally opened, admitting them to the company of the generation, of the men who would defend the tribe until the new group was ready.

It was very annoying to have Yingu staring, eyes wide, mouth slack, listening, yet hardly hearing, but he was a nice boy, kind, gentle, honest. She could forgive him a lot.

CHAPTER TWO

MAMBANGO had a curious effect on white people. They argued about what it could be. The whole country had a queer effect on white people, everybody knew, but Mambango was special, much more definite in what it did to people than the rest of the country. The drinkers drank more, the ascetic became more ascetic, the fleshly more fleshly; those with a tendency to eccentricity became daily more uncertain in their behaviour. What was a quirk became a symbol of mania after a year at Mambango; those who were steady and reliable were found out. At Mambango everyone became

" queer," that is to say, in the old-fashioned sense of the word before popular homosexuality was discovered.

There had been several suicides at Mambango during the twelve years before the club was built. The club reduced the suicides because people could drink, quarrel and argue together, instead of moping in the bungalows, the men wondering if they could risk a black woman or not, the women—well, the club was built when the first two white women came to Mambango. There were only three women now, and two of them, Mrs. Pryce and Mrs. Mooning, hated each other. They had only two things in common, as Mrs. Mooning put it to her husband ; they were both women, and they both disliked Mrs. Tamlin. They despised her, and they envied her too. The manager's wife who should really only be a hag in some small town in the English provinces. Sometimes it was too much to bear, but in this place, as Mrs. Mooning saw it, if you did not love someone, then you must hate. Mooning could not understand that. He was a very tall, thin man, handsome and sick, pale and large-eyed with the malaria which always moved about in him, waiting for a chill. He drank a good deal now, sitting up after his wife had gone to bed, drinking. Sometimes he slept in his chair, one of those huge wood and cane affairs with the long extensions for resting the legs upon ; Bombay-Fornicators, as Major Mallows called them in that sharp, knowing way of the old regular officer.

Mrs. Mooning, bored, having exhausted the safety of marriage, had wondered if she could have one last fling, but with whom, and how ? That had been the problem ; how ? Mooning had been very jealous, once, and when drunk he could be quarrelsome and he would shout at her. " Then go and hawk yourself out," he would cry. " Don't mind me." " One day I might," she had once screamed back at him, feeling the ground. He had eyed her closely after that, swaying, but thinking, cunning, with his thick mouth curling as though he surveyed a doubtful horse which the coper had over-praised.

"I wouldn't do that," he had whispered at her. "I wouldn't do that if I were you. You see, I might cut that bloody throat of yours." Then he had pealed with laughter. She struck him with her fist and he had whimpered and gone to bed too drunk to weep. He had changed after that and she had cut down his allowance of "fun" to once a week, Saturday night, and he became grateful for it, in between moods of sullenness.

Then there were the Pryces. Mambango had had seven years to work on them ; seven years during which Pryce had changed from a well-built man of medium height to a balloon of flesh who gasped if he had to walk up the hill. Each mess had a small truck of its own for carrying the white men to their plantations, to the workshop and the factory. Pryce was cursed often by his colleagues who used the same truck, for he would not, said he could not, walk. He would sit and send notes for the truck. He was frightened about his heart, imagining it encased in fat; fatty degeneration, he thought it was. So worried was he about his heart that he had ceased what he called " relations " with his wife. " 'Aving relations," as he put it to O'Riordan, " 'as got a bit risky so I've packed it in." O'Riordan had surveyed him, his thin bitter face thoughtful and grave. " I think that's a good thing," he told Pryce. " Good for your wife, too." Pryce did not see the twinkle in O'Riordan's cruel eyes as they surveyed the huge ruin of fat which had ceased 'aving relations.

Mrs. Pryce was a small, beautiful woman about to swell beyond plumpness at any time now. The first few years with " him," her husband, had been happy ; they had been spent in Canada, where they had not suffered much because of their accents and origin. It was not until they went to Africa where they met their own race, lower middle-class thrust above themselves by " white standard " salaries, middle-class dreaming of aristocracy and with a deeper interest in the horse than was possible in England, and the genuine article, the aristocrat who either treated Africa as a giant park, or as a place in which to get a living ; it was not until then that they felt out of water. Mrs. Pryce managed to improve her accent until it sounded quite passable, but Pryce was obstinate and would " 'ave none of this la-di-da lark." She could do nothing with him. He did not seem to care, but they had known happiness. Sometimes, in their first two years at Mambango, he had had to go off on long inspection tours of the distant plantations and he was away for days at a time. She missed him very much then, and when he came back he would stand in the doorway first, put out his hands and smile at her and say, " Well, my pet, what shall we 'ave first ? A bit of 'ome cooking or a bit of the old grumble and grunt ? " Always it was grumble and grunt first in those days. Ah, how different it was now. She loathed his huge body and was sorry for him too. She had difficulty with him sometimes and would remind him about his heart, saying, " You might drop dead. Don't, Freddy ! " and he would grow pale and look at her with strange eyes as his heavy breathing grew easier, hunger dead in the wave of fear.

" But tell me you want it, anyway," he would plead, and then she could have screamed, with despair, with hunger, with disgust. Sometimes she wept when alone, especially when they played a slow waltz on the radio in the long, slumberous, empty afternoon of heat, and she felt her prison, tied as she was to a mound of fat.

Many of the other white men kept African women ; shapely, fickle girls of the Chango tribe which lived near the mountains. They were cheap, though the price had gone up a lot in the last few years. That was what education did, Major Mallows often explained. In the old days the girls asked for a hundred cigarettes a week and were happy, but nowadays it was grab, grab, grab. Still, they were good and useful creatures. They loved their work and some of them stayed with their masters for years.

The plantations at Mambango made a bright green waving sea, and from the mountains it appeared as a great verdant square in ·the dreary plains of bush and thorn jungle. The traveller could drive through the Mambango plantations and see little or nothing, usually nothing, of the whites who lived there, or their houses. In all, there were fourteen whites, including those who, with a relief profound, passed as whites, and there were about four of these. " About four," some would say, because one could not be quite sure about those not born at " home," though one was careful to say this only to one who had been born at " home," for people were devilishly touchy about this subject. The straight hair, not too black, the blue eye, the pale skin with, if possible, a touch of pink, these were tremendous things, as only those who did not possess them could know.

People still spoke about " a touch of the tarbrush," but with a faint pang of conscience these days.

The whites had made themselves as comfortable as possible. Many had running water, and the Moonings and the Tamlins possessed fridges, so lucky, so luxurious in the eyes of the others who could not keep meat, or milk, or fruit, but must consume it at once or waste it, for these were the seemingly small things which wore away the temper and the spirit at Mambango.

It was always too hot, even during the rains when the jungle steamed in the sun like drying washing, when cigarettes swelled with damp and green mould formed on a leather hat-band in an hour. People were there because they had to be there ; they found no pleasure there, no sense of victory over the jungle, no pleasure in feeling as pioneers. Mambango was a kind of lonely hell, lonelier because there were fourteen people who had slowly drained one another night after night for years. Now only the individual queernesses remained to excite comment, save when the mail brought something unusual to one of them, which he might share, or when terrible things happened, a suicide, a violent death, a madness, and from time to time these things happened, and were referred to years later as to a calendar.

But now, in the great heat, in the silent hot loneliness, there was talk of Christmas. It was not the Christmas of the newly born child who changed the world that they talked, but of the Christmas of eating and drinking and a little excitement, the Christmas which would fade quickly with the sun in the morning and the hangover of the blazing midday.

Mooning, the life and death of the club, as O'Riordan put it, brought the subject up on Friday night when most of the whites were present. He cleared his throat loudly several times until they began to watch him and then he made his announcement.

" We all know," he told them, " that soon it will be Christmas. The time of good cheer." He heard O'Riordan sneer and he turned to look at him, meaningly, but O'Riordan was examining his glass of whisky. How he hated that Irish clod. He continued : " Even though there are those among us who do not think of it as a time of good cheer, I know that most of us intend having a bloody good time." There was servile laughter, because Mooning was a technician and was one of Tamlin's right-hand men. Mooning, too, had " background " as Major Mallows put it ; one could tell he had been meant for a better place than Mambango. Sometimes he spoke of " Mother " : Mother had gone up to Scotland for some fishing with Lord So-and-So's party and Mooning was worried about her, for she was getting old now. Or Mother had put in rather a large order at Fortnum and Mason's for him. Plume and Major Mallows would nod understandingly, hearing these things over a drink with Mooning, and those others who were present could envy them, for it was of that other world Mooning spoke, the world of good clubs and cars gliding quietly into a London square, late, after a party.

Now Mooning developed his theme. He had had a few whiskies and he felt happy. Already there was in his vision of the coming Christmas, a brightness, a happiness, a happiness which he knew only he could bring to it, for he was unhappy and he wanted a party, a party in which there would be nothing but gaiety and pleasure, blotting out Africa and the nigs and the sweat and heat and the hate that came sometimes when the Africans were stubborn, or stupid, or difficult.

" We all know," he said, raising his voice as the ' vision brightened. " We all know that we are exiles," he paused there. " Most of us anyway." He paused again ; there was an awkward silence, De Gaugin, the curious " French " type, staring at the ceiling, Bakkar, the South African Dutchman with the dark skin, humming to himself, and Carato (Maltese, he said he was) examining his nails. Mooning did not hurry on for their sakes, for he did not know what " most of us anyway " had meant to them. " Exiles," he said, " far from home." He was tempted to develop that thought but he was not drunk enough to follow the faint temptation he felt. Yet he could see that he had moved them ; their eyes had changed, they looked at him fixedly, full of thoughts. " Let's have a good time," he said. " Let's give it a good beating, this Christmas. Let's form a committee to look after the food and drink. Let's have a real party and make it a Christmas worth having."

There was a chorus of assent and everyone began calling out suggestions, and he brought them to order. He wanted them to suggest Major Mallows, Plume and himself, as the

Committee, and it should have one woman on it, but which woman? That was the tricky reef he must navigate, for the women would be at each other's throats over it, and would nag their husbands about it in the small hours. He knew only too well what it would be like.

Mooning watched O'Riordan for that sneer, but O'Riordan knew he was watching him for it and disappointed him, his face expressionless, which was worse, he knew, for Mooning's eyes glittered with meaning. Mooning waited for support of Pryce's suggestion, waving his hands in false deprecation— "No, really, why Plume, Major Mallows and me? Why?" —until they pressed him, and he accepted, resignedly, just showing a doubtful pleasure in their trust of him. And so it was agreed. Plume did not want to be on the Committee, one could see that; he hated the attention drawn to himself, but Major Mallows had flushed with pleasure, for he loved trust, loved confidence to be put in him. He got up and made a graceful little speech, for he could handle language; one had to admit that.

"I think you can rely on us," he said, his blue eyes twinkling. He was just a bit tight, Mooning noted. "I think we know what is good. I think you can safely starve yourselves and get ready for a good blow-out. I've made one or two little arrangements already, as a matter of fact." He waited for the laughter, and it came, some genuine, from the simpler hearts, and some because it was wanted. It pleased him, and Mooning could see he would make a long speech if he was not brought to order. He would give him two minutes, no more.

"You know," said Major Mallows, expanding, after a sip of the whisky in his right hand, "you know I've spent some queer Christmases in my time. Frontier in India, Middle East, France. I was at that queer Christmas in 1914 in the trenches you must have heard about, when the Jerries and

the Tommies danced together. Well, as I was saying, I've
spent some queer Christmases in my time, and although we're
cut off here, we can be sure of one thing, we'll make it a *real*
English Christmas. I can't get you snow, mind you "—he
waited again and they laughed—" but I'll get you the best
we can——"

" I. I. I," thought Mooning. Did Mallows think he was
the bloody Committee ? He cut in, ending it, and Mallows
sat down, quite pleased with himself. Mallows was all right
as long as you knew how to handle him ; otherwise he would
jaw away for hours, the way he did with O'Riordan, until
they began to quarrel.

" There's this matter of a lady," Mooning said, smiling,
giving it that peculiar English quality which had so much
meaning, as if " the ladies " were special people who might
get out of hand, who *had* to be considered, but despite whom,
and of course *with* whom, one would make the best of it.
For they were there ; they were very much there, after all,
were the ladies.

There was a puzzled silence. " We must have a lady on
the Committee, you know," said Mooning gallantly. " They
know a thing or two about prog, food and good things, you
know." If Mother were here, what wouldn't she do ? She'd
show them a Christmas. He felt a great longing for Mother,
but only for a moment. They quarrelled so much, even
though he loved her as few sons loved their mothers. Hadn't
seen her for seven years, and now he loved her more than
ever. Queer, that. *He* would have to choose the woman, he
could see that. He thought of the right woman. Why *not* ?

" I suggest Mrs. Tamlin," he said. No one could disagree.
There was a silence and then murmuring, perhaps of assent,
perhaps just murmurings for the sake of sound. But he was
swift.

" I see you agree with me," he said gaily. " Mrs. Tamlin

is the lady, unless there are any other suggestions." He knew there would be none. There was another chorus of agreement, though Mrs. Pryce, sitting next to her husband, had a sharp look in her face as she turned and spoke to her husband. She was urging him to make another suggestion, but he ignored her, staring in front of him. When she pressed him, he spoke sharply out of the side of his mouth :

" D'you want me to 'ave trouble with the boss ? " he said. That shut her up, as he had known it would.

" Good," cried Mooning. " Now let's have a drink on it."

So it was settled. There were those who were not glad, but it was too late now. They could quarrel about it, argue against it, until Christmas was over, but only among themselves, for Mooning did not care now what they thought, he reflected. He knew people ; people were a bunch of bastards, and there were not many you could trust. They were all right when they knew what was going to be done, and what they thought about it privately, after they had given assent, even a nod, to the plan, did not matter one damn. Mooning was telling this to Major Mallows when Plume came over and joined them.

CHAPTER THREE

MAJOR MALLOWS was fifty-six and, owing to a will of iron, where diet and " feeling young " was concerned, looked forty. He was an honest man, so honest that he had ruined his life. It was O'Riordan who said that to him one night, and so impressed with this view of his life was Major Mallows that he used it ever afterwards when " life " was discussed over drinks. Although he did not realise it, his acceptance of O'Riordan's opinion in this matter was the beginning of his deterioration. From the day O'Riordan voiced that opinion, life for Major Mallows was never quite the same, although he did not know it. He was conscious only of a vague unrest, a feeling of half acknowledged despair, a consciousness of age, and combined with his usual contemptuous affection for O'Riordan was a sensation of dislike and antagonism, and he could not think why. But that swine, O'Riordan, as he often told Plume, was uncanny sometimes, evil in a way, and useless into the bargain, as O'Riordan would have put it.

Major Mallows lived between a desire for the village near which he had been born, and the need to finally achieve success in Africa. He had tried to find the success since he had left the Army ten years before but it had eluded him. Always, he found himself working for someone like Tamlin, or even Mooning, who was his superior. Being an ex-Army officer, Mallows had nothing to recommend him, save " knowledge of men," " used to administration," " ex-officer." He knew this, but he tried to prevent its bitterness, for the world was a civilian's world, and try as he might he could not really become a civilian. A civilian was someone who walked in the flow of the crowd, who had not known " men," men in service, in action, those who worked for a thing bigger than their selfish little desires. Only Plume understood this. None of the others knew what he meant. Plume had had some, too, only a few years, though, and, curious thing, would not use his rank ; he had finished as a captain and may have wished he had been a major, but he was definite. He was just Mr. Plume, and as he told Mallows when they were tight one night together, he had wanted to do " big things " in the Army but was not up to it. He was honest about that, Mallows had to admit, just saying that he had lacked the guts and the brains to rise above captain.

Bound together by their experience as regular officers, Plume and Mallows tolerated Mooning at first, but he had gradually seeped into their life until he had become their friend, though there had been a time when that could not have happened, for Mooning was not quite straight, not quite a good type, didn't Plume agree? Yes, Plume had agreed wearily, for what the hell did it matter anyway? He liked Mallows; they were friends, and if he got malaria, Mallows was always there, tender, thoughtful, like a woman, he would nurse him. They shared the same bungalow. It nestled under a giant candelabra tree, which the mountain Africans tapped at times for its sap. They used it in their arrow poison, so Mallows called their bungalow " Poison Villa," and Plume did not object, for Mallows was rather a child in his way, and affectionately he tolerated these small exhibitions of his childishness.

Mooning was excited after the speeches, and the formation of the committee had completed his day. The extra large whisky had lit that vein of excitement in him which caused him to say over and over again, " I knew I could do it. I knew all the time." He awaited their pleasure, their congratulations, but they only hummed and hawed.

" But don't you think it was neatly done. After all, you know what a crowd they are. That bloody fellow, that so-called Frenchman, didn't like it at all, I can tell you, though I didn't mean anything by that bit about ' most of us '; it was only later I caught on to it."

They both said it was wonderful the way he had managed it. They looked significantly at each other, helping the other when Mooning was difficult, and Mooning could be difficult, bloody difficult. He was such a vain little type. He behaved like the Mayor of a little town, yes, like the Mayor of Mambango, and one day it *would* be a town according to Tamlin, but Tamlin was a simple type; he still thought in terms of

Australia. He did not, never would, understand Africa. He
had come to Africa too late, as Mallows often said. Africa
wanted you young. To destroy you properly, or make you,
Africa needed to find you when you were young. It was a
cruel country, but it gave you something, something no
other place could give you.

Mallows explained this to Mooning. He was trying to get
him over his worry about the choice of the woman for the
Committee, for Mooning was trying to comfort himself on
the choice of Mrs. Tamlin. It might be misunderstood.
People might think he had chosen Mrs. Tamlin because he
wanted to do a bit of creeping to the boss. But it was not
that, not at all.

" We know," Mallows told him patiently. " We know.
We think you did the right thing, don't we, Plume ? " Plume
said, well of course. Mooning was pleased, but :

" There's one snag," said Mallows.

" Oh ? " Mooning grew keen, the keenness of worry
sharpened by whisky. " What snag ? "

" Do you know Mrs. Tamlin very well ? " said Mallows.

" Well, yes. In the normal way. I don't *know* her, but—
well, I know her."

" Does she know about me ? " Major Mallows had decided
not to beat about the bush any longer. " Are you sure she'll
want to be on the committee with me ? After all——"

" Know about you ? " Mooning was about to be puzzled
and then found himself realising what Mallows meant. It was
rather awkward. " You mean about the woman ? " Of
course, Mallows had an African bint. Funny that. It would
not have mattered a damn ordinarily, but Mallows's question
gave it a new quality.

" That's right," said Mallows. " My bint. Does she know
about that ? And if she does, what about it ? After all, I
only know her to say hallo to, but you never know with a

woman. She probably knows I keep a bint and I'd rather not have any nonsense about it. You see what I mean, don't you."

"Well, yes," said Mooning, "but why should it worry her. She may not know. Who'd tell her, anyway?"

There could only be two people who would tell her and both were women. One was Mrs. Pryce and the other was Mrs. Mooning.

"Mrs. Pryce, of course," Plume replied quickly. He thought about Mrs. Mooning. Amy. Amy, he was thinking, how did you ever get married to this little rat, Mooning? And yet, Mooning was attractive. He would be attractive to a woman. The soft dark eyes, the lean face, the thick, nervous red mouth. Amy said they didn't. But what proof was there of it. He hated Mooning at that moment, imagining Amy, who said they didn't, doing it. God, he felt the sweat gathering in the hollow at the base of his throat.

"Yes, maybe," Mooning humoured Mallows. "It might be that Mrs. Pryce has mentioned it, but after all this is bloody old Mambango, you know. You're not the only one to have a bint."

Only one person in the whole of Mambango knew about Plume and Amy, and that was O'Riordan, who had felt it out with his sensitive nerves one night and they had discussed it.

"Watch yourself," O'Riordan had told him. "She's dangerous, that one. She's an old-timer, you know that."

Plume had not resented O'Riordan for that advice. He knew O'Riordan was right, but Amy, it did not matter what she had been, was something wonderful to look forward to ; the whole thing, that was. And it would happen. It would happen. He knew, too, that it was only at Mambango that she could have so attracted him.

If Amy did not know about the bint, and he was sure she

did not know, it was hardly likely that Mrs. Pryce knew, he reasoned, so Mallows was making too much of it. He said so, gently, and Mallows tried to accept his view.

"It's just that I don't want any bloody nonsense, that's all," Mallows told them both. "I'll defend my bint against anyone. I've had her five years and she's a bloody little jewel taken all round." His eyes grew fond. "I never have much to do with our womenfolk and I'm not sure I want to start now. But if you think that there'll be no nonsense, then you needn't worry about me. Sorry to have brought it up, but there it is."

Mooning was all kindness. He understood, he knew what Mallows meant. He laughed knowingly. He assured them there was nothing to worry about. He preferred it white, but every man to his taste. He saw Plume's eyes on him, curious, hostile. Was Plume tight? Plume stared him out and Mooning worried.

"Anything I've said, Plume?" he asked anxiously. "You look a bit queer." Plume cut him short.

"Nothing," he said. "Nothing. I was thinking of something else." He wanted to put his hands on Mooning's neck, and squeeze.

"Well, that's that," Mooning slapped his knees. "It's settled."

"Maybe," said Plume with assumed patience. "Maybe. Anyway, Mambango will be grateful to you for all you are doing. You have that consolation, at least. You're doing something fine for us all."

Mooning believed him and said, "Well, if we all pull together——"

When he had gone back to the bar, Mallows said to Plume, "Why did you pitch into him like that, Plumey?"

"He loves it. He devours it. He gives me a pain, and don't ask me why. I'm not sure myself."

He was sure, though. He knew that pain of jealousy, and each time he saw Mooning he thought of him in possession of Amy, and Amy stood in various attitudes in his mind all day now. Because he could not have her, her beauty grew, and his longing increased.

" You're suffering from ingrowing greens," O'Riordan had told him. " When a man wants greens that badly, he should buy himself a nice piece of black stuff and not go hunting another man's wife, three other men's wife, that is. This is her third, isn't it ? "

" Yes," Plume had replied. " Her third. But I'm what she always wanted and didn't get. I *know* that." O'Riordan stared as though to make certain of Plume's meaning.

" Well, God spare me days," said O'Riordan. " That's a bit of bad news."

" Why ? " Plume had been impatient.

" Why ? " mocked O'Riordan in a high voice. " Because you sound like a bloody schoolboy, that's why. I thought it was just a simple, honest, innocent desire for a ration of greens. But not this. Not this——" He was going to dramatise it, to blow it up beyond lifesize, as he did everything else, and Plume stopped him.

" It's love, you see ? " he said sardonically. " Miss Right has come along at last." That was in the beginning, before it began to hurt.

" *Mrs.* Right, you mean." O'Riordan had thrown his head back and laughed. " It's the grandest thing when you see the love light in a boy's eyes," he had said.

" I'm going to have a good crack at her, anyway," Plume said.

" Are you really serious about her, though, Plumey ? "

" I don't know," he had replied. " I just feel an extraordinary attraction to her, that's all I can tell you."

" That's greens," said O'Riordan simply.

Mallows finished his whisky and said, " What about a game of snooker ? " Plume shook his head.

" Bored ? " asked Mallows in that kindly way of his.

" Bored as hell. Do you ever wonder why we end up in bloody places like Mambango, Mallows ? "

" Often," he said, wiping his thick grey moustache. " Too often. It's not much of a life, is it ? "

" A life ? " Plume's voice was mingled with his sigh. "When I think of Monday morning and those swarms of nigs I could scream. Do you ever get weary of the nigs ? "

" No, I like 'em. They're all right. You used to get on all right with them once. What's happened ? " Mallows probed carefully into his friend. They did not explore each other usually, and this fact was the secret of their friendship in an atmosphere in which two men living together usually came to know too much of each other. They explored each other's minds until a day came when one of them stood sated in the desert of the other's mind, all exploration over, and began to notice all his faults.

It was not like that with Mallows and Plume. They had great reserves of self ; they did not engage in conversations of discovery, and they lived in a kind of dull harmony which suited them. But Plume was somewhat different these days, out of sorts, given to making bitter remarks when none was necessary. Mallows probed softly, sensitively.

" Feeling all right. I mean, not the old malaria again ? "

" No." Plume barred the gate and Mallows said, " Another drink ? "

" We may as well. It's Friday. Shall we get slowly tight, or go home after this ? " That sounded like the old Plume, and Mallow's eyes were fond again as he said :

" No, not me. Got to be sober to-night or the missus will be upset." They both laughed, thinking of the slender girl, Shalanga, as a missus, upset. " Why shouldn't I have one

myself, someone like Shalanga ? "—but he knew he had not
the courage for intimacy with Africans, even the men made
him nervous. He had a feeling that there were dark forces
there which a white man like himself could not control. The
Africans sometimes frightened him. Their savage, unchecked
laughter of white teeth when they were amused ; their mad
dancing to those thudding drums, and their fierce animal joy
in happiness. Sometimes it frightened him when he looked
into it, and often though he wanted an African woman, he
recoiled in his nervousness of that African joy in the world,
the belly and the body. Secretly he envied them their freedom
from their minds.

CHAPTER FOUR

MRS. MOONING lay dreaming on her bed in the burning afternoon. She was naked. The door was locked,
the windows were shaded, and she lifted one long white leg
and swung it gently and slowly up and down. " Forty," she
said dreamily. " Now the other one."

She was thirty-eight and she was worried about her hips
and her thighs ; there was the faintest threat of fat. She had
grown to enjoy her exercise in the afternoon of the half
darkened room. On the sheet stretched firmly over the bed
and already damp with her fragrant sweat, she kicked herself
slowly into a sensual daze, counting quietly, enjoying the long
white glide of her legs in the room's dusk. Behind her awareness of the exercise moved the fantasies born of thousands of
boring days ; a swirl of men, words, hands, voices, unfulfilled
longings, bitter husks of endings, the heat of Mambango in
conflict with her waning moon.

"I love you," she said at the end of each leg exercise. "I love you. I love you." She said it again and again, changing the inflection each time, sometimes huskily, now sharply and passionately, trying to imagine herself a man hearing it. "I love you. You, *you*, *you*," she cried. She pedalled furiously with her legs, her teeth bared, almost demented of a sudden with boredom, with the thought of Mooning who fretted for Saturday night, to-night, when she would have to pretend that she, too, was "rather keen for it," as Mooning would put it in that lust-thickened voice of Saturday night.

"I promise you we don't," she had told Plume. She said the words again now, aloud, those words which had given him such pleasure, for it was still strange to see what gave a man pleasure, still strange after how many men? How often she went over their names. She thought it must be about fourteen; fourteen glorious, wonderful men, until Mooning came. She said the words again, hearing them with Plume's ears :

"I promise you we don't," then after a moment or two— "darling." She had known he had known she was lying, but it made him happy for a moment in his torture, poor dear. She felt that weak, swollen, sore tenderness she always felt when she thought of a man's desire, wanting to smother his pain with flesh. The Saturday night after telling him that lie she had made herself suffer when Mooning came to her room. She had enjoyed it briefly, as usual, but this time there was the splendid pain of her martyrdom for Plume ; it *was* martyrdom, she was sure, and in Mooning's arms she had her fantasy, almost in tears with whipped-up love, a pure love, for Plume who could not have her—yet.

She began to roll on her hips, slimming them, she could almost feel the process, trying to imagine Plume's embrace.

" I'm sick of this bloody subterfuge and hand-holding," he had growled one day. " Sick of it."

" Darling," she said, " soon it will be all right. Wait till Tom is away."

" When will that be ? " he asked, and then he grew angry. " Where the hell can he go anyway ? " he cried. " He never goes anywhere." He wanted to say all the brutal things in his mind to her.

" Oh, please be patient, Plumey, my sweet."

She bowed herself into an arch, feeling the stretch of her belly, the creak in her spine, until she was exhausted. Then she lay still in the darkness, boredom near her, she sighing in the close heat of the dark room.

" Oh, Plumey," she cried in a childish voice. " Dear, dear Plumey. Does it ache, my poor Plumey ? "

When the time came she would tear him with her nails.

She heard the servants quarrelling on the veranda, and remembering, she hated for a moment the Africa she loved. She loved its smell, the smell of dried cow dung and wood-fires, of dying dry grass and the bitter iron smell of the soil in the teeming rain, and the smell of African bodies, like smoke and cut lemon with a tang of ammonia. She was careful of that Africa, but she loved its violence, its pitilessness and its vast, overpowering loneliness.

" Oh, Plumey, I love you," she whispered, laughing at her lie, but enjoying its sonorousness, the almost imperceptible shudder it set up deep inside her tuned-up body.

" It's wrong of us," she whispered. " Wrong. Do you hear me ? " She had not seen a film for simply years and years, but she lived them again, holding Plumey's sweet face in the tender hands of her imagination. " It's wrong," she whispered. Forbidden fruit. Illicit love. The tears on her lover's face as she held it. She felt the actual pang of the dreamed sorrow as she lay there, alone in the dark. " Oh,

Plumey, it's wrong." There was something young, tender and sweet in it all ; she felt a tear forming in her right eye and she forced it out, half listening to Gesuka shouting at the cook. " Evil one, you are lying. You stole it. I saw you." The pride in her knowledge of the language banished Plume from her mind, but her hands on her breasts reminded her of the mirror and she got up and went to it, holding her breasts like an offering.

" For you, my sweet dear," she said. If only Plumey had thick black hair and a straighter nose, like Jack had had. Jack, so long ago now.

Drawn into her own eyes, she leaned forward and stared into them, forgetting all.

These afternoons were like church when she had been young, alone in the incense-fragrant dusk, the gleam of brass and the cough of the sacristan echoing in the nave.

These afternoons were her pleasure, for, as she had told Mooning one day in her temper, " One day I'll go mad here. Mad, mad, mad, with boredom."

" Then why did you bloody well come ? " he had shouted at her and had gone pale when she snarled at him like a beautiful dog.

" Mad, that's what I'll go," she sometimes told the mirror, and then, " Mirror, mirror on the wall, who is the loveliest of them all ? Plumey is my loveliest and I'll give him ev-ev-everything."

The fantasy ceased when Gesuka called, " Tea is ready, Memsahib." Glorious, scrumptious, hot golden scones there would be, she knew. Oh, dear, dear Gesuka.

Mooning was sitting there when she came out wearing a housecoat of black Japanese silk. The leaping golden dragons had faded, but the silk suited her long, thick dark hair and her white skin which was just beginning to wear the faint

sallowness of her twelfth year in Africa. " The day my breasts
sag, I'll kill myself," she would tell her mirror sometimes.
They were her favourite part of her body. It was Saturday
and Mooning was looking at her already in that keen, yet dog-
like, way. She took a swift pleasure in the thought that she
might refuse him after all, but no, she wanted it too. It was
better than nothing after all, save when he was " nervy," or
tight, when he was a damned nuisance. What pain she could
give him if she cut out his Saturday night. There was something comical about a man when one had ceased to love him,
especially on Saturday night.

Mooning beamed with pride when he told her about the
committee.

" Why didn't you put me on the Committee ? " she said
crossly. " Why Mrs. Tamlin ? That hag." How curious a
stupid little committee should make him so happy.

" But, Amy, old thing, you're my wife." He was always
using out of date expressions, like " old thing."

" That's right. I forgot," she said. " I'm your wife." It
hurt him. Out of the corner of her eye she saw his pain. She
felt a great happiness as she crunched the scone. Dear, dear
Gesuka.

" I don't want to be on the damned committee," she said
contemptuously. " But I hate that hag as much as I like her
husband."

" Oh, you like Tamlin ? " he said. " That's new."

" Is it ? " she laughed deliciously, again and again, thinking
of the mirror, and the dark room with pleasure. " Of course
I like him," she said. " He's a *man*. A *man*."

" I was a fool ever to let her start talking to me like this,"
Mooning was thinking moodily. He should have put a stop
to it when it had begun, a year after the marriage.

" A man, is he ? " he said. " Huh."

She did not bother with him any more. She turned the pages of *Vogue*. It was a year old but it was modern, modern, when she remembered she was cooped up in this hole in the middle of Africa. She hated Africa as she looked at the gaunt beautifully dressed women, their costumes of lovely material, rich with colour, or showing their long bodies in the new underwear. What a waste it all was ; her lovely body cut off here, holed up in a rotten bungalow with Mooning when there were men in London and Paris who would give their all, their very all, just to handle her.

She ate another scone thoughtfully.

Into her dream Mooning's voice cut like a sword, like a sudden sword of frightening cold.

" Why is Plume sending you notes ? " he asked.

" Sending me notes ? " she said. She recovered her poise and now she stared him out. " What do you mean ? " she cried angrily.

" I found a note this morning on the veranda, from Plume," he said, less gentle now, yet still feeling for his position.

She nearly said " Which one ? " Which one was it ? Yesterday's ?

" What did it say ? " she asked, interested.

" It said not to forget Christmas," he said, his voice full of meaning, and edged with bitter question.

" Oh, that," she said quickly. " I promised Major Mallows and Plume that I'd get Gesuka to make them some of these scones." He knew she was lying, and she knew he knew. She almost laughed aloud as she drank up his stupid, suspicious gaze.

" Scones," he said. " Scones for Christmas ? "

" Yes," she told him. " Scones. *Scones*. And for Christmas. Why ? Did you think he was going to take me away from you ? " He blushed with anger. He wanted to get up and stalk out, but he remembered it was Saturday night, and in a panic he began to humour her, hate seething in him for her cruel tongue, her pitiless eyes.

"No, Amy," he said hastily. "Of course not. It's just that I don't get on with Plume very well. It's nothing."

She had understood his haste to please her again and she was about to destroy his Saturday night, but she wanted it too, and she contented herself with a few snarling words about men being like children and then turned to *Vogue* again.

Chewing his forgotten scone, Mooning tried to do away with the jealousy he felt, which made him want to do violence to something, but it stayed there ; a slow, burning glow of suspicion, of doubt and of misery. How cruel a thing life was, he brooded. How cruel a woman could be.

"Drink your tea," Amy told him sharply. She knew how to disturb such moods. She was watching him closely, her eyes only slightly narrowed. Her heart was beating normally again now, but she had had a fright, for Mooning could be frightening at times. She had once seen him beat an African until he screamed for mercy.

"I'm sorry, Amy," he said humbly. "I didn't mean what you thought."

"Neither did I," she said in a crisp voice. "It's nonsense."

"I'm getting you something you'll like for Christmas," he told her, waiting for her delight.

"Sweet," she said. She looked round to make sure the servants were not there and then she took his hand and placed it on her breast. He felt its firm warmth, and, for-getting where he was, and impelled by what she had done, and by Saturday night, he began to struggle to his feet, getting hold of her in that feverish way men have sometimes, but she pushed him off, her tongue sticking out of her smiling white teeth.

"Not now," she said archly. "Not *now*."

He breathed heavily and swallowed hard. He reminded her for a moment of one of those bulls alone in a paddock, waiting. She burst out into hysterical laughter and went into the house, leaving him there, panting, puzzled and angry. But it was Saturday, and his heart sang when he remembered that.

CHAPTER FIVE

MRS. TAMLIN was pleased when she got Mooning's note asking if she would agree to be the lady member of the Christmas Committee. She began smoothing her greying hair with her free hand as she read the note again. Such a nice man, Mr. Mooning, and he had written such a graceful little note. Why should nice men have such horrible wives? Of course she would like to be on the Committee. She hurriedly replied to the note in her small, neat writing. When the servant had gone she began to think about Major Mallows and Mr. Plume. Mr. Plume was such a handsome man in a certain kind of light, especially when his thick golden hair glowed in the sunlight; such a strong, kind face. He looked as if he had suffered in that quiet patient way he had. Could it be true about gaol? She hardly knew him, and she knew even less of Major Mallows. There was something rather wicked about *him*. She had heard him chuckling in the Club, and rolling his eyes nastily while talking with that strange man, Mr. O'Riordan. She had been sure they were telling each other those stories which men were always telling when ladies were not within hearing, or did not appear to be within hearing. She wondered what Tammy would say when she told him she had accepted.

He was reading a magazine when she told him and he put
it down in that slow way which meant he was about to say
something sharp.

" Oh, you have, have you ? " he said, but she could see
that he was joking. She knew, too, that he loved her very
much and that he relied on her, and that she had become a
part of his mind and his person, and that without her he
could never be the same man. He had not changed a great
deal in his manner towards her since she had first gazed upon
him as he lay with glazed eyes on the hospital bed in France.
He hated being ill. That was in 1916 when the smashed and
ruined men were pouring in from Guillemont and High
Wood on the Somme, the chaff from the machine-gunners'
bloody scythe. The scars of the wounds still showed on his
chest to-day. His hair was grey now and his figure had
thickened, but the immense energy which had overcome those
cruel wounds was still in his possession.

The trained tenderness of the nurse still showed in her
hands, Tamlin noticed at times when she bathed his eyes
after a day in the glaring sun, or clipped his hair which always
curled out on his neck. They had survived a great deal
together. They had known a kind of passion and they had
survived its normal death. They had overcome the trials of
poverty, and of misunderstanding of which there had been
much owing to the stubbornness which Tammy showed
when his bosses had tried to exercise their will, as Tammy
had often thought, wrongly. She had had to stand by him
when he had been wrong, so often wrong. She had experienced the pity of women, and of men, who had thought
her married to a fool. In some things Tammy *was* a fool, she
knew. He was a fool about money. He spent it like water,
and when they had been poor he had said he hated money.
He grew impatient with bosses who would not give him his
head, for he always knew he was right. Now, he was contented

in his bosses. They lived in London and did not trouble him, and all day he worked like an engine : in the heat of the plantations, or in the steamy gloom of that horrible office in which they had killed the puff adder one morning. She felt that they had come here to a job which would hold Tammy for good. It was a job no one else had been able to do and Tammy was doing it. He was tough and daring and courageous, and she was so proud of him when she saw him standing with legs apart, his battered sun helmet on the back of his head while he watched the tractors rattling and grinding along the horizon which quivered in the heat. He had never had malaria. She touched wood when she thought of it. How lucky he was when so many men here were wrecks, deaf from quinine, grey faced in the heat. If it were not for those two months each year which the women spent at Chombo in the hills, the women would die, but would they ? How did Mrs. Pryce stand it ? She never went away, and though Mambango had pulled her down and had run its hot fingers across her doll-like face, she was still lovely to look at as a woman. Thinking of her, Mrs. Tamlin began patting her hair. There were times when she wished she had been beautiful, too, but this wish came less frequently nowadays. She did not even long for children any more. They had just not come and one day she had realised they would never come. " Just write them off," Tammy had told her absent-mindedly. " You're not cut out to be a mother."

Mrs. Pryce had no children, and Mrs. Mooning had none either. It was just sheer wickedness on their part, she was sure, just selfishness ; she was afraid all women these days were rather selfish.

She was thrilled to think she was going to be on the Committee for it gave her a feeling that she was going to matter at Mambango, even for a short time.

Tamlin came in late, biting his lower lip. There were one

or two things going on that he did not much like the look of, he told Maisie when she said he looked " done up."

" What kind of things, Tammy ? "

" Labour." He said it with a baleful far-away look in his eyes. He said it as though that one word should explain a volume of misery, a tangle of rage, frustration and suffering. " Labour," he repeated.

She rushed to hurry Songo with the tea. Better to leave Tammy for a while with his worry in a good comfortable armchair. It was wonderful what tea did for him when he was tired.

Labour. It was on his conscience, always had been. He, for the sheer pleasure of work and achievement, would work for his food. They could keep the rotten money. It was his wife who nagged him into financial effort. But it was different for " labour." They had no vision of work for work's sake, they worked for money and the small things it could buy them. There was something sad about them. And here, at Mambango, the Africans were restive and he could not blame them. They were raw, in many ways savage and primitive, but in others gentle and trusting and honest. But they were discovering the sweet corruption of money, of gain and possession, though as yet in the humblest way. The cutters on the plantations got ten shillings a month and a daily ration of maize flour. He had warned London. He had tried several approaches ; he had appealed to the heart with no result. Then he had tried to frighten them, and that had failed too.

Now, someone was working among the Africans. Someone was telling them that they should be dissatisfied, and he did not know who it was. There was no trouble, but there was a certain something in the faces of the Africans on pay day, a questioning look, an expectancy as though the *Bwana* would speak to them about something dear to their hearts. He had looked solemnly into their eyes as they filed before him but no man spoke. They laughed together and shouted as usual. But there was something in the atmosphere that warned him. A kind of intuition was sharpened by close contact with simple and primitive people, and Tamlin did not doubt that he had this intuition.

Then he was told that De Gaugin had been struck on the head from behind while serving out the flour ration. He went across to Number Five plantation in his ancient car and he found De Gaugin in his bungalow. He was sitting in a cane chair, pale and seeming shocked. He believed De Gaugin was stupid in his treatment of Africans and he had made up his mind that if De Gaugin had provoked trouble among the Africans, he would discharge him. De Gaugin was one of those men who could not find it in him to give an African the benefit of the doubt, who suspected impudence if an African ventured to correct one of his, De Gaugin's, mistaken impressions about what had been or had not been done over some piece of hoeing, or planting. De Gaugin would seek for a lie, for some hidden meaning, until the Africans under him were afraid and began to be as secretive as he had mistakenly suspected.

He was a small thin dark man of about forty years of age. He was something of an amateur boxer and he wore one of those thick broad wriststraps, a badge of vanity and a token of muscular strength. He drank a good deal of the locally brewed rum and he was a favourite with what Major Mallows called " the off whites." De Gaugin was a hard worker, scrupulously honest, and with an ambition to prove that he could be relied upon in any situation in which his work placed him. He was of Mauritian origin, but he was proud of being a Frenchman. He read a good deal, particularly of history, and it was one of his theories that if Dupleix had been able to keep his foothold in India, the Far East would have been a happier place. He would tell this to Moti Ram, the sick Indian who kept the general store at the edge of the Mambango plantation boundary, and Moti Ram, subtle and resigned, would nod sympathetically and wonder what manner of man was this.

De Gaugin was nervous when he saw Tamlin enter his house. He respected Tamlin, and often when studying his build would make secret guesses as to their respective physical powers. Another thing he liked about Tamlin was his freedom from that sense of superiority which the other Britishers at Mambango displayed, without realising it generally, but at times studied and deliberately insulting.

Tamlin sat down near him and without greeting him, said : " What happened ? " His seriousness disturbed De Gaugin, who was in some pain and still affected by the physical shock no less than by the immense blow to his athletic pride. By a nigger, too, and from behind.

" From behind," he said angrily. " I was hit from behind."

" I know. But why ? What was going on ? "

De Gaugin would not, or could not, say. He waved his hands and spoke of the treachery of the niggers.

" Now listen, De Gaugin," said Tamlin brutally. " The labour's not in a very contented state of mind at present. I'm very sorry you've had such a bad knock and I'll find the bastard that did it if it's the last thing I do. But you must have done something to provoke it." De Gaugin began to protest, but Tamlin said, " I know what goes on round here. I know you sock the odd African and I'm telling you that that time's passing. You can't get away with it these days. The local District Commissioner is pretty hot on running in Europeans who beat up Africans, and apart from that, it's bad for the labour. I'm just telling you to go easy with your fists."

De Gaugin turned pale with rage and was trying to contain

it. He moved his lips and his dark eyes had swollen, as it were, in the sockets.

" That's all," Tamlin got up. He seemed very agitated. "I'll find the African who did it," he said. "And I'll fix him."

" African," De Gaugin was thinking. African was Tamlin's new word for a nigger. It had an unusual sound ; " African." He should be beaten with a *kiboko*, he wanted to shout, beaten until he begged for mercy. But he was silent. There were other ways in which to win back his position among the " Africans." He stood up and thanked Tamlin for coming to see him. Tamlin brusquely said good-bye and went off again to the compound.

" No more rations," he told the assembled Africans, " until you give me the man who struck *Bwana* De Gaugin." There was a great mumbling among the hundreds of black, shining men who stood before him, full of trust in him because he had frightened them, and because he knew they placed reliance on him. He gave them no time to think but drove to his bungalow.

He won. When he had finished his tea the African *Neapara* in charge of the labour for De Gaugin's plantation came to see him. He reported that he had found the man who had struck De Gaugin. What would the *Bwana* do ?

" Do ? " Well, the matter would be taken to the District Commissioner, unless——. Here Tamlin paused and gave his thin ironic smile, unless De Gaugin's assailant preferred twenty on his behind from the *Neapara's* rhinoceros hide whip ; the six-foot *kiboko* which he handled so well. The *Neapara* nodded, solemn as became the ex-sergeant from the far Sudan. He knew what was liked.

" I have already put that to him, *Effendi*," he said. He never called any white man *Bwana* who had been a soldier. The proper term for the white man who had been a soldier was *Effendi*, and Tamlin, after his fashion, while appreciating this, fought against the pleasure it gave him.

" And what did he say ? "

" He said better to be beaten by you, and I have prepared his mind for two weeks' cut in his pay, *Effendi.*"

Really ? Tamlin was impressed. Twenty on the arse. It was a real beating to get. He agreed about the cut in pay but gave the *Neapara* faint praise for his forethought, for it might spoil him. He knew that the African could be as hard on his fellows, if allowed, as the most cynical and hardened of disillusioned Europeans.

Because the next day was Sunday, about which day Tamlin was very particular, he decided that the punishment should be meted out at once. He gave orders to this effect, and by half past five, as the sun was beginning to struggle in his rosy veils of flame below the mountains, the assembled Africans, big-eyed and still, watched the *Neapara* swish the long stiff whip solemnly and frighteningly.

De Gaugin's assailant lay prone on his face, a wet sack laid over his bare buttocks, quivering, as the *Neapara* intended, to each long sibilant swish of the whip before the beating. This swishing was done gravely, like some slow but deliberate ritual, and the hard-lined face of the ex-sergeant was grim, for this was a parade, and a moment of pride, and of moment for those savage ones who were assembled for this lesson on things and their order in a man's life. Then sharply he pivoted on his feet, magnificent in his lean height and in the long pull and tightness of the muscles in his black, shining legs, and under the thin cotton vest. The *kiboko* came down fast, was allowed a moment's somnolence after the blow, and then raised again. Pitilessly, remorselessly, it rose and fell, the loud crack of the blows evoking a faint jerk in the silent crowd of onlookers as though the earth jolted with each impact of the *kiboko* on the victim's body. The beaten African uttered no sound for he came of a tribe which did not answer aloud to pain, and he was thinking of this as he rose to his feet and drew up his ragged shorts. The *Neapara* had drawn his whip to his side, like a sword, and stood proudly and arrogantly looking down on the smaller man whom he had beaten.

"Go," said the *Neapara* with a jerk of his head. His medal ribbons of the terrible war against the Germans were on his left breast as they always were when he beat a man. "Go," he said again, and the man smiled and joined the crowd who edged away from him, for this one had angered the white men and had been humiliated, and for some days he would have only his intimate friends as companions.

"It is finished," the *Neapara* roared suddenly, like one who hated men of this country, so far from his own, who hated all who had not known what it was to be a soldier.

Tamlin nodded and the Africans broke into a great mumbling and chattering as they drifted away in their groups, many laughing in their high-pitched way of delight as they imitated the scene which they had just witnessed. One, the clown of them all, seized his own behind and screamed like a woman, in mockery of this one who had been flogged, and those near him bent with the laughter which was so great when this one, the clown, mimicked, as was his way daily, in rain, in heat, or when all were sad. Forgotten were their fear and their gravity. They began to run in long lines, their lope slow and steady, singing the song of the homecoming, which they did whenever they left the plantations, and in his pleasure at this sight, Tamlin forgot his regret for the beating. They forgave everything, these Africans, and once again they had shown him the basic goodness and warmth of their nature, bringing the familiar pang of guilt to him as always when he had been hard to them. It was soft of him, he felt, but he could not help it. There was something in them that he had learned to love, and sometimes he was afraid it would conquer him, but he was saved from this when he witnessed some scene of callousness among them, or saw them hacking an animal to death, as though it were wood. They had to be saved, saved from their sad life from which they had never stirred in a thousand years. To-morrow, he would try again.

Tamlin kept God in a special compartment. God was for an hour on Sunday, for it was a man's duty to remember God, especially when he had charge of lost savages. He was not one of these Sky Pilots, as he had told O'Riordan several times during those bloody annoying arguments which that fellow always provoked. No, he just felt it was the right thing for a man to speak his mind about God to a crowd of savages who had not known Him, and he enjoyed it, for they were thrilling moments when he saw the awe and the wonder his words produced. He spoke the language fairly well and when he was in a difficulty he used English, and not understanding, the mass of Africans would nod vigorously, helping the *Bwana* on lest he should stop this fascinating series of cries and movements of his hands and eyes.

The *Neapara*, emotional with pride and pleasure in a task well done, saluted Tamlin and said, " The matter is finished, *Effendi*." He was dismissed with a curt, thoughtful nod, but it was enough to please him and he stalked off with his long swinging stride to his hut.

CHAPTER SIX

BEFORE the Committee had its first meeting, Plume found that his hunger for Mrs. Mooning was too great to bear, and Major Mallows would sit watching him while pretending to read. Plume would jump to his feet and stride quickly across the room and stare from the window, seeing nothing, chewing his lower lip, and sometimes he would utter a sound between a sigh and a moan. Then he would find fault with his servant, his voice rising as the African showed his silent bewilderment.

"You see, you cunning bastard?" he shouted one hot afternoon when he had returned exhausted from the plantations. "You see what I mean?"

The African was silent, his head lowered slightly, yet watching Plume like a cat, for a man never knew what might follow such great anger. He was confused. The *Bwana* was asking about why it was that black men had no brains, why they forgot what was told them again and again.

"Do you *see*," shouted Plume. "Do you *see*?" Then in English he cried, "I loathe you and your bloody rotten country. All of you. All of you." He vented his despair until he raised his trembling hand in a threat to strike, and the servant slid away to the door, his face turned to the Major, his eyes large with appeal for help. He seemed to sense a permission to go and he went and all was well, for Plume did not call him back.

After a silence which Mallows tried to break by some rustling of his paper, as though to show his deep interest in it, Plume said "I've had enough." He had said it to himself, aloud, so Mallows waited until he said it again and then he put down his paper.

"Look, Plumey," he said in a kindly voice, "I know what it's all about, but I'll only mention it if you won't get mad with me."

This touched Plume and he said, "Why should I get mad with you?"

"It's a woman, isn't it? It's *her*."

"Her?" Plume was going to make Mallows explain himself, but changed his mind and said, "You know about it? How?"

"I'm surprised the whole place doesn't know about it,"

said the Major with just the right touch of brutality and good humour which robbed the sentence of a possible wound to the other's sensitive state. For Plume was trembling slightly where he stood. He wanted to tell Mallows all about it, all about the yearning which possessed him like a malady, and about the pain with which the thought of this woman filled him all day, and about whom he had begun to dream terrible and humiliating dreams. "For me," he wanted to say, "it is worse than for anyone else, because I've kept free of this kind of thing for years. A woman? Yes. But not this awful feeling of despair and misery which gets worse and worse." Instead he said, "I don't know what to do."

"Is it that bad?" Mallows got up and put his hand on Plume's arm. "Christ, I'm sorry it's like that, Plumey. I wish I could help. I was going to recommend a nice piece of black stuff I know of. Fresh, too. But what's the use of that?" he added hopefully.

"No use at all," Plume told him, and then he began to laugh and as quickly stopped again. "It's like the bloody toothache," he told the Major gravely. "It's there all the time and you don't know what to do with yourself. Sometimes I think it's the climate or that I'm cracking up, or that I need a woman. But it's not that. I just love this woman, that's all, and I can't deal with it." His face wore an expression of fierce despair when he added, "I feel I could do myself in sometimes, because I know she's a bitch in a way, and doesn't really give a curse for me, and despite this I find myself telling myself that if she'll only give me a chance she'll grow to love me. And that is the worst humiliation of all." Mallows murmured his sympathy and Plume's eyes narrowed and he said, "How did you know it was *her*?"

"By the way you hang around when she's in the Club. You're beginning to show it, you see. And that's a pity."

"Yes, yes, a pity." Plume strode to the window again

and stared out at Africa, sad Africa with that silence of sunset over it, when the birds were quiet and the sky began to swim into soft riotous colour which changed from a mist of fire into a fusing of green and purple haze. There was a kind of huge and tragic loneliness in these moments of sunset, for the immensity of the continent could be felt in that deep silence of the fast approaching darkness, and Plume felt its magnificence and its obscure malignant threat as the darkness covered the forests and the mountains and reached to the window at which he stood. A few chilled stars glittered, and the realisation of the endless vault in which they hung completed his despair. What pain was there to equal the knowledge that, after all, it did not matter whether one existed or not, whether one had come into this world or not, and yet, knowing this, to be obsessed with longing for some woman who did not suffer for lack of him ?

He put that to Mallows, who knotted his forehead and brows and replied, " But that's just the point. You're making it all into something it just bloody well isn't, see ? You're making it into a rhapsody when it's really only glands as that fellow O'Riordan says." The Major came and looked into Plume's vacant eyes. " And he's right, you know. It's just bloody glands driving a chap on, only you've made it into a poem and it's only greens no matter how you put it. Greens and no more."

" Maybe," said Plume sullenly. " But that doesn't help me much. It may be greens but I've never had this misery before. I think I need a good booze-up. A really good booze-up and smash some furniture. What d'you say to that ? "

" I agree save for the bit about the furniture."

" I'll get myself oiled up to-night." It was like a threat, thought Mallows. Plume vaguely hoped he might meet Amy when he was drunk. He would then tell her to clear off to hell out of it. No, no. He felt sorrow for that when he remembered the touch of that firm springy flesh under the silk dress. He shivered with lust and tenderness. It was not like the love he had had for Julia—ten, no eleven, years ago. That memory kindled feelings which would never quite die ; feelings of remorse for having pushed her aside in preference for adventure. Julia seemed even more obscure nowadays when he thought of her, for he burned for this other one, and the flesh, the uneasy, tormented envelope, had shrivelled the memory of Julia which had grown kindly, regretful and in some curious way, holy, for he had surely wronged her. But had he ? He could never make up his mind. He was not unhappy enough yet to do so. Amy, in her body, had brought his routined life to a standstill, a standstill that was full of indecision and hunger, and with a force which dragged him from humiliation to deluded hope, and he knew it was only flesh. That was the galling part of it, he told himself. Why not just cut her out, forget her, simply wipe her out of his mind and get on with life ? But it was impossible. She was there, and there was hope. And life now appeared poor and ugly and dull.

Perhaps he should have married Julia, but she had only wanted a piece of the giant suburbia which grew round London like a red creeper. When he thought of that he knew he had been right to go on with his adventure. " Leave the Army," Julia had said, " It's the Army or me. I'll make you happy here." And Daddy had arranged a job for him in the firm, in one of those grimy buildings in a narrow street in " the City."

Mallows had gone and Plume smelt the heavy scent of the frangipani blossoms which always filled the air of the living-room after dusk, as though the blossoms outside the opened window sighed each evening after the day of heat. Smelling their perfume, he was glad again of Africa, any Africa, even Mambango, rather than the life Julia had nearly wooed him into. And yet, he regretted Julia. He was forty-five now. He had left the Army eight years ago, disappointed. He had enjoyed the war as a young regular subaltern on the Western Front. He could not understand why he had enjoyed it. He had read a good many of the flood of war books which had begun in 1929, and they were all true. The bloody murder of battalions, the lice, the fear when the ration of courage was gone, the battering down of the youthful spirit into a cold lump of dull lead as the war had neared its end. He had seen it all, but he had enjoyed it. There had been complete release for him in the great machine of the war. And then one day he had found himself shuddering uncontrollably, his lips out of control, his spirit rammed up into his heaving chest by terror as the enormous hammers of the German bombardment struck the earth about him. It was 1918 and the Armistice saved him from one day screaming aloud before the troops. It was a private hell, those last few months, which he could share with nobody, and even now when he remembered those months he wanted to clasp his head and moan.

He had not even realised that over one million British men of his own generation had been killed and nearly five millions wounded in the war he had survived. It was O'Riordan who told him when they were all arguing together one night :

" The best we had went west," Mallows had said after O'Riordan had astounded Plume with the figures. " We can never be the same nation again."

" No, that's true," O'Riordan had agreed. " Just look at us sitting here. What bloody right have *we* got to be alive ? A gang of boozing bums who should have gone west too. But we were spared to bring culture to the dark continent." He knew he was making Mallows uneasy and he enjoyed it. O'Riordan had fought in the war, too, but he was proud of Ireland's struggle for freedom, and as he told them when

they quarrelled about the Irish question, " Englishmen could
never understand that, for you've never had to divide your
loyalties. And that's why you'll never understand India's
struggle either." Then they would fight.

Plume laughed to himself, thinking of O'Riordan.

In his quiet room Mallows stroked Shalanga's warm
velvety shoulder distractedly.

Shalanga had taken off his shoes and stockings and now
she sat beside him on the shabby, sagging sofa in Mallow's
bedroom. Mallows wanted to read the latest newspapers
which had reached him from England, but he was distracted
by Shalanga's closeness. He had found that he could not be
cruel to her. Once he had shouted at her and she had stared
at him with soft, frightened eyes like those of a pet antelope
he had had years ago and had forgotten. That look had
touched his heart and he knew that in his possession he had
someone who relied on his goodness, who loved him in a
way he could not quite understand, and which had begun to
turn him into that which he was not ; a thoughtful, gentle
owner of a gentler being. There were times when he felt the
growth of this responsibility, for she had found a softness in
him which, he knew, had begun to win over his Anglo-
Saxon armour. He worried about it and he wished to talk
about it with Plume, but he had never asked for advice in
his life and he had a mania about privacy into which only
Plume could occasionally intrude.

Mallows's room was lined with books. He was a happy man.
He had these books, Shalanga, and a drink when he required
it. He was one of those white bachelors, as O'Riordan put
it, who preferred a black bint whom he could control, and
who lost nothing of his own personality as he would have
done in marriage. When this was passed on to Mallows he
had nodded brightly and said, " That's true. That's a fact.
I never saw it like that before." It explained all the liaisons

between white men and black women. It gave them freedom and supplied the body's solace which was marriage's reason for the young. When they were tired of it, they sacked the woman until time came for another.

" You can't do that," said O'Riordan, " with a white wife, unless you are willing to pay." He went further and said, " The Christian principle is right, in principle, about marriage, but it's a bloody bore for a man, and sometimes for a woman. Biology has struggled with Christianity for centuries and now the struggle is at its bitterest. The woman will win when the promiscuous stage is over."

There was a row in the Club after he had said that. Everybody quarrelled, argued, fought against each other over what O'Riordan had said. Many cursed him. But for Mallows, who earlier in his life would never have consorted with a woman who was not of the white race, it had become simple. He knew that any woman was a solace if she was not a nuisance, had not too sharp a tongue, did not get in the way and was happy when she was wanted. He knew, too, that the easy-going master-and-maid relationship he had with Shalanga had ruined him for marriage with a white woman, for this relationship was without the Christian ethic which gave a woman her true freedom in marriage.

Shalanga never interfered when he was reading. He would sit there, smoking, his book on his knee, scratching her small warm ear absent-mindedly while she knitted, a thing she had been taught by a woman of her tribe who had been to the mission at Kyongo.

" Why don't you knit me socks ? " Mallows had asked her.

" First I must learn to do with the two needles. Only when I know the thing fully can I do a sock," she told him. " It is this that the woman has told me."

" Oh, all right," he said in English. " If you're happy, go on making these absurd cushion covers of yours."

Mallows was fifty. His natural kindliness found little at Mambango to ruffle him, but he was conscious of a feeling of waste which he would not have felt in London or Bombay. At Mambango men toiled while the jungle waited at the plantation's edges. Mallows was conscious of that quiet hostility, and it depressed him to think that that battle would never truly be over. At night the jungle grew while Mambango slept and in the day-time it was slashed down, driven back by the Birmingham blades of the Africans. So he could not feel truly at peace here as in a civilisation, for it would take many people many years with machines to destroy that life which waited to envelop the ordered plantations, the neat bungalows, the rows of African huts and the factory. He admired Tamlin, who had brought order and effort to this place which had beaten other men, yet even now there was that sense of decay in the atmosphere of the place, that quiet lostness which made a fellow thoughtful when he drank alone. Like now, his book forgotten, his whisky in his hand. Shalanga was not anybody. She was a part of this place, a child of the fierce sun and the bloody ceremony from which he had bought her. She did not and could not give him comfort for that strange deserted feeling which he experienced when he thought that he might one day die here. And at Mambango a dead one had to be underground a few hours after death, so that it was like planting a potato. He knew ; he had seen several buried, not here, they were never buried here, but at the mission cemetery fifty miles away.

He sucked in his breath sharply and called for his bath.

CHAPTER SEVEN

THE Committee met on Wednesday evening at the Club.
Mooning had arranged things rather well, thought Mrs.
Tamlin. Thoughtfully he had ordered coffee and cakes for
Mrs. Tamlin, and a bottle of whisky for the men. Mallows
and Plume were not at their ease, she quickly noted, and she
said :

" Major Mallows, I hear you're a great reader."

Mallows coughed and said he was, but added that the
biggest reader at Mambango was Mr. O'Riordan. Mrs. Tamlin
was about to say, " He's a strange man, isn't he ? I'd love to
talk to him," but instead she told Major Mallows that she
was arranging a supply of books from the Y.M.C.A. at Chugi.
" They won't be religious books," she added hastily, and they
all laughed so that she coloured and said, " I don't mean
that. I mean they'll be books all can read. Not that you're
not religious, Major——" she floundered until Mallows said :

" Very good of you, Mrs. Tamlin. No one's ever thought
of doing things like that before."

Mooning coughed, that kind of cough which signals that
it is time for the main business.

" I like this little woman," Plume was thinking. " This is
what Julia would have been like when she'd weathered a bit.
Cool, kind, efficient, with that touch of innocence which no
curious knowledge could blight, and Mrs. Tamlin must have
seen a bit of life in her travels with Tamlin."

They discussed whether it was advisable to have a dance
with only three women on the place.

" Definitely not," said Mallows. " It would be a bear

garden, if you'll pardon me, Mrs. Tamlin. We've got some queer cards here in the way of men and I don't think a dance is a good idea." But Plume suddenly seized the idea. He saw himself holding Amy to the tune of the radiogram, and he said :

" But can't we get some ladies to come from Chugi ? "

" Chugi, my dear chap," Mooning told him in his new voice of authority, " is one hundred and sixteen miles away."

" Sorry," said Plume. He sulked for a time, thinking of Mooning and Amy. " I'll never have her, I know," he told himself morosely. " Never."

There was the question of turkeys and geese. Where could they be found in this god-forsaken country, Major Mallows wanted to know.

" There just aren't any, that's all," Mooning told them. " Some White Fathers about two hundred miles away have got geese, I'm told, but we can write that idea off. But," he told them triumphantly, " I've made one or two little arrangements. I've ordered two whole pigs. Two fat beauties. Monsters." He was pleased with their reception of this news.

" Good show," said Mallows. " How did you do it ? Who the devil breeds pigs in this climate ? "

" There's a German I know living about forty miles from here. Good type, all told. He was in the last war and came out here to manage somebody's land. He breeds pigs, and a few weeks ago I did a bit of business with him and ordered two pigs. There are fourteen Europeans here, counting the doubtfuls, and we can easily get rid of two pigs."

" Trust a German to think of raising pigs in a place like this," the Major said, and Mrs. Tamlin, all smiles, said :

" Why, I think that's awfully clever of you, Mr. Mooning. You saved the day. Oh, just imagine ! Roast pork ! I can get some apples for the sauce, *and* the stuffing too."

" He's fattening them up," added Mooning. He was now very happy. He had told no one of his forethought, and to-morrow the news would be discussed in every bungalow. " Now what about the actual dinner, the actual arrangements ? "

They differed sharply about this, especially when the Major said, " Let's be orderly. Let's start with Christmas Eve. The dinner comes on Christmas Day."

" Quite right," Plume put in with his hostile eyes on Mooning, who agreed rather than spoil the effect of his triumph over the pigs.

" I think Christmas Eve should be a kind of jollification in the Club," Mrs. Tamlin was saying, when Mallows punched a small brown fist into his left palm and said :

" I've got it. Just the thing. What about a *n'goma* by the nigs on Christmas Eve. They'd love it, and we'd enjoy it too."

" What exactly will that mean ? " Mrs. Tamlin wanted to know.

" Dances. Tribal dances," the Major told her. " With drums. Ever seen one ? " He was as eager as a boy. Mrs. Tamlin caught his eagerness and she said, " It sounds a good idea."

Mooning and Plume agreed, Mooning more enthusiastic than Plume, who was, he felt, rather pointless as a member of the Committee after all.

" We'll have to ask your husband, Mrs. Tamlin," said Mooning. " After all, he's the boss." He gave a servile laugh and Mrs. Tamlin told them she was sure he would agree.

As to the Christmas dinner, that would be held the night after the *n'goma*, they all agreed. Tables for six people would be laid, and there would be a table for the Bachelors' Mess.

The Bachelors' Mess had a bad reputation. It held about

six youngish men who kept to themselves and there were stories of orgies and drunken parties being common there.

When the question of drink came up, Mooning awkwardly hinted that they would need " a good quantity," and Mallows interrupted and said :

" We'll need a great deal more than a good quantity. We'll need all we can get." He turned and told Mrs. Tamlin in a soft, persuasive voice, " We may as well face it, Mrs. Tamlin, but Mambango is pretty much of a hole and nearly every man here likes his liquor. And I'm afraid Christmas is going to mean quite a party as far as liquor is concerned."

" But of course," said Mrs. Tamlin. " What would Christmas be at Mambango without plenty to drink." She saw Major Mallows' eyes admiring her, saying, " What a capital little woman," in their blue brightness. She felt an innocent flutter in her throat ; she had forgotten what it was like to be admired by a " man," for a husband was not really a " man."

They cleared up point after point, Plume justifying his presence by some suggestions about liqueurs and wines. Arrogantly, when he saw Mooning's interest, he proved that Mooning knew little or nothing about good wines, and Mrs. Tamlin was impressed with these signs of breeding in Mr. Plume, as she thought of it.

Before they rose Mrs. Tamlin said, " There's one thing I must say. It's about the pigs. Now pigs are terrible animals for worms. The pork will have to be well cooked, really well cooked, or everybody will have worms. We must see to that."

" I think I may say," said Mooning, turning from one to the other, " that I have the best cook in Mambango in my house. Let him do the pork."

They agreed with him. Even though Mrs. Tamlin felt some annoyance with Mooning's claim, she knew that it was a fact. Mooning's cook was famed among the Europeans at Mambango for his skill. He could make meringues, scones, and fruit salads with real cream, as all knew. He was clean, too, compared with the other cooks, some of whom were so bad that their masters feared to visit their kitchens, afraid of what they might see. There was that revolting beast whom Mrs. Pryce had employed and whom she had surprised one day shaping dumplings by squashing them under his armpit before throwing them into the pan. Mrs. Pryce had not eaten for days after that, bewildered by the generous white smile of the cook who had known his offence, and ill with fear for what she had eaten in the past.

"Mine is a horrible cook, but he's the best I can get," Mrs. Tamlin told them. "I envy you yours, Mr. Mooning."

"My wife discovered him, not me," he told her proudly, so proudly that Plume thought, "Amy lies to me. He would not feel this way if he was unhappy with her. She's a liar. A liar." He hastened the breaking up of the party after Mooning told Mrs. Tamlin, "Why even Plume here has asked my wife to let the cook make him some scones, haven't you, Plume?"

Plume sought playfulness in Mooning's face but could find none. The fool suspected nothing. And what is there to suspect, anyway, his bitter thoughts asked him.

Mrs. Tamlin would have liked to ask them to her house for a drink, but she never knew how Tammy would view such an action without his nod of agreement. She felt rebellious for a moment, but agreed that Tammy generally had his reasons, maddening though some of them were at times.

When she said good night to them, she felt sorry for Major Mallows and Mr. Plume going back to their lonely house, no wives to receive them. She wondered who darned their socks and sewed for them. Men managed about these things, she knew, for they were unimportant to a man when single, and when married he demanded these services from his wife as a token of affection. The more she thought about men in general, the stranger she found them. Even Tammy had his little slynesses which she never would have believed were there at one time, saying one thing to her to please her and doing the opposite. Once he had told her a lie, a deliberate lie. He had said that he did not approve of white men having native women, and then she had found out that he had arranged for some of the Europeans here to buy rations for their African mistresses. It was a great shock to her, but she got over the shock in time, yet she wondered if she had not, after all, made an idol of him. Then, as soon as she was in his presence she felt a weakness for him, a weakness which flourished in the aura of his energy and his gentled animalism.

He mixed a drink for her when she got back and she felt guilt for remembering his lie which she had never discussed with him.

CHAPTER EIGHT

" HEAR this," said the stranger in the dark glasses, " hear this all of you," and it was noticeable that men were quiet when he spoke. He told them a story of the willing, stupid bird which worked for the crocodile who told this bird that such work for one as fierce as he brought much honour to a bird, especially to a stupid bird for whom no other beast had found use.

" And hear this," the stranger told them. " One day that bird was cleaning the teeth of this great crocodile with his beak, and the bird coughed. So angry was the crocodile that he closed his jaws with a snap, but the frightened bird had escaped and he sat on a branch in his fear, watching the crocodile.

" ' Come back, O small bird,' cried the crocodile. ' I did not know you were there or I would not have closed my jaws.' This was a lie."

"And hear this. The bird is still sitting on that branch and the crocodile is watching that bird in sorrow, for when other birds come near and the crocodile offers them the work of the teeth cleaning, the bird on the branch cries out, ' Do not go, O fellow bird, for this cruel one tried to eat me while I did the work of the teeth cleaning. So do not go to him,' and this stupid bird has thus become a clever bird and the crocodile weeps for that which is past."

Men listened in fascination as the stranger talked.

" I am that bird," he told them. " And who is the crocodile ? Can a man answer me that riddle ? "

No. Men could not answer. " Then I will tell you," he said.

He was a tall thin man of the warrior's age, with a skin not so black as that of the men who listened now at his feet. He had a grave face which the white-rimmed dark glasses had made shapeless, as would white glasses make the face of a white man. These glasses gave him a blinded look. Ask any man who had read, or any man who had lost his gentleness and his fear along with his tribe. They all knew, these men, that the white man was the enemy of the black man. And yet a man did not feel this thing. " That," said the clever one, " is because you are a fool and cannot read and cannot think. Like an ox you are here at your work and your brain is that of the ox. But the white man has a clever brain, like a spear-blade sharp from the stone. This white man is like the crocodile with the bird. He uses him but would eat him in his anger. And hear this ; I was that bird and now I sit on the branch and I will no longer work for the crocodile."

" And does this crocodile, the white man, call for your work ? " asked Chopa, the clownish one who imitated all he saw and who made all laugh when the sun was hot. He did not smile, but men knew and they laughed aloud to see this clever one remove the black glasses and stare with angry eyes at Chopa.

" The crocodile would like me to work," said the stranger in a thin, buzzing, fierce voice. " But I will not. Never. I will not."

" What tribe are you of, strange one ? " said Chopa. " You mouth our tongue but you are not of us."

" I have no tribe," he shouted, not looking at them now, but looking far off at nothing, like *Bwana* Tamlin calling to the God. " I have no tribe. There *is* no tribe. It is a trick which is over and done. All black men are one tribe, one people, one African people."

" What is African ? " asked Chopa. " What is this thing which you tell us we are ? "

" Africa is a country," cried the stranger, " the biggest country in the world, and it is now in the power of these white men for whom we work."

" For whom *we* work, strange one," shouted Chopa. " You do not work for the crocodile now. You have told us this with your mouth."

Then the stranger was angry. " Fool," he shouted. " For whom *you* work. But I speak of the Africans."

" Then what are these Africans ? "

All men now threw themselves about in laughter, slapped each other, squealed, and made gestures of pain in their laughter.

" This one must go if I must talk," said the stranger quietly. " This one is a fool who has no brain. He is a snake's *Kuma*."

" You who have no tribe can not call me that," said Chopa in anger. He walked towards the stranger, a stick in his hand. " I will beat your skull with this if you mouth these things to me." He showed the strange one the stick. Men were

divided in their minds by the tribal oneness with Chopa and
the spell of the strange one's tongue of which there was much
to be heard.

" Rub your hands in the soil," said Chopa to the strange
one. That was the tribal courage call before fighting, but the
strange one would not make it. He stared like a snake into
Chopa's eyes until Chopa called to the men, " He is afraid.
And now I will sit down and hear smoother words." And
smoother they were from that time on.

" I am trying to tell you about the land and the people,"
said the stranger. " I am trying to tell you that we have all
been as slaves of the white man."

" We were slaves of the Arab man not long ago," cried a
grey-haired man who cooked for those men who sat there
listening to the words. " We were slaves of the Arab men
who killed here and chained here in the time of my youth.
What manner of slave then am I now in the time of age when
my belly is filled and I am in the land of my tribe ? "

" It is a different kind of slavery now," the strange one
told him.

One day these old ones would be dead with their memories
and the young would have no sign of that other time.

He told them of Africa which they could not imagine. He
told them of great seas of water which they could not imagine.
And he told them of many kinds of white men who had come
to the land, and the most powerful of these were the *Angrezi*
for whom they worked in these days in which they lived. No
one could understand what he meant. He cried out to them,
his eyes on a book, telling them that this was the holy book
of the white man which bade them that all men were alike
but which the white men denied.

" This book," he called out, " this book was read to me
for a long time by white men at the Mission. It is a book of
strength and of truth, and the white men lie in their mouths

to us, for if you read this book you will hear the word of the spirit in the sky, and yet white men are cruel and are liars and would spit on us as slaves of another time."

Then the strange one became like one mad with drums and dancing, his eyes wide and staring, and he cried out in tongues which none knew. And when he had done with that, he called out again in their tongue that he had come to save them.

" But you have no tribe," shouted Chopa. " You have told us this word. You have told us you have no tribe. How then can you save us, and from what thing will you save us ? " He began to imitate the strange one's voice and men rolled about again, their eyes closed and their mouths opened with laughter.

" You are not as some," screamed the strange one, and all were silenced by this. " You are not as some who have lost their land to the white men. You have lost nothing because the white man cannot live in your country. Those white men here are sick or are always eating medicine. This is no land to steal. Work for you is not what work is for those who have lost their land. When you are tired of the white man's work you can go home to your land and village. But one day the white man will find a way of making you work always, every day, all your life, for you will have no land."

" And like you we will have no tribe ? " shouted Chopa.

" Yes," hissed the strange one in his snake-voice. " Yes. Like me, you will understand all."

That mystery in those words made all men sit quiet and think. " I will go now," he told them, " but I will come again when you have thought of this thing of the crocodile and the bird. And there is one thing I must tell you. I will work for the crocodile again and I will work here so that I shall be among you and can give you the words which will tell you who you are and where you live, for you do not know these things. And hear this—do not tell of what I have said to you, or of me, to any white man, or to any black man who loves the white man, for if you do, you will hear a stone crack." And all men marvelled that he knew this expression of their tribe which meant death, and when they had marvelled they felt a fear and a wonder that such a one as this strange one could promise a talker death. He left them then and men fought to speak first until Chopa cried " Silence " in the voice of the strange one and while they laughed he began to speak as they had not heard him speak before.

They were sitting in the clean-swept compound in front of their rows of huts, clean-swept like a village in a country where the bridal price was low. Sitting there they could look down the hill to the great burned plains of rank yellow grass studded with the withered thorn trees. On the right, below them, the green plantations began and they could see the dark bungalows of the white men. And between the plantations' nearest boundary and the compound where they sat was the hut of the *Neapara*, that lean hard one, Yussuf, from the Sudan, " The Whipper," as men called him. And now, out of that hut, he came. He walked towards them, frightening, yet of a kind of walk that men admired ; proud, yet of a kind that men would wish to be. This one hated dirt and he would grip a man by the ear and twist that ear if that one had cast dirt in a wrong place.

" Pig," he would say, " pig," and then he would say, " Pick up that dirt and place it on your head, pig," and when that one had done this he would know what next to do. He would walk before the women with his dirt on his head and would bear with their jeering laughter and with his shame.

So now, when this one came walking towards them there was a great scramble of those who must look for dirt, lest this one should be displeased. The setting sun glowed red on him as he came, like shining paint at a ceremony. They sat quiet when he stood before them. He looked quickly at them, one by one, reading each face, and they were afraid lest he smell a lie or a wrong thing, for this one had that terrible knowledge of the things behind a man's face if that man had fear of a wrong thing done. All men sitting there showed innocence in calm wide eyes which were strange to see and which were only seen when this one stood before them.

"Who was that thin one in the white man's suit who went from here before I came?" he said. No one replied. No man ever replied until this one pointed at him. "You," said The Whipper, and he pointed to the old grey one who remembered the time of the Arab men. The Whipper, like white men, believed that an old man told more truth than a young one, and in this he was right, for the old grey one said, "He was a stranger with a mouthful of words."

When The Whipper said, "What words?" Chopa said, "He has come for work. He seeks a task for some money like us all," and they were all glad that the old one was silenced, for to Chopa The Whipper said:

"And what task could that stranger do who wore a white man's suit? Did he think he could wield a steel on the plantation dressed like that? Did he think that?"

"It is not known, that thing," said Chopa. "But he is a clever one and perhaps will write things in a book in an office, for he has learned from white men at the Mission. That is what he said about the Mission, yet he did not say about the book or the office. Those words are mine."

"Be quiet now," said this one to Chopa. "You will break your tongue if you go on in this way. Let another speak. You." He pointed to Sumbu, a quiet man who sat alone always humming to himself like a bee on a flower.

"Me?" said Sumbu.

"Yes. You," this one told him.

"What shall I say? Tell me what I should say?"

" Have you not been hearing what has been said ? Is your brain dead in your skull ? " The Whipper's deep eyes were fixed on Sumbu.

" No. I have heard all. I saw only his suit." He then told The Whipper every detail of the stranger's suit, remembering things which other men had not seen, a tear here, a patch there, the colour of an odd button, the colour of the cloth and the price of that cloth as he had discovered it when last he had been to the Indian's store. All this, and the manner in which the stranger moved his hands, when talking, he described. The Whipper nodded, carried away like other men by the talk of Sumbu. When Sumbu stopped talking, this one said to him, " And did you not hear his words ? "

" Could a man hear words when he has studied so much of a man's clothes and hands ? " This Sumbu was either cunning, like a crow, or stupid like a pig.

" Enough," said the *Neapara*. " The talk is finished." He left them, going to pray as he did each evening at sunset, washing himself, and crying out like an animal, alone, for no man here had a God like his. He had once told them of this God and had sung a prayer to them and was sorry for that, for when he had done he glared at them and cried :

" Pigs. How would you know what that means in your darkness? And yet Mohammed had hopes of you all. You are black, like me, but you are lost in a darkness from which no man can drag you."

Men talked about this one's God. Was it the same as that of the white men ? No. For at sundown white men did not pray as The Whipper prayed. They rushed like antelopes to the verandas and opened bottles and poured from them into glasses and drank like beasts at a river which might soon dry up. Some drank on into the night until senseless and were dragged from their chairs to their beds by those fortunate ones who worked in their houses.

When The Whipper was gone to his prayer, Chopa said :
" There is some trouble in this thing for men like us. This
one knows in his clever way that this stranger has words
which disturb men in their minds. So let us forget him. Let
us be silent."

" That is a wise thing to say," shouted the old grey one,
and he got up and went away. One by one all got up and went
away, for it was a trouble to be together now.

They could hear The Whipper crying to his God in that
thin voice like a sad woman who tells. They went into their
huts and shut out this voice and all thought of the stranger
and what he had said.

CHAPTER NINE

O'RIORDAN lay on his face in his dark room. It was
nearly midnight. His hands were pressed under him
against his stomach and he moaned when the pain became
unbearable. He tried not to move and the sweat poured from
him on to the soaking sheet.

" Holy mother of Jesus," he whimpered. It was like a
crab inside his belly. It seemed to sidle and he would hold
his breath, and then would pant as the two hot pincers closed
and flooded his body with glaring electric pain, the pincers
shuddering in an agony which seemed to shake his mind,
making him afraid he would begin screaming aloud in his
pain and in the terror of its remorseless struggle in his body
in this dark lonely room.

It had been going on for ten minutes. It must soon stop.
It usually lasted about ten minutes. It must stop soon or he
would die, or cry out until people came running and found

him. It stopped and he collapsed inside his body and mind, drawing long gasping breaths of gratitude and exhaustion, his mind partly unhinged. He lay there panting for another ten minutes, and when he began to think he wondered why he had not prayed. He had vowed he would when the pain came again, but he had forgotten. He had not prayed since his last visit to St. Colman's Cathedral with his mother twenty-three years ago. There had been no reason, no pain, no fear, until one night some months ago, these claws had clenched in his belly, bringing him to his knees in agony and then on to his face. After the pain came the fear. What was it? He half knew but evaded it. It was low down, below his navel. He had two medical encyclopædiae on his bookshelves. Tempted to study them, he burnt them in the stove of his kitchen, the cook wondering what was this thing of burning these books in his stove.

He did not want to find out what this tearing pain was. He never knew when it would come. When it did it was usually night. After the second attack he starved himself, but the pain, when it came, seemed to be fiercer. He drank more whisky and one night when it came on in waves of fire through his whole body, he was drunk and the pain had to cut through a deep fog before it brought him quivering on to his face. He began to drink heavily, something which he had not done since the end of the war. He kept his fear to himself but he became apprehensive in the evenings, his green eyes sharp and nervous, waiting for the sudden onslaught which might come at any moment.

Now he dragged himself on to his side in the dark and he saw a figure beside him.

" It is I, *Bwana*," this figure told him. " It is I, Yamanga." O'Riordan could not speak. He waved his hand, lying there on his side, dragging air into his throat which seemed to have atrophied.

" You have pain, *Bwana*," said Yamanga softly. He could see O'Riordan's eyes shining in the darkness, rolling in their sockets. He had not seen his master with this beaten expression in the seven years he had served him. He had watched O'Riordan in this agony after hearing him crying out for Jesus in a voice of pain. He knew Jesus from the Mission of long ago, but white men like O'Riordan, when they called aloud on Jesus, were in anger or pain.

" Whisky," whispered O'Riordan. He tried to say it again and could not, but he saw that Yamanga had understood and he felt a great affection for the small quiet African who now appeared so full of understanding and gentleness. He drank the whisky neat and then lay on his back.

" Cigarettes," he said. " Light."

In the white glare of the Petromax he lit a cigarette, comforted by the thick blue haze of smoke he blew into the bright streaming light.

" What is it, *Bwana*? This pain." Yamanga was kneeling by the bed, his eyes huge and soft with fear for this master to whom he had grown attached, who was kind to him and not like some others he had known. There were only two others as kind as this master at Mambango, men said, and they were *Bwana* Major Mallows and *Bwana* Plume.

O'Riordan began to remember the world he had inhabited before the claws closed in him. He had been lying, not drunk, but with his mind accelerating from nearly a dozen whiskies. He had been thinking of the fall of the Alcazar of which he had heard through his radio, and from the disappointment of that news his mind had been going back and forth between *Mein Kampf*, which he was reading, and the argument he had had at the Bachelors' Mess with Glebb about the abdication of King Edward, or as Glebb called him, " Teddy." They would argue for years at Mambango about that, as they had argued constantly since it had happened. He had been in a

bar at Chugi in 1936 when the news had come through. One
of the women, a lean, tired greyhound with huge mascaraed
eyes, had burst into tears, saying :

" So he's gone. Driven out by a pack of Bishops. Driven
out."

It meant more in Africa than it did in London, O'Riordan
knew. It increased the sense of their exile in that bar away
from it all, with the yellow heat pouring ·down on to the
plains outside. He was thinking of that crying woman when
the pain had come.

He heard himself talking to Yamanga, telling him it was
only malaria, and he knew that Yamanga knew he was lying
to him.

" It is a pain, *Bwana*. It is not like a malaria pain in the
bones. It is a different pain."

" No. It is a pain that comes from the drink." He shook
his whisky glass, and he could see Yamanga trying to believe
him.

" Shall I call the *Bwana* Major ? " he asked, for the *Bwana*
Major Mallows was the master's special friend. All evening
they would talk excitedly sometimes like women in a market-
place, waving books and crying out in the English words,
" No. No, no, no," to each other, their drinks forgotten.

" No. All is well," O'Riordan told him. He could now
hear his voice, and strange it sounded after the daze of pain
and the beaten feeling in the body after it.

" You must see the doctor at Chugi, *Bwana*," said Yamanga.
Gloomily, O'Riordan agreed. He had put it off again and
again, but now he must see a doctor. He feared he was beyond
an operation, for that was what they would recommend, but
no knife could remove such a pain. He saw death, death in
pain. He had the Irish worship of death in him, but not his
own which could not have grandeur, but only a terror and
an agony and in the end a hole in the hungry African soil.

He tried to think it was not necessary to see the doctor. How could a doctor stuck away in the bush and jungle know what these claws inside him were made of? But he *would* know. He knew himself. Cells gone mad and straining to eat their way out of their prison into his blood, into his whole frightened organism. It *was* that, he was sure. In terror his mind ran away from the thought. He sat up and poured another drink.

" You can sleep now, Yamanga. Good that you came to me as you did. Good." Yamanga said good night and went reluctantly to his hut outside O'Riordan's window.

When he was alone, O'Riordan stared at his smouldering cigarette, his body thankful for its release, but his mind already forgetting the pain it had known. He began to think about the Spanish War. He had bet Mallows that war was coming, world war. He had worked it all out, but Mallows would not have it. Hitler did not want war. He could get all he wanted without it. " He wants Europe," O'Riordan had said, " and he won't get it without war. You'll see."

He wished Mallows could be here now so that he could forget the fear which had become his companion in these last weeks. Often the fear was so great that he feared he would run about desperately, or shout about it, especially when in the Club he saw them all, free of fear and pain, confident and sure of their plans and their life. He was no longer sure. He lived in fear of death which he had thought he did not fear. There was a fear which made a man want to grovel and call out to God, not for forgiveness, but for more time without pain and fear.

" Out of the depths we cry to Thee, O Lord, Lord hear our prayer." He tried to remember it but it would not come. Black curtains and the gold splashes of candlelight on the dark polished coffin of Da, the father of the family which always quarrelled, and which quarrelled even when he lay there in that other room, dead, his waxen face among the flowers which hid the great bruise where the tram had struck him in his drunken wandering.

The death he feared would pull him through seas of burning pain until it finished with him and crushed him down like a rag. He began to walk up and down the room, then he switched the radio on, switching the dial for music. Voices shouting hate and lies and denials of half truths, the radio world of that other truth and that other lie which was not truth and not a lie and yet had become everything to the world.

" We will show the world," a German voice was shouting, " what Germany is made of. We will——" Switch. Then, " An official spokesman denied this morning——" and then the screaming voice of hate and the bands, throats of crying brass for the blood and the mystic soil of some sacred land, some holy flag. " Ah, bugger you all," O'Riordan shouted into the radio. " Bugger all of you." He switched off. He had forgotten his pain and his fear in his excitement, in his hatred of Hitler and the gang who were about to fall on Europe and destroy it, but this emotion passed and he found himself thinking about the doctor. He had not seen a doctor for years. He disliked consulting doctors, as much as he disliked asking for advice. He looked after his own malaria, and, though Plasmoquin and things with names like that were creeping as far as Mambango, he, like most others here, still used quinine. Since the swift death of Jackson some years ago of black-water, he had always drunk a glass of bicarbonate of soda in solution with his quinine, for it was said that all Colonial officials were advised to do this in order to prevent black-water. He, like the others here, had strong views and firm theories about malaria. His teeth were discoloured by quinine and he had grown slightly deaf from it, but not enough to discourage the conversation which was meat and drink to him.

Ought he to see this bloody doctor or not ? He could not

make up his mind and he knew why. He was afraid of his
fears being confirmed. He remembered an aunt in Queens-
town (Cobh if they insisted) who had died, gnawed into a
crying wreck. Was it the same thing which lived inside *him*?
He shivered and switched on the radio again. He wanted to
pace up and down but he was tired. He lay back in an armchair and fell asleep, stilled, fallen deep into a dark chasm of
fearless dream.

At dawn, Yamanga made his way across the ridge to Major
Mallows' bungalow. The Major was doing his breathing
exercises on the veranda after having sat silent and still, watching the dawn and drinking in the cool, quiet silence of those
moments before Africa was revealed, grey and shabby, and
dwarfing him with its size before the sun rose on it in a whirl-
pool of garish fire. He did what the Swami at Benares had
taught him, his diaphragm pumping the clean, sharp air which
soon would be warm and impregnated with wood smoke and
the smell of scorched grass. He longed for an Indian dawn
again, the dawn that flamed on a land crushed by history,
where every stone had seen valour, or cowardice, or cruelty
or a god walking. Not the dawn which raced across a savage
land which had sat silent and sick on the edge of history since
time began. From the great Sud south of Egypt to the Cape
was the Africa which had defied men until only a handful of
years ago. He saw the sun rise on its poverty, its scrub, its
scrawny soil, but there was a something here which India
could not give him. It was true that Africa had claws and
she dug them into you, and you could go far from her, but
you would come back. The nigs said that to him often, and
he knew it was true.

Yamanga sat waiting until the Major lit a cigarette and put
on his pyjama jacket.

"Well, Yamanga?" he said. "Come to borrow the iron
this time, or a new fork?"

" No, *Bwana*," he said. " But my *Bwana* is sick and this time it is not fever."

" Does he know you have come to tell me this ? "

" No, *Bwana*. I came on my own, for he wishes to keep his sickness secret."

" What's this sickness ? "

" It is a pain," said Yamanga hoarsely as though he felt the pain himself. " A pain that is like a knife for he cried out in this pain and I came and watched him and he did not see me. He held his stomach like this, lying down, and whining like a shot animal."

" Ulcer, by Christ," the Major thought, something he feared himself. " Must cut down this drinking—after Christmas though."

" He must see a doctor with this pain, *Bwana*."

" Yes. I will speak to him and will not let him know how I know this thing. Go back now and give him his tea."

" He is asleep in a chair. He has been up all night." Yamanga had some tears in his eyes, and, seeing these, Mallows turned away. Jesus, when would anyone ever know the Africans, who could laugh at another's pain but who could cry for a man who was good to them ?

" Now clear off, Yamanga," he said in English. " Go and give the *Bwana* a bloody good cup of tea."

He sat down when Yamanga had gone and thought of an ulcer. When he was afraid he got up and called for breakfast. There were burned tinned sausages, tinned fat bacon and sour bread, but before this there was the one good thing that Mambango could offer; fresh papaya, its smooth yellow-orange flesh bedewed with cool juice. He sprinkled it with lemon and scooped up the fruit in his silver spoon. As he ate it he thought " Pepsin. Papaya is full of pepsin, which is good for the stomach and good for an ulcer—if a chap *has* one—and yet if you put a piece of meat between the two halves of a papaya, the meat would be digested by the fruit. That was what everybody said, but, like the bloody rope trick of India, no one had seen it done yet. Must try it some time."

He ate all the food brought to the table. Plume was still asleep. Torpid chap, Plumey. He slept like a dead man, and after a booze up he slept on the next day until midday. Not fit, stale and torpid.

" Thank God for a bloody good appetite and a sound constitution," said Major Mallows aloud.

When he was dressed he walked across to O'Riordan's hut.

CHAPTER TEN

IN the mess where the " off-white " bachelors lived, De Gaugin told the story of the attack on him, and they discussed the punishment which the guilty African had received. Because these men did not receive the same respect from the Africans as that given to Englishmen, they were more afraid of the Africans and therefore more aggressive. The Africans knew that Englishmen did not mix with these near-white men much, and they knew too that Englishmen made jokes about them, or in other ways showed a sort of contempt for them. They drew lower pay than Englishmen, worked harder, and, it was noticed, lived poorer lives than the Englishmen.

The "off-whites" knew the Africans saw all this and though they accepted it, for that they had to do, they showed their resentment by a concerted antagonism to the Africans under them. The Africans worked hard for them, for behind these masters stood the Englishmen who backed them up, though it was said that many hard words were spoken by the English overseers to these men when they had, through fear of losing respect, done stupid or cruel things to the Africans.

" It is not enough to beat them and cut their pay," cried a poor South African Dutchman who in his heart despised these half-castes from Reunion, from Madagascar and Mauritius. He was a huge uneducated, half-savage and innocent man named Bakkar. He had thin yellow hair and dark, coarse skin. He was a man of great physical strength and he was so poor that he lived on the same diet as the African labourers ; maize-meal porridge and tea, though he was able to afford cigarettes. He was from one of those South African Dutch families who, hungry for another wilderness, had trekked north out of the bush from which the British had driven them in the Boer War. He hated Englishmen and suspected that only Irishmen understood why the Boers hated the English who were cruel because after the cruelty came progress. But the Dutch did not want progress, his mother had taught him ; they wanted their wilderness and their privacy.

Now, like many of his kind, Bakkar hired himself out to manage ox-teams, for none in Africa could excel the Dutch in the management of oxen. For two years he had been in charge of the ox-herds at Mambango. These oxen, when he had trained them, did work which the tractors could not do. He did not earn much money but he had now had the first real freedom he had ever known. He had his own small shack to live in, with a table and a chair, and, being a South African Dutchman, a well-oiled, perfectly kept rifle. He did not, like the others in the mess in which he argued, keep an African woman. He hated and despised Africans, and much as he longed for a wife, he never gave in to the black temptation. He hoped one day to marry the daughter of a poverty-stricken Dutch family called Van Rennen, who farmed a piece of cruel land near Chugi.

" In South Africa we would shoot them if they attacked a white man, but under the English the Kaffir is ruined and he stands on his hind legs and gives cheek. Christ, man, I'd kill him with my bare 'ands ! " Bakkar fascinated them all in his huge muscular anger. When he got drunk on rum they liked to hear him sing " Suikerbossie " and " Sarie Marais," and they could see the hard, cold pride of his peculiar nation, the greatest shots and the hardest masters in Africa, shining in his eyes.

All agreed with him, even those who did not agree. De Gaugin flexed his wrists as he imagined himself punching Africans into unconsciousness as they attacked him in crowds. In this fantasy he was driven against a wall and the mob could not down him. He lived each blow he struck until all lay unconscious around him. He looked at Bakkar towering above him and he knew that he could not beat him in a fight, but he would not admit it. He had a sudden dream of how, finally, after being mauled by Bakkar, he got through by superior boxing skill, and with a left hook to the body bent the gasping giant towards him. Then he swung on the balls of his small feet and brought his right fist up—— The Dutchman would sway, unconscious, and then fall like a tree at his feet, and then, remembering where he was, he stared up at Bakkar and knew that the dream could never become flesh and truth.

" There's going to be trouble in this country," De Gaugin said, interrupting the Dutchman. The others voiced their agreement. Of course there was going to be trouble. The blacks were beginning to get out of hand. Teaching them the Christian religion was part of the trouble, but here Bakkar had something to say which would not wait.

" The Christian religion is for us. It is a white man's religion and cannot be understood by blacks. They pick on the worst parts of it and use them to argue with us. But there

are some parts of it which are meant for blacks and they
should be taught those parts only. To hew wood and to bring
water is the true work of the blacks. My father told me that,
and the longer I live 'ere among them, man, the more I
know 'e is right."

De Gaugin did not like the way in which the Dutchman
had said that; he spoke as if none of those present really
understood the situation. It was not what he said, but the way
in which he said it, and De Gaugin was irritated. He took
pride in his reading and in his brain, which he felt was meant
for great things if only he could escape from this company
into which his origin and his name had thrust him. He looked
at this illiterate giant and said :

" Can you read, Bakkar ? "

The small grey eyes of the Dutchman moved slowly round
until they met the bright dark eyes of this little dago who had
found this tenderest spot of all.

" Read, man ? Christ, what do you mean ? "

There was a tense silence among the five men who sat,
stood, or leaned under the Petromax lamp hanging from a
beam in the roof.

" I mean read. Can you read, that's all ? " De Gaugin had
removed all hint, all nuance from his voice. He could hear its
innocent, good-natured tone after he had spoken. Two others,
small, lean Madagascan-French, who resented this Dutchman's
size, took courage from De Gaugin but could not conceal
their venom.

" Aye. Can you read ? Have you read the Bible ? " one
asked meaningly, and the other added, " Christ, he is only
asking you a simple question."

Bakkar looked at them all silently and they could hear his
heavy breathing. His big red fists were clenched.

" I got to go now," he said. " Christ, man, but it's late,"
and he nodded to them and left, his drink unfinished.

De Gaugin's vanity would not allow him to speak after this victory. He sat with his eyes half closed, smiling and nodding his sleek dark head as though he had known this would happen. The others gave him their praise, telling him they had seen nothing like it for years, that that would shut that Dutch bull up for a long time, and that who would have thought of such a question but De Gaugin.

The delight in the discomfiture of Bakkar lasted for a long time, until De Gaugin had used up all their praise. Then he said :

" But what we was saying's true. We have to watch out on the plantations now. I think there is some trouble among these niggers. I don't know what it is but someone is getting at them. If another one goes for me, I kill him. I kill him stone dead, job or no job."

They agreed in unctuous chorus with this, fired by the difficulty of their position, poised between black and white. Unlike the Indian, who was willing to endure all for the sake of making money in peace and slowly gaining the real power, these men would not fall back into the place of menials, and yet they did not know how they could advance and stand beside the Englishman who stood above all, cool, arrogant, unafraid, confident and clever, and cruel when it was necessary, with kindly words and a new law.

" Just fancy that big bugger not knowing how to read," said one, a small, hard-working man with shifty eyes.

" Yes," said De Gaugin. " That is why the British beat them in the Boer War. They were only a stage above the Africans, those Dutchmen who lived in the bush. They lived by the Bible and they are narrow men. My brother lived among them for a time and preferred the poverty in Madagascar."

" Have you heard about the Irishman, O'Riordan ? " said Morcery, one of the foremen in the factory.

" No, what's up ? " They could smell gossip of which all at Mambango were in constant need.

" This morning he was in great pain with his stomach. I got that from one of my niggers who is a relative of O'Riordan's servant and do you know that his servant was in tears when he told his relative about it ? "

" Lies," said De Gaugin. " Who can imagine one of these savages weeping about a white man's pain ? But this pain, what is it ? "

" It is appendicitis, that's what it is." Morcery described the whole process of appendicitis with all the legends attached. The others, in morbid silence, listened, imagining it all.

" Have you seen Mrs. Mooning lately ? " asked another. He bared his teeth and rolled his eyes. " Ah, God, what I could not do to that woman if I had the chance. Have you seen her walk ? " He got up and imitated her walk, swaying as he crossed the room, almost a woman in his urgency to show them what drew him to her. They watched in silence, thinking of what it meant, of what this woman could do for them, their eyes fiercer with the new subject which always came up whenever there were men without women of their own kind.

" He has it once a week only," said Morcery. " I got that from a man who knows her cook. The cook told him as a secret but I got it out of him. I could not believe it. Mooning, the all-powerful over us, who must beg for his portion. Is it possible that a man in possession of such a beautiful package of woman must be starved in this way ? "

" She has other thoughts."

" She is not pleased with him. She is anxious."

" She is a bitch who could do a man in with that body and that face."

" She is something none of us will ever have. We must

be content with a local whore and with all the risks thereof."
They laughed loudly.

The air was charged with their longing and their awakened
lusts. Another bottle of rum was produced and De Gaugin
began to tell them about a woman he had known in Antana-
narivo when he was training to box a sergeant of the French
Army. The choice was between this lovely woman who would
fell him in his strength, or fitness and victory in the ring. He
won both, but only because he knew himself. It was like
this——

CHAPTER ELEVEN

YUSSUF, the *Neapara*, sat with his child on his knee. It
was a small fat son with cropped hair and firm healthy
cheeks. Yussuf had already spoken to the Regimental Sergeant
Major of the 8th Frontier Rifles about him. He could join
as a drummer in about ten years' time and could travel on to
sergeant-major, not like his father, who had ruined his life
over a carelessness and never got beyond the rank of sergeant.
From that day of the terrible punishment read out in the
Orderly Room when he was broken down to a private again
he had sworn never to trust another, for it was through
trusting another that he had been flung down from his place
near the shining crown of rank upon which he had almost
had his hands. Flung down among those whom he had
mastered and taught, and it took him years to climb back
again, but never beyond the rank of sergeant. His pride never
recovered, for all men knew of it, and in the black steel box of
the battalion records which he had so often loaded on to the
baggage camels had always lain the record of his failure. Now,
retired these seven years, he hunted slackness and dirt. He

would stand over a man until the task was completed. Suspicion was in his eye, for he had learned men, and had tasted failure's long drink because of an hour's slackness when he had trusted another.

His father was a savage who had embraced Islam during service with the Madhi against the Egyptian " Turks " and the English in the Sudan. His father had perished among the piles of dead who broke like waves on the British fire at Omdurman. Years later he joined the ranks of the men who had slain his father and he found them good masters for the soldier.

He fought in German Africa with the 8th Frontier Rifles and had killed many men.

When his time came to leave the Army his company commander had got him the job at Mambango. He had much power, being the highest of all black men, for between him and the masses of labourers there was nothing, only a gulf which he knew could never be closed. When he saw these men in their savagery he saw what he had been and he saw his saviour as a mixture of Prophet and British officer. He had adopted as many European ways as he could afford. He took quinine, smoked a pipe, read simple English, pasted pictures cut from magazines on the walls of his hut, for when could a man afford a frame ? Over the doorway of his hut was a large picture of the King in Army uniform. Each day he saluted this before beginning the day's work. He had fought for this King whom he had never seen, who was abstract, like God, and with all the power of God because of that aloofness and of the knowledge that he existed despite that aloofness.

The King was good. But what of these white men ? They were not all good. Some were good, but many were poor stuff and he looked beyond these to the King in order to forget those thoughts. The first time he was cheated by a white man was six months after leaving the Army. This white man had employed him while he awaited news of his application for work at Mambango. This white man had gone back on his word after agreeing to pay him a certain wage, and at the end of the third month, when called to Mambango, he had counted the total and yet it was not that which the white man put into his hand. Never before had that happened to him.

The white man said, " You are mistaken. I said this, not that." Yussuf examined the man's face and it was not a good face, so he agreed and said, " As you have said then let it be," and had given him a certain look which made the white man say again that he, Yussuf, had made the mistake. That was a new kind of white man not seen before in the land.

And here at Mambango there were some white men who had no strength in them, but who were like women and had no gift but that of being able to tell a man to cut this tree or bring that sack here. The world was changing fast and with it black men, and white men. There was a young white man in the mess of the unmarried who had one day cursed him because he had not understood a difficult instruction quickly enough. He had smiled and taken his reproof, but seeing the smile the young white man shouted at him, " Don't you laugh when I talk to you, you bloody savage. You're not in the Army now. You're working for your living. Don't forget that." He had not forgotten.

He put the two-year-old son down and watched him play with a heap of clean stones which the women had washed for him. Yussuf made them wash everything and he knew they thought him mad.

He saw the man whom he awaited now approaching. He was an old man in rags. They greeted each other in the local tongue and the old man sat down.

" It is the one I thought it was," he told Yussuf, who grinned and clicked his fingers. " But," added the old man,

" he is mad and we have nothing against him. The *Bwana* Inspector of Police, when he got your message, said it might be one Chombo who is telling men in this country that they must attack the white men. But this one is only known as one of the madmen who cry out about God and evil and have caused tears in many villages. This one has done nothing yet to anger the police."

" How is it known that this one who has come here in the black glasses has not come to make evil here ? Why does he put on these black glasses ? To hide his face ? And why should he hide his face ? It is because he does not want men to know him."

The old man had hunted murderers, sellers of bhang and the killing liquor of the Navambo, and had learned much of the fierceness and terror which was part of the growing detribalised mass spreading like a rash on the country. Knowing what he knew, he pitied this soldier who thought that a harmless madman wore black glasses in order to hide his face. He knew these soldiers. They were simple men who lived in a world of their own.

" No," he said, " this one is a hunter of the White Man's God. The *Bwana* Inspector will be happy you have told us of him for he is interested in the talk of these men, but he does not fear them."

Yussuf was disappointed and unconvinced. He knew these policemen. They thought they knew all that was in the world. A platoon of soldiers would tear these troublemaking men from the soil of the country and men could live their lives again without their brains being scalded with words and thoughts of hunger and money for all.

" I cannot believe this thing. One who wears a white man's suit and black glasses and walks slowly and proudly as though he were a chief's son is a man to be watched by the Government's eye. Old one, do you not think this ? "

" I do not think. I do what I am told," said the old man. " I am not given money to think but to obey."

Yussuf could understand that and he said, " It is enough then. I will watch this one with the black glasses and if I find he has words to mouth about money and rage and the justice of work, then I will seize him in these hands."

" That is the right thing," said the old man. He rose and spat into the sun for luck and bade Yussuf good-bye. He walked away like a poor old man on the way to his village.

" I will go and see *Bwana* Tamlin about this thing," thought Yussuf. " He will listen to what I must say of this thing. He is a man who has done things."

When he reached the door of Tamlin's office the sun was blazing like a torch, throwing pools of cool shadows from the trees on to the soil which was baked to a dead grey where the ploughs had not torn it. The crows were tapping back and forth across the tin roof of the office building. Sometimes Tamlin rushed out, red with temper, and fired at them with an old shotgun. They bounced into the air and wavered there patiently until he had gone back inside. Then they dropped back on to the roof and began tapping and scratching their way across the tin again.

" They drive me mad," Tamlin would shout to anyone who would listen.

Yussuf looked through the window and saw that *Bwana* Major Mallows and *Bwana* Plume were sitting with *Bwana* Tamlin and *Bwana* O'Riordan. Why did this *Bwana* Plume not use his military rank when men knew he had been an officer for years ? He sat down in the shade and watched the flashing machetes of a line of labourers as they cut a crop nearly a mile away. His eyes were still keen and he could spot those who rested too much when their machetes ceased to flash. It made him restless. He hated idle men.

Tamlin had been concerned to hear O'Riordan's description

of his pain, so concerned that O'Riordan felt afraid again, and when Tamlin frowned and said, " That sounds serious to me, O'Riordan. You'd better get looked over quickly," he shivered, sensing a conspiracy of pity and apprehension for him among his friends. Tamlin was a serious man and his gravity as he looked into the green eyes of the sick man was too much for O'Riordan, who said, " I'm not dying, you know, Tamlin," and he tried to believe it.

" Well, go to the doctor. The Major can take you into Chugi in a lorry and take all the time you need. And don't back out, will you, when you get there ? " He smiled, his hard face youthful for a second or two. " Well, you can both go off as soon as you like. It's only ten days to Christmas, remember."

They went back to their bungalows to pack suitcases and on the way up the hill Mallows said, " Cheer up, old boy. You mustn't worry." He missed the brightness and edge of O'Riordan's conversation. He could feel the other's fear and worry. " I *am* worried," O'Riordan replied. " As soon as I know the worst, I'll take it all right. It's this waiting and wondering what you've got chewing your inside up." They both thought of what they feared the thing to be but neither mentioned it, and Mallows thought, " If I got it I'd do myself in." O'Riordan was seeing the pale voracious crab again which sidled about inside him and which might close those terrible pincers again at any moment. They walked on in silence, O'Riordan trying to think that after all his pain and its terror, could it not be indigestion ?

" So it's you," said Tamlin as Yussuf came to attention and gave the exaggerated salute which always nettled Tamlin, though he could not think why. There was something about Yussuf which annoyed him and he could not name it, and yet he prized him and knew he could trust him. There was a shrewdness in Yussuf which sometimes appeared like cunning, as when Yussuf put out feelers on one subject while planning to approach another.

He listened to the sharp voice telling him of this strange one who had come, of his suspicions, of everything save the fact that he had sent in a message to the police post, for no one at Mambango knew that Yussuf was a police agent when needed, for if there was one thing the police could be certain about, it was the loyalty of ex-non-commissioned officers.

" So what, then ? " said Tamlin sceptically. " What has this strange one done that you must come to me about it ? " Irritated, he played Yussuf's suspicions down. Interested, he waited for further news.

" This one is one of those who go preaching about God in the village."

" And what's wrong with that ? " asked Tamlin sharply.

" You preach on Sundays, *Bwana*," said Yussuf solemnly, still at attention, " but this one is a black man. Why should he go round preaching of God ? "

" He can do what he likes so long as he does not interfere in things that are not his concern."

" Yes, *Bwana*," said Yussuf, accepting the fact that the *Bwana* was not going to be convinced. From now on only yes and eyes front.

" So leave it at that."

" Yes, *Bwana*."

" You can keep your eye on him."

" Yes, *Bwana*."

" How are your children ? "

" They are happy, *Bwana*."

" Good."

" Yes, *Bwana*."

" Good-bye."

" Good-bye, *Bwana*."

Yussuf saluted again, turned curtly on the heel and toe of

his sandals and stalked out, saying to himself, " God who knows all will understand what I have tried to do, even though the *Bwana* will not listen." He had the long-service n.c.o.'s distrust and suspicion of men with " ideas," and he knew in his bones that this strange one was such a man. Yes, he would wait, by God. Most white men whom he had known all his official life had been like Tamlin, unwilling to believe a story of intrigue, though interested, until it was almost too late, and yet he knew that when he had found a white man who was suspicious, who was' ready to hear of intrigue and of certain feeling in certain men, these kind of white men had made everybody unhappy until the unity and happiness of men was destroyed. Despite this he was certain that this man in the black glasses would cause a trouble at Mambango and *Bwana* Tamlin would see that black men were not like white men.

Yussuf, because of his long Army experience, had the habit of service deeply ingrained. He did not question the reason for his part in the panorama; his small part. He had not discovered that he was unhappy and only a cog, as would his sons. He had not heard a radio broadcast in his own language telling him of canals, dams, cheaper clothes, better medicine, and the pursuit of happiness, or the way of hate. To be detribalised in that special Army way was not the detribalisation of the rusty tin-roofed shacks, the twopenny whore and the loneliness of bitter dirty men and snarling women. He had seen these growing camps of the detribalised on the edges of the city, the city in which white men could forget that they were surrounded by the great breaking African tribes. He had seen these men shouting back at African policemen who seemed to lose their voices if they were alone, and who went quietly away. And he had heard men preaching to them, some of God and the paradise to come which was better than this place in which they heard him, and others of things that were not quite clear, but which gave the listener a thrill of fear and anger, for these spoke of their rage to undo what had been done by white men.

Everywhere the tribe was breaking up and the chiefs were arguing with young men who said " that is an old custom and we will not do it." A woman was a different thing for these young men. For them an old man was an idiot, and to be able to read a book was a sign of the coming world.

Like all his kind who had learned not to question the way, Yussuf had closed his mind. His loyalty to what white men did and said was sufficient for his guiding light and as yet no one had laughed at him for this. He had seen a new kind of white man coming into the land, only a few, but they had surprised him with their values which were like equipment for a struggle and not quiet habits for a time that was gone. Used only to white men who ploughed a quiet furrow gradually, Yussuf was not ready for the fever which was coming upon his world, and it did not hurt him to see de-graded groups of his race who had fallen below even their tribal status, who had been knocked out before they had begun ; and who were a bitter threat to comfort, a brake on progress, and who would smash the lazy machine which the white men had only begun to build. He did not know this, but he felt disturbed by something. It was like the strange worry he had felt before a mutiny which he did not know was coming, and yet which was like an oppression in the air of the camp. It was not here at Mambango. It was not there at Chugi. But it was in many men's faces, men who did not yet know what they felt ; who did not know of the dying world order which was imperceptibly deserting them after infecting them with its disease, like a kind well-meaning doctor with blunt instruments.

CHAPTER TWELVE

FOUR days after O'Riordan's departure with Mallows there was a strike. Nearly two thousand labourers put down their machetes and, looking puzzled but interested, waited to see what would happen. The shock to the Europeans was intense and the atmosphere of the plantations, the Club, the offices, was wound up tightly and swiftly like a guitar string. The great heat did not help and irritation was like electricity under light but nervous control. They struck at midday, but the Africans who worked in the factory stayed at their work.

Burkington-Jones, one of the younger members of the Bachelors' Mess, brought the news to the office where Tamlin was holding a production conference with Pryce and Mooning.

Burkington-Jones had been in Africa a year. He was twenty-three and had been intended for "The Church," but had given up his studies at twenty-two and had begun to quarrel with his father, a God-fearing man with plenty of money, who was used to obedience, for he lived in the country, where the local people had not been ruined by the profit motive. He hated the city and the town. He had a mystical love of the soil and of toil, honest toil by honest men, as he would put it, who have not sold their souls for gain.

It took a year of his son's argumentative company to convince the old man that Africa was the place for a time where his son could " rough it " and later, when a suitable piece of land was bought for him, he could " make good in the colonies."

Burkington-Jones discovered that Africa was a place of

freedom, a great continent which beckoned a man to enter-
prise from every side. A colonel, an old friend of his father's,
resident in Chugi, put him up for a while and then got him
a post as labour overseer on one of the Mambango plantations.
The pay was not bad, but the power, the position, and the
company were good. To sow wild oats from the Bachelors'
Mess in Mambango in the company of Glebb, Happer and an
ex-policeman called Clemmison, was like living a book about
Africa. Plenty of shooting, lion, too, a few miles over the ridge,
and jaunts into the nearest town when drinking at the Club
palled.

This morning he jumped off the lorry when it stopped at
the corner of his plantation and shouted "Cheerio" to
Chessing and Glebb, who worked farther afield, and then he
called for the head labourer in the snarling voice which, he
had learned, made Africans come running. But nobody
appeared and that was very strange. He called again, his
voice louder, his snarl sharper, and the heat poured down
on the bright green jungle near which he stood and on the
yellowing waving sea of the plantation. He grew angry at
once and the sweat came faster from his skin as he began to
stride along the overgrown lane towards the labourers' huts,
forgetting his fear of snakes in his temper.

"Hey, you bloody bastards," he yelled in English, "where
are you?" The compound near the huts was empty. It was
as though every African, man, wife, and child, had vanished.
Then he heard the half-whispered sounds of men talking in
low voices, and with fury he understood that they were all
in their huts. Used to instant obedience from people for
whom he felt a kindly contempt and about whom he had
learned to possess only a mild curiosity as to curious customs,
he was now almost beside himself like a rich man in a hotel
when poor snivelling waiters have struck for money, as though
money was everything.

Burkington-Jones strode up to the first hut and kicked in the planks which served as a door. He could not see into the black smoke-scented interior after the sun's glare, but he could hear two or three people moving. In his temper he forgot the little he had learned of the language and shouted, " Come out, you bastards. Come out." There was no reply.

He did not know what to do next. This was the first time in his life that he had met with what people called " trouble." He had never clashed with the wills of men who were not of his order. His experience of " trouble " was confined to one or two youthful quarrels. And now he thought that this strange silence, this unusual inactivity, this insolent disregard of his shouted anger, must be the " trouble " which all the old hands discussed in the Club when they spoke of their past experiences or the gloomy future of Africa which the officials were ruining by kindness.

" The French know how to handle their bloody wogs, take my tip. Make them citizens and then bash them if there's trouble."

" What about the Portuguese ? Know what they do ? " Mallows had told him one night. " If they have a cheeky nig they use a special instrument to show him his place. It's like a big wooden spoon with holes in the actual spoon part. The nig has to hold out each hand and the *Bwana* bashes away at each hand with the spoon. The holes prevent the hands from bruising or swelling. Some chemical or whatd'youcallit law of Nature, I suppose. But it makes the old nig sit up and take notice, I tell you."

" The Belgians have got their wogs taped, too. No bloody nonsense there about no right to punch a wog, no nasty cruelty to the poor black brother. No. Just smash them down if they get stupid. After all, *are* we giving these wogs a better Africa or aren't we. If we are, then no bloody nonsense. We either know what's good for them or we don't. If we do, then make them work and keep quiet."

And so on. It was all very well, but what to do now? He was seething and he went crouched into the dark hut and seized an arm and dragged an African out into the sun. He was a young and muscular labourer and wearing only a pair of ragged shorts. He tore himself free from Burkington-Jones's grasp and stared at him with what appeared to be a mixture of fright and hatred. Burkington-Jones, in this, his first encounter with those lower ones who held a curious menace which he had always suspected, took the right decision. He stepped back, his heart beating faster and his throat full with fear and anger. There was so much which urged him to throw himself upon this young African, so much history, so much unthinking acceptance of the state of things, of men who obeyed and did, and who were there to perform the tasks allotted them by Nature and by other men who had been put above them. He knew this, but he was afraid, for this was the first time that the reins had turned in his hand, and he was not merely humiliated, he was desperate, but intelligently afraid. They stood watching each other, and with each second the young African felt this mystery, and while retaining his fright of the white man, his life was changed for him and he did not know it. He knew only a feeling of doubt and awaited punishment which he was afraid now he would resist, but fortunately the white man only glared at him, shaking as if with fever, slightly bent forward, his hands clenched.

Burkington-Jones had an idea, and it was the right one, saving him trouble, and, in a way, testing the strained thread of his authority. " Go back into your hut," he shouted. He heard his voice shaking. The African said, " Yes, *Bwana*," and scuttled back into the hut. Burkington-Jones swallowed the large, almost material hardness in his throat but he could not control the excitement of shock and the pleasure of at least being obeyed which shook him within. Then he hurried down to the office to tell Tamlin of this extraordinary thing which had happened on the plantation.

Tamlin knew already. He listened to the young excited Burkington-Jones, nodding every now and then, and amused secretly by the young man's solemn amazement at this thing and by his trembling anger with this collapse of things as they had been.

" What does it mean, sir ? " he asked. " What does it mean ? "

" Mean ? It's a strike, youngster, that's all. A strike. You were right to keep your hands off this chap you mention."

" But do we have strikes here ? Has there been one before ? "

" No. This is the first. But there's always a beginning." Tamlin offered him a cigarette and watched the young man's trembling hand take it.

Puffing at his cigarette and grateful for its almost forgotten boon, Burkington-Jones said, " But *why* ? Why, sir ? "

" Probably money or rations," said Tamlin. " We'll soon find out. You can go and sit in the cashier's office. You'll find other fellows there. We may need you, so stand by there." Although Tamlin was obviously not a frightfully well-bred chap, a bit of a rough diamond, Burkington-Jones felt a rush of loyalty and gratitude for him. He was so steady, so tough, so calm, and had even remembered he'd like a cigarette when he, Burkington-Jones, had forgotten.

" You can rely on me," he said, young and moved.

" Well, I hope so," said Tamlin with mock surprise. " Go and find a cup of tea in the cashier's office."

In the office near Tamlin's, Burkington-Jones found Chessing, Glebb, that revolting little dago De Gaugin, and Plume. Plume was doing a crossword puzzle in the Overseas

Times, and Chessing was cleaning his nails with a long sharp spine from a thorn tree.

" Hallo you," said Chessing. " Had a shock ? Your chaps revolted on you after all you've done for them, too ? " That was just like Chessing. Always trying to stand on his enthusiasm and spoil his enjoyment of new things.

" I know what I'd do if I had the power," said Burkington-Jones, but before he could describe it, Plume turned round and said :

" Well, don't tell us. Just sit down and keep quiet, son."

Son ? Who the hell did Plume think he was ? He was not all that old himself. But Burkington-Jones sat down and exchanged a look with Chessing, who gave him a smile of affectionate disdain and then turned back to cleaning his nails. It would not have been so bad if Plume had not said it in front of that greasy little swine, De Gaugin, who had smiled and looked out of the window.

De Gaugin wished to speak out, but not before Plume, for whom he had a respect as for an Englishman who was set in his ways and who had made up his mind as to where various men stood and what he would take in the way of opinions from them according to their status. De Gaugin was saying to himself, " I knew this would happen. I told them." He had not told them, but he felt certain that he had. He had seen it all coming. He was feeling two emotions. One of fury that the wogs had downed tools, and after one of them had attacked him, and another of exultation to see the Englishmen flouted and to know that he had seen it coming. There was also the comforting knowledge that what came next depended on the will of the Englishman and not on his. He would do what they told him, but he could feel aloof, as if silently making his protest and yet doing their foolish will.

Chessing did not care at all. There was a time when he

could have called out a squad of policemen, surrounded the area, made the right paralysing arrests, and then back to the office for a cigarette and a cup of tea before the interrogation and the report. A wog was a tricky thing, half child, half savage animal, at least that was his experience, as he always added if an eyebrow was raised among listeners. Chessing was thirty-six and had resigned from the police after a difficult case involving a European woman and an African, a rare case of its kind. The European woman had been rushed out of the country before Chessing could say knife and there was a hush and a difficulty. He liked Mambango. Good money, good quarters and plenty of time to himself. He collected plants and sent them to London, and occasionally wrote learned articles on the subject for magazines with strange names. Let Tamlin do what he liked. The country was going to hell, no matter what the Colonial Office boys said. You could see it before your eyes. In another two years or so he was getting out and he would settle in Cornwall and forget Africa, which had been all right in its time. But for him it was over.

Glebb, an elderly but still fit man, had once had a big farm and a good wife and two children. But it was well known that he only dreamed about gold, for which he had wasted most of his life. The third time he went off after gold, on the basis of a dead certainty this time, he was away for over a year, and when he got back his wife had gone and the children too. They had gone back to England and that was the end of his marriage. It was the end of the farm too. He was penniless. He mortgaged the land but there was East Coast fever among the cattle and that finished it. Somebody got him a job at Mambango and he worked quietly in the tractor shed. He was a quiet, heavy, bald man with sad, vacant eyes. He gave no trouble, liked his drink, and would never interfere with the " goings on " in the Bachelors' Mess in which he lived.

He would always give a helping hand if he could. He still thought he might find gold if he was only a bit younger. He was sixty-three but not as fit as he looked. He did not care what they did about the strike as long as there was no violence. There was a time when he could have taken any nig on, but he had slowed up and he never crossed words with a cheeky nig now ; easier to report it and leave it at that. No one ever asked his opinion about anything. He was just old Glebb and was there ; that was all. Now he sat at the cashier's table and played with a piece of paper, thinking about a dog he had once had.

Tamlin had sent Yussuf with a squad of reliable men he had picked himself. They patrolled the whole plantation area by lorry. Every labourer had a machete and that was something to think about, as Tamlin wrote in his meticulously kept daily diary which lay on his desk when it was not in the safe. The first report which came in from Yussuf said that all was quiet. Every man was in his hut and there was no sign of movement.

There was something queer about this, even in his experience of Borneo, Samoa, Australia and Africa. This quiet orderliness ; no shouting, no threats, no mob, no spokesman. Nearly two thousand Africans split up into five villages, silent in their huts.

At ten o'clock Pryce came in, in a lather of sweat as usual, his fat yellow face with its ragged brown moustache wearing a kind of fixed look of awe. His white shirt was plastered to his body and he was breathing like a tired dog as he took the chair which Tamlin offered him.

" Know what it is ? " said Pryce with an air of foreboding and almost religious solemnity. Before Tamlin could reply he said, " It's bloody witchcraft, that's what it is. There's an 'orrible gloom over everything. I been round with the boys and I've 'eard one or two things, though I 'ad me own suspicions from the start. It's bloody witchcraft, that's what it is."

"By Christ, I believe you're right," exclaimed Tamlin. Fancy a fellow like Pryce spotting it, a fellow who would be more at home running a pub in some London back-crack. But Pryce was a good engineer, no matter about the aitches as Tamlin often said if he heard someone laugh at the fat, balding man's pronunciation. Tamlin had been long enough in Australia to dislike certain British prejudices. He was fond of Pryce, and, like others at Mambango, he often wondered what Mrs. Pryce saw in him.

"I know I'm right," said Pryce. "I been out 'ere a few years among these blackies and that's what it is. Witchcraft."

It must be witchcraft, thought Tamlin. It *felt* like witchcraft, this mysterious strike without a voice.

"Send that youngster, Burkington-Jones, to bring in one of the Africans from the factory, an intelligent one," Tamlin said. He saw Pryce was reluctant and knew why. Pryce would not like to give an order to Burkington-Jones, who *might* resent it from an "oik" like Pryce. Burkington-Jones was a bit 'igh-class in his manner. It was one of those things that had to be understood but which could not properly be explained, and Tamlin hated it for a moment or two, his rage with British curiosities of class, high, middle or low, fuming as he regarded Pryce, who was saying :

"I'll call 'im in 'ere if you like, Mr. Tamlin."

"Yes, do that, please," said Tamlin. "If it's witchcraft," he thought, "I'll give them hell on Sunday morning. I'll give them sheer bloody hell for this. The poor bastards." What a life. Could anybody ever really know what was going to become of Africa, when you thought of its size, its diversity, its peoples, its long stagnant wait on the very edge of thousands of years of civilisation to its north and east. He forgot who had said that to him over a beer one night in Chugi and he often thought of it.

Burkington-Jones brought a rather scared African boiler tender into the office. Because he wore overalls he was a cut above those others who slaved in the plantations for a dozen or so shillings a month. There were only three boiler tenders in the factory and he was one of them. He was an intelligent man who was only beginning to dimly comprehend that if a man could read and write and was what white men called honest, he could go up until he might get nearly Indian scale wages. But he knew, too, it was too late, even if there had been the school, the time and the opportunity. Knowing all this, he had a respect for white men, insane though they were in many ways, and he had a contempt for his own kind who were nothing but slaves and brutes. But despite this he was suspicious of white men. Their only idea in life was to get work out of men, any men, and he knew they knew there was plenty more where he came from.

He looked at Tamlin with careful eyes. He had never been so close to him before, and had only seen him rushing past or through the factory once or twice. This was the master of them all, white and black. He drank the white man up into his memory, his eyes, his hair, skin, clothes, hands, and he searched for a trick or a habit which he could describe later at one of those long talks the factory workers had at night over their last meal in their compound when they discussed the white men and their ways. During these talks there was always something to discover about white men. The men who knew most were servants who worked in their houses, but these would not sit down with one who worked with his hands, in dirt and noise.

" Do you know anything about witchcraft ? " the white man said quickly, so that it was like a blow. Tamlin used the local words " magic medicine " and he saw the African's eyes stare and widen as he heard the question. Tamlin was irritated. He expected the African to repeat the words and when he did he almost lost his temper.

" Yes. Witchcraft. Witchcraft. Witchcraft," he said loudly. This repetition of the words three times puzzled the African, as did the angry face of the white man. Then it cleared in his mind and he found he did not know what to reply. He became afraid and Tamlin saw it and could not control his temper. He seldom lost his good nature with the Africans, but sometimes, especially when it was urgent, they drove a fellow almost out of his mind. He began to speak slowly, deliberately, sardonically.

" I said do you know anything about witchcraft ? I think someone is using witchcraft to stop the men coming to work. Do you understand *now* ? "

The man understood and he closed his mind like a clam. Tamlin had to assure him that he in no way connected him with what was afoot among the labourers. He only wanted to know the custom in these matters. It was necessary to know something of these customs for there was good reason to believe that someone was using them to prevent the labourers from doing their rightful work. Did he understand that ?

The man nodded, dumb, worried, anxious to please and yet afraid to say too much. He knew, as did all the other Africans, what was going on, but there was a loyalty of fear to his own kind, as well as there was a longing for normal conditions to return, and yet the problem was how much to say. If one said too much one would be pointed out as an enemy of the people, and if one said only a little the white man would spring on him and force him to tell all. Would it not be best then to tell all at once ? No, better that it be dragged out by the white man when all men would know that he had not willingly opened his mouth. He had a fear, too, of the men who had made this witchcraft, and though he had, during the last few years, lost his fear of it after long work among the machines of the factory, that fear had come back again now and was connected with his fear of sharper minds, of violence, and of a darkness which he hesitated to face.

So Tamlin began to bully, to shout, to threaten. He made the African stand in the corner while he wrestled with him from the desk. He knew that locked in that shaven black skull was a knowledge, and a fear. He began to terrify him with threats which, if they were challenged, could not be carried out, but the time had not yet come for an African to challenge them. Before Tamlin's assault, before all the harsh and frightening words, he quailed and then he began to cry, for the African heart was touched and afraid, used as it was to generations of chiefs and of the chiefly power in concert with an iron tribal code. He was reminded of so much that was gone and was going, of power in the hands of one who knew how to wield it, and of a humility which had all but lost its way on the thousand roads, which had opened.

"I will tell," he said, his hands clasped, tears in his eyes. Tamlin fought with a mixture of triumph and shame, for though anxious to be what he thought was righteous, he could hardly bear the sight of the pathetic man he had created in the corner of his office.

"All right, all right," he snapped. "Do not be afraid. All is well. Just tell me what these men have done, for I see that you know all."

"It is because of the Klismas *n'goma*, *Bwana*," the African whispered, his tears shining like silver beads in his eyes and on his black cheeks. "It is because of the dancing for the white people at Klismas."

Klismas? By God, so that was it. The Christmas Committee had made a balls of everything as he had been afraid they would, though he had to admit that he had raised no objection when told of the plan for the African dancing on Christmas Eve. But why should they object ? They loved to dance. They would dance whenever asked. They knew there would be perks, an extra ration, say, or a free issue of maize to make beer. Why ? He turned on the African again, saying " Why ? " forgetting his pity and once again fixing him with those pale, searching eyes.

" Why should men fear dancing at Klismas ? " he said with menace. " Who has done this thing ? " He knew now that there were voices at work, voices which had terrorised the Africans. Send for the police ! No, not yet. Flog somebody ! No, not yet. He was anxious to act, and like all white men in a time of African crisis, torn between justice and clemency, and fury and injured pride, for the whole thing rested on African acceptance of the white man's superiority—in all things, and it was necessary to act and to act with great speed. It might all crumble, all his work at Mambango. He might be beaten like those others. Never, by Christ, never. He kept his hands off the African, fought the longing to shake him.

" Well, come on," he roared. " Come on and talk."

In the cashier's office they could hear Tamlin's voice and Plume said nothing, lifting his eyebrows only and lighting another cigarette.

Burkington-Jones said, " God, he's in a hell of a temper. He's usually so quiet with the nigs."

" With the *Africans*," said Plume. " The *Africans*." He could not help saying it, and he was sorry when he had done so, for he had a loyalty to Tamlin and not any reason to amuse this half-baked kid. But Burkington-Jones did not understand anyway what he had meant, thinking it some kind of gentle reproof.

CHAPTER THIRTEEN

MOONING, at heart, was one of those men who, when in authority among dark-skinned people, tend to panic in a curious way if the order of things is upset, when there are white women present at the scene of threat. The white woman assumes a kind of sacred quality when the darker-skinned population is disturbed, a sacred quality which, in Mooning's case, destroyed his sense of proportion while appealing to the public schoolboy which was in conflict with the grown man. O'Riordan had mocked him in the past for this tendency when they had discussed such things, though O'Riordan, by virtue of his reading, knew that the ghastly shambles of slaughtered Englishwomen at Cawnpore and Agra lay at the half-forgotten root of it. He knew this, while he knew that the bloody and savage biblical revenge which had followed the triumphant British bayonets had been forgotten, if ever known. It was the agony of the whole Imperial thing, of skin loving and hating other skin. The white woman behind the white men who faced the screaming dark ones destroyed the sense of what was truly in the minds of the white men. The presence of the white women denied the biological fact that white men, to justify their presence and their message, should take their wives from the dark ones. The white women denied the fact, and deepened the snarling, half-insane racial chasm.

The " colonial problem " had been solved privately in bed from Lagos to Singapore for a hundred years, but this was denied in the clubs where white men could " get away from the black faces." When O'Riordan had said this there was a furious row in the Club, and Mooning had not spoken to O'Riordan for weeks after it.

As soon as the news came that " the labour " had struck, Mooning all but lost his self-control. He saw his wife in the hands, the black hands, of the mob, and hysterical rage filled him.

" It's Tamlin's fault," he told Amy. " Tamlin and his bloody Sunday morning revival meetings. They'll go for the women, that's what they'll do. I know the nigs and I know what they'll do." He knew a sudden tenderness for her.

Amy laughed, but her laughter was a sneer to her husband. " You won't laugh if they get hold of you," he said, his face white with annoyance and emotion.

" How do you know ? " she mocked, and was surprised with his reception of this little harmless joke. He bared his teeth and shouted, " Don't you make cheap jokes about a thing like this. What about Mrs. Pryce and Mrs. Tamlin ? Don't you care about what they might feel ? "

" But, dear, what are you going on about ? No one has done anything. You've said the labour is in its huts, quiet. What's frightening about that ? "

He could not tell her of what he suspected, of what he divined underneath the childish African life as he saw it ; of that dark cruelty and those suspected lusts which that childishness hid. She saw that he was going to be a perfect menace if there was any trouble and she despised him, her lips hardening, her flesh drawn towards Plume, who could not be like this stupid idiot who was her husband every Saturday night. She wanted to hurt him with the right words, and she dredged for them, fighting with her habit of prudence which had always curbed her tongue.

" And what do you propose to do about this terrible

danger ? " she said, allowing her voice to convey only a hint of her contempt for him, but in his nervous state he read her deeper meaning and he lost control of himself. He took two steps forward and struck her with his open hand, knocking her to the floor. She got up immediately and faced him, her face dead white, wishing she were a man. She was weeping with hate. The sultry heat of the day and the emotional storm which had caught them up, had formed a bead of perspiration on her upper lip so that it was perched, glistening, in the arch of lipstick. It fascinated her husband, reminding him of desire, but unable to overcome his sudden antagonism for what he saw as her coldness, her heartlessness, her use of him and of his toil to preserve her comfort. All the meanness, the smallness of hopeless marriage took hold of his reason and justified his wish to beat her until she cried for mercy and knew him as man, the only man, and he knew this was not possible. It was a dream.

"You hit me. You hit me," she was hissing at him, her voice a whisper as in a sacred place, or in the presence of death. "You hit me. You swine. You rotten, cowardly swine. If I had a revolver I'd *kill* you, you swine ! " It was the way she said *kill* that almost broke him, but he was quick, he knew that nothing could undo what he had done. He had only been trying to save her from what she mocked at on Saturday nights as " a fate worse than death," that had caused all this, and she could not understand it. She was only a woman after all. That thought gave him a kind of comfort, but it could never overcome the vicious, the merciless look in her eyes as they faced each other in the sunlit room. He sought for something to say and, finding nothing, he sat down in one of the deep armchairs and hid his eyes with his left hand. He could hear the swift fruff of her silk housecoat as she stepped towards him and continued her cries of hate and recrimination. Things he had forgotten, or had never known were being thrown at him in a passionate scream which he had never heard before. "It's the climate," he kept saying to himself, "it's this bloody awful —— place that's done this to us," and yet, the things he was hearing now from that horrible voice told him it was not the climate, it was not the place. It was *him, him, him.* The way she snarled *you* was almost unnerving. He waited under this rain of hatred which he had mined, a lode which seemed inexhaustible.

"When I picked you up," she was shouting, "you were a little drunken rat——"

"Picked me up," he cried. "That's what you did, like a tart," but her torrent swept his brief triumph away and he lowered his head again, scared by the beautiful trembling statue of rage which stood over him.

"A *rat,*" she yelled, "that's what you were. Everyone said I was a fool. Everyone knew you were just a bloody drunken little bastard and I stopped you drinking. I made some kind of a man of you and came here to this back-water and served you——"

"Don't swear," he shouted, hurt. He had never heard her swear. It gave him a pain which he did not understand, and when he had said that she began to scream foul words at him which he had thought women did not know. Where had she learned them?

"I made you into something," she cried, lost in the deep human pleasure it gave her to remember and to cry this. "I made you. I gave you a beautiful house and taught you what a decent life could be. Everyone here knows what I did for you, everyone. But you're a bloody rat, that's all. You're no good at bottom. You're a bloody remittance man whom *I* saved, and it's been a humiliation to see you strutting about as if you were the cock of the walk. You rat," she howled. She could hear the servants whispering and muttering outside the door, and it added to her ecstasy. "I don't care

who hears me," she screamed. " Everyone knows what I've
gone through. When I think of some of the men I've known.
When I think——"

He got to his feet, his face dull with a hundred memories
she had clawed into life again; drunk on a soiled bed with
her tending him, long ago, in debt and lying left and right
and lying to her and being found out and being forgiven,
and for this, now, he loathed her. But not that alone was it
which had got him to his feet. It was when he thought of the
men she had known——

" What about them ? " he said in a low voice. " What
about these men you have known ? " Then he shouted, staring
above her head, " You're a whore. A whore, and everyone
knows about it. I gave you respectability. I took you on
when no one would look at you. I gave you a home and I
gave you everything you have to-day. I've got a good job
and people respect me, and I gave you my name——"

" *Mooning,*" she sneered, and then shouted in his face,
" *Mooning,* I've had better names than that twice before and
better men that came with them." That hit him again, she
could see. She chuckled, her right hand fixing her hair, her
eye on him, cold, and again in control of herself.

" I know you've had a lot of names," he said, glum, beaten.
" And I know you should have had more, but you lay on
your back instead of legalising it. I know all that and everyone
else knows too. They don't say so, but they know it. You
can forget, because you did it. I can't forget because I'm here,
with it, with you. You bloody, dirty little tart. Do you
hear ? "

" Of course I hear. Your aboriginal mind is easy to understand. Sometimes I wonder if you can really read and write
——" He cut in, still dull.

" I've done my best for you. I never complained when
you cut my greens down to once a week——"

She screeched with sudden laughter at this. "You should have done," she spat at him. "You should have taken what you wanted. Not like a rat, whining and whimpering for it." She could not imagine Jack standing for once a week. No, Jack was like a raving lion for it. Those hands! Those—— If only she had not let Jack down he would have been here now, master of her, his black hair tight-brushed on his small neat head, his beautiful tall body——

"Should I ?" he was saying. "Should I have taken what I wanted?" It was the most terrible thing of all to hear. But she was quick. "Not now," she sneered. "Not now. You've had all you're going to get from me. It's over. For good." She went to the couch and lay down on it, and lit a cigarette, taking the scene into a new phase, a quieter tone, a more reasonable and enjoyable antagonism. To finally destroy the marriage she needed a better atmosphere, quieter tears and more piercing recriminations voiced through them. He did his part. He came and half knelt, half sat beside her, hoping to stroke the long beautiful wounding white leg which was revealed through the opened silk. But, well trained, he resisted this longing and turned his racked face to her, saying :

"Amy, what are we doing ?"

"Doing ?" She blew cigarette smoke from her small nostrils, and flexed her leg, lifting it so that he could still see it and want it. "We're putting an end to this idiotic arrangement which *you* call marriage. That's what we're doing."

"No," he said. "No, Amy, no." He was going to lay down his head on her body, but before he could decide on it she squirmed away, showing him what he had only vaguely wanted to do, shaming him again. He wanted to get up and fight on, shouting and being the man, but he knew that was not the way. He would have to whimper and something told

him that that, too, would fail, but he could try, and she
knew he would try. She half-bared one breast, as though
forgetfully, so that he would know the full pain of what he
was to lose, and seeing it he broke up altogether.

" Amy," he whispered. " No. Don't end it. It's me. It's
my fault. I know it is." He was thinking, " Why can't I be
strong and courageous with her as I am with other people,
with men, with niggers, with people ? Why must I have to
cringe like this ? Just because of Saturday night and the
possibility of a bit more if I'm good ? " She saw him thinking
but could not guess what it was he was saying to himself.
He was not dangerous, she knew, but he had hit her, and for
that she would make him suffer. No, not just for that, but for
being what he was, for everything, for being a last hope as
he had then seemed, and for having helped her to be mistaken.
How many turnings there were in the road, and how many
wrong ones of them she had taken, and yet she had meant
no harm. She had only wanted to enjoy her life and look
what it had come to. She watched him implore, her eyes
hostile, contemptuous, but interested.

" I was only thinking of you," he was whispering, coaxing.
" I was only thinking of you and the women, and you went
for me——"

" I didn't go for you," she said, bored, turning her eyes to
her cigarette.

" You did." He urged, " You did, Amy."

" *I didn't*," she snapped at him. His face flooded with
despair. " All right, you didn't," he said, glum again. " I
suppose it was all my fault," not meaning it, but hopeful.

" Yes," she said, hard and mean, " It's all your fault.
Every bloody thing is your fault. You're a fool. The labourers
lie in their huts and you come whining about the women
and the danger, trying to get round me "—she had an
inspiration—" trying to impress me. You thought you'd get

me into bed, that's it. That's it," she cried, " you thought I'd be a little woman and get soft about you."

" You bitch," he shouted. " I didn't. I didn't." He grabbed her hair and dragged her on to the floor, trying to beat her head on it, mad, big-eyed, driven over the edge, but she was too quick for him. She pushed her cigarette into his face and he yelped, struggling away, his hands pressed over his eyes, nose and mouth, in pain, in deep despair and, as he saw it, swaying there, in degradation.

He could hear her sharp breathing, he could feel her apprehension, but he was finished. He sat down, still hiding his eyes, and she said :

" If you touch me again, I'll kill you." He just shook his head to and fro as though in a denial.

" You can leave," she said. " I won't live with you. I just won't any more."

" Leave ? " His voice was fogged behind his hands. " Where shall I go ? Where shall I go ? This is my house."

" It isn't your house," she shouted. " It's the company's, and as much mine as yours. You can go to the Bachelors' Mess and stay there until I've cleared off."

" Cleared off ? " He removed his hands, showing a blister beside his nose. " Amy, no. Don't ask me to go. Think of what people will say. It'll be the talk of the place." He begged, he beseeched.

" If you don't go, I will," she said.

" Where can you go ? You can't, Amy."

" Then go," she said. She could have Plume in for a night, she had suddenly realised, and though there might be difficulties, she waved them away, seeing Plume there, waiting. Oh, Plumey. She could feel the great melting beginning, the pain, making her brusque and sharp to this rat in the chair before her now.

" Go," she said. Every time he protested she said " Go "

until it was a shout. "Go. Go. Go. Go. For Christ's sake, go." He got up and left her.

"Are you going?" she called, and ridiculously, so that she laughed, genuinely amused, he called back, "Yes, I'm going. Aren't I?"

CHAPTER FOURTEEN

IF people were not talking about the strike that night, they were talking about the row between the Moonings. Mooning in the Bachelors' Mess seemed an amazing thing when one thought about it, didn't it? After all, he had such a lovely looking wife and it seemed queer for the owner of a beautiful job like that to be celibate in the Bachelors' Mess. What could it all be about? And just on Christmas, too.

"Just think of her alone there," said one man to another in the Club, and they thought of it, wistful, calling for more Scotch.

"Such a sweet woman," said one, not wishing to be misunderstood, for gossip was swift at Mambango. "Yes," said the other, smiling, understanding. "Really sweet."

When Plume heard the news about Mooning moving into the Bachelors' Mess, he closed his eyes for a moment, a tremor in his heart and throat. "I'm a fool," he said to himself. "A fool."

He was in the Club when he heard the news. He was missing Mallows, just as the group near him at the bar were saying they missed O'Riordan and his talk, and they wondered how the poor bugger was. A pain like that was something to worry about.

"It seemed to knock all the life out of him," said Burkington-Jones to Chessing. "He wasn't the same man when he went off with Mallows."

Chessing nodded. "He wasn't the same man," he said. "He's finished." Burkington-Jones with the young awe and veneration for death, which had not been seen, which was so far off, said, "Finished? Do you mean he'll die?"

"Yes, he'll die," said Chessing softly. "It's a certain look a chap gets, you know. But *don't* tell anyone I said so."

"No, no, I won't. Christ, poor old O'Riordan." Burkington-Jones put down his drink and said solemnly, "It must be horrible to be old, mustn't it, Chessing. You know, to know it's all over." It was all so far off, really, when he thought of it. Chessing smiled again. "O'Riordan seems old to you," he said, "but he's not really. He's not fifty yet."

"Fifty's old," said Burkington-Jones firmly. "When a man's fifty he's finished. There's nothing left to do."

Plume, standing with his back to them, his crossword puzzle forgotten, heard the young confident voice. He was forty-five, nearly finished, he thought ironically, and yet he burned for this woman. He was a fool, a fool. He could not concentrate any more. With Mallows away and being alone in the house, he had for some reason felt quieter. He had begun to read again, browsing through the hundreds of books which Mallows had got together. He had been able to think about his desire for Mrs. Mooning, and though there was something contemptible and pathetic in it, as he saw it in that quiet house, alone, it was still there. There was something in the woman that required him, he was sure. There was something in her that drew him, for though everyone knew she had gone through two husbands before Mooning, and that there had been "men," he could not get it out of his mind that behind all that there was a real woman whom he alone could understand. He knew, too, in a shrewd way, that all men felt this about all women they wanted, and for a few it lasted beyond the dulled palate of possession. Yet he desired her, not just desire, there was something more. Sorry for her, he was too, and conscious that there were quiet, gentle depths in her into which no man had been, the depths beyond the body and the appetite. " If this is love," he thought, " it's not only hell, it's stupid, utterly stupid." It was stupid because it disturbed him and made him what he did not wish to be, a man who wanted Mooning's wife, and Mooning was not somebody whose place he wished to take, and yet it was what he ached for. It was a crisis for him, he knew. Quietly, over a drink, he would think it over, so often, and would despise himself and yet burn for her in this terrible way which broke the end of everything he did, making it pointless, making life a slow, agonised marking of time. He was elated to hear that Mooning had left. He had severed all contact with Mrs. Mooning some time ago, and she had stayed silent, but now that Mooning was gone, he might go quietly along and see her. It thrilled and worried him, and he could feel the hope, and the whisky, sweeping away the worry, the trepidation and the doubt.

When he had gone, Burkington-Jones said, " What do you think of that chap, Plume, Chessing ? He's a queer bird, isn't he ? "

Chessing knew all about Plume, knew about the cashiering in India and the stretch Plume had done later for a curious deal in ivory. That was years ago when Chessing had been a much younger policeman. Technically, Plume should have been chucked out of the country after his stretch, but he was related to the right people, it turned out, and there were extenuating circumstances; a decent Englishman snared by a dirty foreigner. There was, though, the cashiering, but that was very straightforward and not at all criminal. A punch on a general's jaw, at Simla, as far as Chessing could remember, over a woman ; tight, of course, and one or two other charges which could be brought against most officers, but which were not chargeable unless an incident, like punching a general's jaw, excited the official machine.

" Yes, he's a queer chap," said Chessing. " Nice chap, too." Plume was not his real name. That had come after gaol.

" You know, they say he's been in trouble. I even heard he'd been in gaol."

" Absolute bull," said Chessing. " How could he be in the country if he'd been in gaol ? "

" Yes, of course," said Burkington-Jones. " I forgot that. But how could such a rumour start ? "

" Plume may have been in gaol," Chessing replied. " He may have been a warden." They laughed, Burkington-Jones loudly, boring Chessing, who was tired of him.

" What about the witchcraft thing, Chessing ? " Burkington-Jones went on to the new tack with his usual zest. There was not possibly enough he could learn, thought Chessing.

" It's true," he told the younger man. " It's quite common. It's a big part of wog life, you know, but we're not supposed to recognise it, the officials that is. It's not supposed to be there at all, but it's very much there. The tribes all believe in it." He wanted to use the word " Africans," but could not bring himself to do so, for it sounded strange at Mambango, and strangest of all from the mouth of Tamlin, who used it always. He always felt guilt about using " nig," but it was a habit.

" What'll Tamlin do ? "

" We'll know to-morrow. It'll need handling."

" Why don't they put you on to it, Chessing ? You've had experience."

" They have," said Chessing. " I'm starting on it to-morrow morning."

Burkington-Jones was full of admiration. " That's great, Chessing," he said. " Great. What'll you do ? "

"Forget it now," Chessing told him, calm and firm. "Have another drink."

It was five o'clock before Tamlin got the whole story from the African boiler-tender. Sweating, he had dismissed him and had sent for Chessing. They had a long argument. Tamlin had a considerable respect for Chessing, whose tall, dark and neat figure always caused him to think, "If I could, I'd like to look like that."

As if someone of taste had advised him, Chessing sucked a pipe, which suited his quietness, and regarding him, Tamlin thought, "Just like one of those adverts in *Punch*"; and he was right, for Chessing had taken years to arrive at the correct choice of tweed jacket, which he was wearing now, despite the sweltering heat. He wore good hand-stitched shoes, not slung together by some Indian copyist, as he would say, but from London, and the right shade of silk scarf tucked inside his dark blue, cellular, cotton shirt. He occasionally gave a short lecture to the other members of the Bachelors' Mess about clothes and their value in daily life. Chessing had once had a wife, but after the fashion of the country she had gone off with another, and he had settled down into celibacy with little regret once he had known that she would not come back.

He listened now to Tamlin, pipe in mouth, nodding occasionally. When the other had finished, Chessing said, "Yes, I think the chap is quite right and is telling you the truth. You see, there are all kinds of new things going on, not just in this country, but all over Africa. Africans who have accepted Christianity are, in many cases, as nationalism gets hold of them, inventing new religions. They keep the Old Testament and varnish a lot of the tribal stuff on top. They do this, because, some of us think, they grow proud of the worst aspects of their tribalism once they get the nationalist bug."

" Why ? " said Tamlin. " Why should they grow proud of the worst aspects ? "

" Because they're African, that's why. For a nationalist, anything African is good, especially if we whites taught them to be ashamed of it. And we may have one of those boys here among the labour."

" Christ," said Tamlin, impressed. " Do you mean to say that's going on in this country now ? "

" Oh, yes. It's only started. Later it'll be a big thing. A really big thing."

" And what can be done about it ? "

Chessing shrugged his neat shoulders. " I used to worry like hell about it once, when I was in the police. But I don't now. I only hope the boys at the top are watching it." He looked up, his large blue eyes sharp and focused on Tamlin's. " It's big, you know. Really big. We started something in Africa and we mustn't complain if it gets difficult."

" What do you think is the angle here ? "

" I suggest you let me creep round the huts a bit with the *Neapara*, Yussuf and one or two stalwarts, and I'll let you know. Do nothing to-night save put a couple of listeners among the huts."

" Right," said Tamlin. " We'll give it a try. What time d'you want to start in the morning ? "

" Dawn. If I can have the *Neapara* and the chaps at my house at dawn, we'll give the thing the once over and let you know."

It was very seldom that Tamlin asked for advice, but he was glad it was of Chessing he had now asked it. He felt a confidence in him. He was sure he would help to smooth all this over.

" One thing more, Chessing. Are they likely to be dangerous ? "

"Oh, yes," said Chessing. "Quite dangerous if they've got many Holy Joes among them."

"What's a Holy Joe?"

"Sorry," said Chessing, remembering the Sunday mornings. "I mean chaps who've been to the Mission and have discovered Africa with the help of agitators. That's how it goes, you know. You should take all the usual precautions, as though there was a real trouble. It does no harm and costs little. And it saves the police a job later." He gave Tamlin a cold, knowing smile as he mentioned the police. "I've had some, you know," he added.

"Righto," said Tamlin. "As you say."

He had told Chessing of the spells laid on the labourers, of the spell which would kill them if they left their huts before permission from the spell-maker. It just did not make sense to Tamlin, with all his experience.

He had noticed the way Chessing had said "Africans," and he liked him more for that. It was little things like that which gave you a clue to a fellow's character. He never objected to a fellow using the expression "nig" or "wog." After all, a chap had the right to think what he liked about people, black or white, and his expressions were his own. He would only object if a fellow handled labour badly, for a labourer was a labourer whether he was "nig" or African. Yet it was nice to hear a fellow like Chessing speak of them as Africans.

There were moments when he thought: "I've come a long way from the reformatory. Who'd ever have thought I'd come this far, handling all kinds of chaps, some from Oxford, I've had even." This was one of those moments and he tried not to enjoy it. Not even Maisie knew about the reformatory. Would it make any difference if she did? He put it back in its secret hole and began a fresh entry in the diary.

Taking off his dark glasses, Samuel Yonamba stared into

the sun for a moment and said a prayer. "O Jesus," he said, as though addressing an acquaintance, "make me strong for what is before me. Make me clever so that I make the right choice in this thing which confronts me. Make me cunning for your sake so that I can bring fruit from the words. And you, too, Twamba, my tribal one, I do not forget to ask strength of you. Make me sharp as you made the old chiefs who have gone sharp. If you make lightning give me some of it. If you make thunder, put some in my voice. Jesus and Twamba, help me to enlighten those in the darkness of the white man's ways."

He was standing at the mouth of a cave overlooking Mambango as the sun flooded it with red quivering light, the trees turned to flames, the plantations to beds of glowing crimson ash. Then it softened as the darkness fell softly like a grey veil turning to a dark blue mist. Far out a grass fire near the horizon flamed like a long golden red scar, increasing in fierceness as darkness gave it prominence.

Samuel was waiting for two men whom he feared, and soon he heard them approaching. "Yonamba," they called softly. "It is I, Paul," and "It is I, Luka."

They sat over some red coals with him while he made black tea and mixed it with sugar. While they drank, Luka, a young man with big projecting teeth and dark glasses, said:

"You see, then, what we can do? Every man lay in his hut, afraid. Do you understand, then, what we can do?"

"I came to teach these men, not to frighten them," said Samuel, wondering if they would resent such directness. They did not reply for a moment and he was fearful. Then Paul, older than both of them, and who had actually been in Europe, the land of the white men, said, "I go soon. I should not be here. Because I have been in Europe the Government watches me and I must go to the town and wait. I can do little here. But you, both of you can teach. Luka is right to show you

what he can do with these people. They have to be taught
that they are not slaves, that there are some things the white
man cannot force them to do. You, Samuel Yonamba, you
do not know what you wish to do. You want men to refuse
to work for the white man and you are afraid when Luka
shows you how it is done."

"It should not be done by this evil medicine. It is a bad
thing and should be let disappear. But Luka has used it,
though he says he does not believe in it." Samuel did not
care now. He would have his say.

"Do you believe in it, Samuel, this medicine?" Paul's
voice was clever, soft and playful. Samuel did not reply.

"We all believe in it." Paul's voice was harder now. "We
all believe in these things, though we wish not to. Then we
should believe in what is in our nature. We are not white
men. You and Luka believe in God and so do I. You cannot
see the wind, nor can you see God, but they are there, and
God is there to help us. I want these men down there to
refuse to work. The word is ' strike.' " He used the English
word. " White men in Europe use it and so must our people.
When men ' strike ' the white men respect them."

"They may shoot them," said Samuel.

"They may. But if they do they will make those who live
hate them, and in this way men become stronger. Teach
them about God and about justice. God is on our side, I
tell you."

"It is dangerous, but it is good," said Luka. To Samuel
he said, " We will work here together. I am one of the men
in charge of the oxen here and I will get you a job with me.
They fear me, these men down there, and they will fear you,
too."

"When will you break this spell you have laid?"

"To-morrow, when the white men know that there are
men who will not dance for them on the eve of Klismas."

"Because they want to. Because it is pleasure for them. And because it is a test for them to refuse. Why should the white man stand and enjoy seeing our men and women dance for them?"

Samuel was afraid of the hate in the man's voice. Samuel was against working for the white men but he had not the quality of hatred in him. He was bitter about the white men's selfishness, but he was not one who wished to fight them. He only wished to teach men to think and to question, and to know God, in whose eyes all men were equal.

"They *will* dance at Klismas, for the white men," said Paul. "They are not ready for such things as you plan, Luka, though you can but try. You know little of ' politics,' but when you do you will learn that it is necessary to fight with true bitterness and the way will be hard. My God is not like your God. My God is a hard, clever God, and even I have much to learn. These men down there are children. They get excited and cannot control themselves. It is best that you speak slowly to them, teach them to protest against injustice which they have grown used to. Teach them that the white man is not God. He is only a man with a government, money and guns. That is all you can do until there are more of us who can awaken the people."

Luka and Samuel were impressed. They were silent in their agreement.

"There is one thing that angers me," said Paul. "I have learned to drink the white man's drink in Europe, and in my own land I am forbidden to drink it. I have had education and I cannot go into the cinema in the town. It is for Indians and white men only. This is injustice to me, but it is not to those down there who have not known and do not want these things. If you remember these differences among men you have begun to learn politics."

Samuel had wanted to be a preacher like one of those

white men at the Mission, but he had failed. Now, hearing
these men, he felt danger and wished he was back at the
Mission, but it was too late for that.

Luka was the man who had actually struck the white man,
De Gaugin, and another man had been forced to take the
punishment. That was another thing which had worried
Samuel when Luka had told him of it in glee. Luka was of
this tribe and could do these things, but it was a lying and
mean thing to do, in Samuel's view of it. He knew, too, that
despite his prayers to Jesus and Twamba, he could never outwit these two, nor, when Paul had gone to the town, could
he outwit Luka. He was very afraid he had done the wrong
thing in coming here. He should have gone to his own tribe.
He remembered his pride the day before when he had
addressed the men and the clown, Chopa, had argued. It was
later that Luka had come to him and had frightened him with
his laugh and his cruel lies. He decided to go home and not
work here as he had planned, but as though he had read his
mind, Luke said, " You are one of us now. What I have
started here, we will finish together."

They were all disappointed mission boys who had found
life hard after the mission. Other mission boys had got jobs,
had found positions, had been rewarded by God for their
belief in him. But these, of three different tribes, had failed,
and had come together, as others were coming together, to
ask questions, to make mistakes, to arouse, and to be shot,
imprisoned, or exiled. They were only the pathetic beginning
of what might one day be an understanding group who would
choose, or be beaten down. They vaguely felt something of
this, and it frightened Samuel.

CHAPTER FIFTEEN

BEFORE seven o'clock the next morning, Chessing, with Yussuf and three powerful Africans from the tractor shed, had toured the villages of the labourers. They were still in their huts and it was obvious that they were in difficulties. They were short of water, they could not get firewood. Chessing was appalled when he thought of the power of superstition, seeing what it' could do to simple people. It made him angry and he said to Yussuf:

"Do men in your country have fears like this?" and Yussuf said, "*Bwana*, we are all afraid of this thing. I am not afraid now, but I do not know even now if there is not a magician who could not cast a spell over me. A man can never know that."

"You are wrong, Yussuf," he said. "No man can cast a spell over you if you do not believe in him." Then wearily he added, for he had said it to a thousand Africans, "It is only fear in your mind. Only fear which the magician knows you believe in."

Yussuf lowered his eyelids and said, "It must be that, *Bwana.*"

"Go to that hut and ask who is the cleverest man in all the villages. Ask the name of the cleverest man, the man who is not afraid. Do not ask about or mention magicians, or you will frighten them."

Yussuf came back after ten minutes and said, "They do not know, *Bwana*. They are afraid. There are chicken bones laid out in front of the huts in a certain way. That is the spell, *Bwana*."

" Come and we will take them away," said Chessing, watching Yussuf's face closely, but Yussuf laughed and said, " It does not frighten me, *Bwana*. *Our* spells are from the Holy Koran and it would only be those I would fear, not these savage playthings."

" Good for you," said Chessing.

They found the chicken bones laid out in small patterns of squares.

" Look," shouted Yussuf, " we lift the spell." Heads appeared at hut doors, many dull black eyes staring as Chessing kicked the patterns away, and Yussuf picked them up and placed them in the pockets of his shorts.

" See them, fools," cried Yussuf. " They are words which have frightened you. There is now no spell."

A few men came and sat in their doorways, looking dazed and weary. They had not slept. They wanted to believe in this white man's power and this black man's contempt for the spell.

Chessing called one of them, using a commanding tone, and what he hoped for happened. The man forgot everything and came to him, but when near Chessing he stopped, having remembered, but Chessing said jocularly, " You see, the spell is broken. All is well." A smile grew slowly across the man's face, a smile of joy, and he put his hands to his mouth and called, " It is finished. Come out. It is finished. It is I, Omanga, who call you, who tells you it is finished."

People came slowly from the huts and stood in the young morning sun. Children began crying and calling and, like dark water, the people flowed between the huts and stood before Chessing and Yussuf. The men eyed Yussuf covertly, for they had broken the law and here was The Whipper.

Chessing began to lie to them in the way he had learned

during years of dealing with suspects. There was the initial exploration to be done, and he began :

" We know the man who did this thing, and though he is a clever man he is not as clever as I." He paused, drawing them, feeling their flow to him. " He said you would stay in your huts but I have brought you out of them. Now, who is the greater magician ? "

They were very impressed, for what this white man said was the truth.

" We know the one who put this spell on you," Chessing was racking his brains for some way of trapping one of them into naming the magician, and he talked on, the words coming easily to him, on subjects such as food, the difficulties for the women, the pointlessness of listening to magicians, when suddenly he found what he thought was the way.

" This magician," he cried to them, " this magician uses one name among you, but we know his real name and you do not. Knowing his real name has destroyed his power. That is why I do not fear his spells. You," he pointed at a young man, " when you saw this magician did he say he was afraid of me ? " The young man shook his head as though it might fall off, his eyes fixed on Chessing, hypnotised. " No, he did not say it, but he was and is, and that is why I caught him and broke his spell." His voice grew soft again and he walked up to the young man and said to him, "What did this one call himself and I will tell you the real secret, young one?" He sweated with strain, willing the young man to obey him, to answer him.

" Luka," said the man, " Luka," then foam formed on his mouth and he fell senseless at Chessing's feet. Chessing had to think swiftly for a wave of shock rippled through the crowd like a wind through standing corn. " You see," he shouted, " he is relieved of his burden. He is resting at my feet." He turned to Yussuf and said quietly, " Luka, do you

know him ? " and when Yussuf nodded, he turned to the
crowd again. " You are free of the spell. Do not fear again,"
then, turning on his heel, he went quickly back to the lorry,
Yussuf and the tractor men following him.

" Yussuf," he said, " where is this Luka ? We will have to
go quickly after him." He knew how swiftly news travelled
in Africa, like the wind it went, in a way that at times seemed
supernatural, for Africa *was* queer no matter what you said.
None knew better than Chessing, how queer. He had seen
things in his police service which had made the hair stand on
his skull and he was not as sceptical as he liked to sound
about witchcraft. He knew there were powers in primitive
men which his own race had lost among the buildings, the
watches and the engines. Drums called them up, for the drums
of Africa were truly its voices.

" He is a herdsman, *Bwana*," said Yussuf, " and he lives
near the boundary, about a mile from my hut. But you will
not find him there."

" Why not ? "

" Already he will have heard."

Chessing knew that Yussuf was probably right. " Has he
a wife ? " Yes, he had. " Then leave me at *Bwana* Tamlin's
office and then go quickly to Luka's hut and if he is not
there bring in his wife, his child, his brother, anyone you can
find." Yussuf rubbed his hands together in the manner of a
white man. He was pleased with his task, as Chessing was
pleased with his morning's work. He was not too experienced
or hardened to look forward to announcing his news to
Tamlin and to hear his praise. He was surprised at his fortune,
for it was not often that a man could pierce the African darkness so easily. He felt again an old affection and a pity for the
nigs who had such good hearts which were so easily frightened
by the darkness.

Tamlin had been brooding in his office. He had hurt poor

Maisie when he blamed her for starting all the trouble by planning the tribal dancing on Christmas Eve. She had even cried a little, protesting that she had not done it. It was the suggestion of Mr. Plume as far as she could remember. Tamlin had forgiven her despite her denial of culpability. " I still forgive you," he had said and they had laughed. " It's a strain for you, I know," she had said.

" It's not a strain," he had lied. " It's not a strain at all. It's pure routine."

But in the office he had been thinking about the attack on De Gaugin and now this witchcraft. It was never possible to know what was really going on among Africans. Only an African could know. It was that knowledge that depressed him now while he awaited news from Chessing.

" Well ? " he said, when Chessing stood in the doorway of the office. " By God, he's really worried," thought Chessing, when he saw Tamlin's intense eyes.

Chessing told him what had happened, watching Tamlin's growing exultation, for it was nothing else. He threw praise about lavishly. " Bloody wonderful, Chessing," he said. " You're a wizard. Now let's hope Yussuf gets this bloody Luka. I think I know the fellow. He's got buck teeth and he's quiet, very quiet. A good herdsman, too, I know that. Do you really think it was he who did this ? Do you think perhaps this fellow lied to you and fainted with wind up ? "

Chessing had been too long a policeman to enthuse about a suspect. " You may be right," he said. But Tamlin was wrong, obviously, for half an hour later a young woman came in to say her husband was dead, stabbed through the heart. Yes, he was the young man who had spoken with the white man. She gave Chessing a long, keen look from her black eyes while he examined her beautiful bare breasts thoughtfully. Poor kid, but did they *really* feel ? He had never satisfied himself about that. They accepted catastrophe even when they howled and wept over it, and this young girl said nothing of her tragedy; she only looked at him with eyes like a healthy animal which watches something strange.

Tamlin was upset about the news, more upset about the girl's loss than about the import of the murder. Chessing did not seem to care, he noticed and Tamlin said, " Bloody rotten, eh ? Murdered because he tried to help us. *You* must feel pretty rotten about it, Chessing ? " Chessing was short with him. " It's sad," he said, " but it's proved who's who. We want Luka, that's certain," and Tamlin nodded, knowing Chessing was right but wondering if Chessing had any heart. Chessing had caused the man's death and yet you wouldn't think so to look at his coolness, Tamlin thought. He sent the young woman up with a note to Maisie, asking her to give her a cup of tea "on the steps of the veranda and be good to her."

" What do we do now ? " said Chessing. He lit his pipe slowly and luxuriously, puffing the fragrant smoke into the sunshine where it hung in a gauzy haze.

" Send for the police," said Tamlin.

" Oh, God," said Chessing.

" Why ? What's the matter ? It's the obvious thing."

" I know," said Chessing, " but you don't know the bull that it will cause. Still, it's our duty. But while we send for them, let's have a look round ourselves."

Tamlin already saw himself leading a man-hunt, all the Europeans spread out across Mambango, combing the place. Against his will he liked it. It quickened something in him. He suggested it to Chessing, who agreed. " Why not ? " he said. " We've got a good start on the police."

" Righto," said Tamlin. " You're in charge of the show. Just give your orders and pick your men. You can make my office your headquarters."

He left Chessing with a large-scale map of Mambango's plantations, hutments and general geographical features.

By midday the Africans had left their huts, and once again the smoke of their cooking fires hung in thin ragged aromatic clouds over the villages. By two o'clock they were all at work, singing in gangs as they moved to the plantations, not knowing that they had made a " strike," or that they had given Mambango its first fear of concerted action, and that from now on their master would think more often of them and of what they were feeling in their villages.

Yussuf had come back with Luka's terrified wife. Luka had left his hut shortly after Chessing had broken the spell in the village. He had been out all night, the woman said. He was often out all night. Chessing questioned her for hours until she began to tell lies from weariness. Then, on Tamlin's instructions, her cooking pot and few possessions were brought and she was locked in one of the tool stores. Tamlin then called a meeting at the Club that evening, to be attended by the European men only; no women, he was definite about that.

While they were talking Mallows drove up in a cloud of dust, thinking he was the bearer of important news for the back-water of Mambango.

He took off his dusty slouch hat and said to Tamlin and Chessing, " O'Riordan's got cancer."

" Christ," said Tamlin. " I knew it, didn't you? Where is he? "

" In the hospital at Chugi. The poor devil took it hard."

" So they told him? "

" Yes. He's pretty far gone. He's got to make a will. Do you know, when he came out of the specialist's room I bloody well cried. It was heartbreaking to see a chap like O'Riordan after the terrible news. He was just crushed, absolutely. I'm going back to be with him. I've come for his things, some books and papers. I'm going back for Christmas Eve with him."

" How long do they give him ? "

" Only a few weeks, they say. They didn't tell him that, only me."

" Well," said Tamlin, " only we three know now, you, me and Chessing here. We just shut up about it, eh ? " It was an order and all nodded. Chessing was pale, for he had more imagination than Tamlin, and he was thinking how treacherous life is, how swiftly it turned to death. A white death was not like a black death.

" He wanted to come back but the docs said they had to make certain examinations, so I left the poor devil in the hospital." He did not attempt to tell them about O'Riordan's frozen eyes following him down the ward, like the eyes of a man just after being wounded.

They sat in silence for over a minute. Tamlin cast down by the news, the manhunt forgotten. He had liked O'Riordan more than he had realised. He was dreaming now about death, and God and about the wrath to come, for there would be wrath, of that he was convinced. The living God awaited all men and had weighed their lives. What would he say of O'Riordan's life. With a name like that an Irishman must be an R.C., and he knew the power of that awful religion over its flock. Idolatrous it was, and the great whore of the world, as his father had taught him. Would it claim O'Riordan again ?

" Did O'Riordan say anything about his soul ? " he asked Major Mallows. Mallows stared at him for a moment and said, " Eh ? "

" I said did O'Riordan say anything about his soul. You know what I mean. Is he preparing for his end ? "

" Good God, I don't know," said Mallows. " I never thought of it. You know what O'Riordan is. Always mocking everything."

" But he didn't mock after the news, did he ? " Tamlin's voice was thinner and somehow waspish.

" No," said Mallows. " He didn't." He felt uncomfortable as always when a man spoke seriously of religion. What a queer mixture Tamlin was. Tamlin brooded for a while and then said, " I'll pray for O'Riordan myself. A man only dies once and it's O'Riordan's turn now. Poor fellow."

Chessing got up and said, " I'll announce the news about the meeting to-night, if you like."

" Do that, if you will," said Tamlin. He seemed to have lost interest, his mind far away with God and O'Riordan.

Mallows coughed far too much, Chessing thought. " Why don't you come up to the Club with me for a drink while I write the chits about to-night," he suggested.

Mallows sprang at this invitation, saying, " *Rather*. I could do with a cold pint all right. Well, excuse me, won't you ? " Tamlin nodded and they left him staring across his desk. Then he ran to the door and shouted, " Hey, Chessing, you won't forget to put out a few people to look for Luka to-day, will you ? We *might* get hold of him to-day if we move."

" I'm putting out a few spies of Yussuf's," Chessing called back. " But we can't really do anything until to-morrow, you know."

" Righto. Only for Christ's sake keep at it or he might do someone else in." To Mallows, Chessing said, " Tamlin's actually bowled over by your news about O'Riordan. D'you notice that ? It's worried him. I'll bet you he's terrified of death."

" Death by sickness, I should say, but not violent death," said Mallows. " I've known him a long time and he's a cold-blooded chap about death."

" Probably got a horror of cancer then."

" So have I," said Mallows. " You get the wind up about those things when you're a bit older than _you_ are now."

Chessing became thoughtful. " M'm," he said, " my worry's prostate and stone in the kidney. It fascinates me, stone in the kidney. I find myself reading about it, against my will, scared to death of it."

" I'm like that about cancer. It's all these bloody magazines we read about health and calories and cancer."

" If I get something incurable," said Chessing, taking his pipe from his mouth, " I'll use my pistol on myself. It's about the only bloody right we'll have left soon in this world." They began to talk about politics, and Mallows said that every politician should be imprisoned after two years in Parliament, automatically, and Chessing laughed as though amused.

CHAPTER SIXTEEN

AMY had put the alarm on for four o'clock and when it rang it was dark but not cold. It was never cold at Mambango, only too hot or pleasant. Now it was pleasant. She put out her hand and woke Plume, who sat up in a confusion saying, " Holy smoke, where am I ? " Then he saw her and she could read the conflict in his face, of gladness, of worry, of further desire and of the need for flight, soon.

" Time to go," she said, smiling. He knew at once that she did not care and he began to fret aloud, though he knew everything.

" What is it ? " he said. " What's the matter ? "

" Nothing," she said, waiting to be pressed further. He took her in his arms and tried to kiss her. She lay still, as though dead, and she felt his muscles go hard as though in strain. He released her, yet his pride driving him on to the end.

" What have I done ? " he asked her.

" Who said you'd done anything," she said.   " Now,
Plumey, come on. You had what you wanted. What more
can I do ? " So he'd had what he wanted. The words were
like a cold plunge. He felt better after them, but his pride
would not let him accept them.

" Is that all it meant to you ? " he said. He still felt something of that yearning and that tenderness for her, as though
only he understood her. He knew there was a dumbness in
his flesh.

" That's all," she said, her smile friendly.   He could see
her naked shape under the sheet. Should he take her again,
pretending passion ? But he did not feel it as he had felt it
for those long weeks of dementia. He had a feeling of disaster,
as of something important which had changed his direction,
like a lost fortune, or a treacherous friend. •

" You didn't feel that when I turned up last night," he
nagged. " Did you ? "

" No," she agreed. " Now, Plumey, you'd better dress or
the servants will know their Memsahib is a whore."

Plume bent down to her and she could see into his eyes.
She scratched the bristles on his jaw idly as she looked at him,
warm in her bed, waiting to return to sleep. He thought of
her curling up with a sigh after he had gone, and he knew
longing again, but now he knew it was his pride.

" You *are* a whore," he said. She smiled, regarded him
with a slight frown, the tip of her tongue between her teeth.
She felt friendship for him, for his quiet stolid honesty.

" Yes, Plumey," she said in a low voice, " I'm a whore.
A whore ! " He smiled sadly and then he saw her mouth
twisting slowly and her whole face contorting, following the
pull of the mouth, and the mouth quivering in the strange
force of grief, or hurt, or sorrow, or whatever it was she was
feeling as the tears welled in her eyes. He did not touch her

but sat watching for a while. Then he got up and began to dress, enormous silence between them, her wet eyes staring at the ceiling.

" Are you trying to tell me I was no good ? " he asked in a distant voice, not looking at her. He could hardly hear her whispered assent as he stood still, one hand holding his shirt, the other the top of his khaki drill trousers.

" I thought so," he said and went on with his dressing.

" You think too much," she said as if to herself. " You think all the time. I didn't want that. I wanted to be hurt, to be overcome, but I could only feel you thinking about him and about how you were appearing to me, and I didn't feel what you felt. I only wanted you, like a meal. I admit that. You didn't enjoy it either."

" It's years since I climbed into bed," he said coldly. " That may mean something." A bash in Grant Road, Bombay, and a swim at Juhu afterwards.

" It means nothing," she said, heartless. " You don't need a woman at all now. You're cured, aren't you ? I remember how you used to tremble when I was with you. You only needed me, not my body. You're a bit queer, Plumey."

" Trembling like a young boy," he sneered. He was surprised to find how this pain he had known had gone and in its place was an affection for her, an understanding. He went and sat beside her, his eyes bright with what he had to say. He stroked her face.

" Do you know," he said, " that I could get in there beside you and start a real love affair with you that you would enjoy." He wondered if he could.

" Could you ? " she said, looking at him and smiling. " Could you really ? "

" Yes," he told her. " I could, because I'm cured, as you say. I *am* cured and I could be the kind of meal you wanted now, quite free from any sentiment. But I wouldn't, even if you wanted it."

" Plumey, I really think you could," she said. " Why wouldn't you ? "

" I don't really know," he told her. " But it may be because it's over for me. Sex, I mean. It never did mean much."

" Did it ever begin ? " she asked, turning her back. He bent down and kissed the hollow between her shoulders, the flesh warm and fragrant against his mouth.

" No," he said. " I don't think it ever began. You've really been a great help, Amy." Without turning, she said, " Plumey darling, you can have me whenever you want me. I mean it. You're sweet. You understand me and I'd hate another man to understand me. Because you understand me you were no good last night. If only you were more brutal you'd be the most wonderful man in the world."

" Bye-bye, Amy," he said. " I'm off. And thanks."

" Bye-bye, darling," she said sleepily. " *Don't* let the servants see you." She heard him tiptoe along the veranda and his breath sharp on the morning air.

" That's that," she said. She thought about the real reason for the death of Plume's passion. She had been too skilful and had revolted him, who had, she saw, never known that this was what he had yearned for from her and was overcome by it, seeing in her avidity the thing he had never known and would not want again, like a man discovering that he did not like tennis during his first try. She curled up as he had known she would and went to sleep, free, and happy. It was as though Mooning had never existed.

CHAPTER SEVENTEEN

THE non-English, or, as the English called them, the " off-whites," had a sort of club of their own. It was a shack which had been thrown up by the company years before and called " The Mambango Arms." It was intended as a reason for refusing the non-English entrance to the real Club up the hill, and it worked. The meeting advertised by Chessing therefore did not include the off-whites, though they were to figure in his plan for the hunting down of Luka. In fact, he had great hopes of them for he knew they would enjoy it to the full. As he saw them, they enjoyed a chance of hunting down a lesser being. You couldn't beat a half-caste sub-inspector for sheer devotion to duty, and a bit more. It had worked in India. He was anxious to prove his loyalty to the English who would not accept him, and his suspicion of the other half of him, the dark people who had supplied the woman for his discredited father. Chessing knew they would love the hunt. They could prove, for themselves, their knowledge of the rightness of the racial arrangements, the arrangements which imprisoned them and which they could only justify by doing to the lesser ones what they felt the higher ones did to *them*. That amused Chessing, who had a deep respect, and at times an affection, for all human nature, he thought.

Plume was in the Club, sitting with Chessing, when people began to stream in. He was perched on a bar-stool, drinking from a tankard of beer. He spoke to most people who came near him. He was almost jocular. They thought it must be because Mallows was back. Partly it was, but even Mallows remarked on this change in Plume.

" Plume, old chap," he had said, " I've never seen you so cheerful. Is it my absence that's done it ? "

" No," Plume had told him. " Maybe it's your return." He loved Mrs. Mooning now, he knew, safely, for good. He would never have believed it possible. She was a good sport. Could a chap say more than that. " You can have me—any time you like," she had said. Once that would have been a terrible thing to hear from a woman, but from her it was like the bond of friendship, something offered which she who offered it knew would be claimed. That was the true friendship. Happy, he thought he had learned a lot in a night. It was something that Mallows would not be able to understand, so he did not tell him, and now there was a loyalty to Amy. It was amusing, and touching too, to think he could dash across to her house and have her, like a meal, and it was warming to know that he would never do it.

His happiness made room for true sorrow for O'Riordan. He sat in silence letting Mallows tell him everything about O'Riordan's responses to the sentence of death by cancer. Mallows had drunk a lot while telling, had breathed heavily, moved almost to tears, not drunken tears, but those of a man who had understood O'Riordan. " You would not know O'Riordan now ; all the fireworks gone," only an occasional bitterness, but without that light sunniness which had masked the barb.

" Gentlemen," Chessing began, pipe in hand. " I have a job to offer you. An exciting job. I want you to catch a murderer." His voice was clear and powerful and he captured his audience at once. They had not realised that this quiet member of the rowdy Bachelors' Mess had this quality which rang in his voice and caught their interest. He spoke to them with a kind of good-hearted contempt, like a commanding officer addressing new recruits in the depot theatre, thought Mallows.

Chessing made his suggestions. One man, one Englishman that was to say, and one of the other chaps from the Mambango Arms (laughter) would pair off and take the lines on the map he would indicate. He explained the circumstances of the murder of the young labourer. He had been found stabbed in the long grass near his village. It was almost certainly because he had given Luka's name, and there was good reason to believe that Luka had killed him. He tried to under-state the matter but soaked in the detective story, one or two of the audience were already talking about clues, and Burkington-Jones stood up and asked if he might make a suggestion. Chessing put his pipe in his mouth and eyed the younger man thoughtfully for a moment. He was annoyed, but he knew Burkington-Jones, who might one day represent the area in politics, for Burkington-Jones had leanings in that direction. He was much concerned about the way in which the Colonial Office was ruining the country. Chessing indicated his assent and Burkington-Jones, in a clear and, to Chessing, irritating voice, turning his head skilfully right and left as he spoke, said:

" There is the matter of this suspect's wife. Has all possible been done to establish that she was not an accomplice ? Has she been expertly questioned ? Could it not be that this whole plan of combing the country is unnecessary and that the man's wife can supply us with the whereabouts of her husband ? "

It was quite a reasonable question, but to Chessing, and to many of the older men, it was maddening to hear this young voice bringing the air and the solemnity of the parliament into the club. Chessing became more popular than ever. There were grunts and growls, and one or two " hear hears "from Burkington-Jones's friends. Tamlin, sitting near Chessing, was squirming about in his chair preparatory to rising. He stood, stocky, and compared with the slender, moustached Burkington-Jones, he appeared coarse, even uncouth with his shirt opened to reveal his hairy chest.

"That's all under control," he said directly to the young man in a curt and ill-mannered way, for he was very put out. "We've got the woman and she's been questioned, by an expert, by Mr. Chessing, who was years in the police. She can't help, but she'll be kept under lock and key until Luka is found. That quite clear?"

The question at the end of Tamlin's statement, with its contempt, brought all Burkington-Jones's social pride to the top. True, Tamlin was the manager, the boss, but he was an ill-bred little bugger too, standing there asking him if it was quite clear in that particular tone which was meant to show the crowd that a fool had questioned his wisdom. Burkington-Jones forgot himself and said in a louder voice than before :

"If you don't mind my saying so, that's not playing the game." No one spoke or moved. They watched Tamlin, who had moved back an inch or so and was examining the brash young man with icy, hostile eyes.

"I do mind," he said in a low, deep tone which carried with curious resonance through the big room. "I do mind," he repeated. "I think you should sit down, son, and let us get on." Someone tittered and Burkington-Jones's face was scarlet. "I still think it's not playing the game," he shouted now, his judgment gone. "It's not right that——" but many voices shouted him down and he began shouting back. Tamlin got up and roared in a way that drew every eye to him, "Sit down!" but Tamlin had lost control of himself too, for he added in the same roar, "We don't want any of the young gentlemen telling us how crude Mr. Tamlin is. Now sit *down*." In the silence that followed this the fans whirred and strained. One or two men puffed at cigarettes, and Plume put away his crossword puzzle with an angry shove into his coat pocket, and Burkington-Jones sat down, far back in his chair, flushed and trembling.

The meeting was over. Chessing told Tamlin he would work out what he called the syndicates of man-hunters by personal arrangement at the bar. Tamlin just went on nodding, his eyes fixed on Burkington-Jones's table, so that Chessing could not judge if he heard or not.

The gabble of conversation as men drifted in twos and threes to the bar filled the room with echoes. Burkington-Jones stayed in his chair, uncertain of what to do, wondering if *anybody* present had understood and sympathised with his effort. Tamlin *was* crude, by God, but it was mortifying to hear from his own mouth that he knew it. It took the taste of the whole gesture away.

"Come on, Socrates," called Chessing. "Don't mope there. You've made an ass of yourself but no one minds. Come and have your leg pulled over a drink." Burkington-Jones saw Tamlin smile at this, but it was a friendly smile. He had an impulse to rush over and make it up, but his caste stopped him. Apologise to a bloody little "oik," never. He got up and flung away to the bar, his short years like a badge of uncertainty on his over-jaunty manner and fixed, nervous smile.

By the morning of Christmas Eve the whole plantation and forest area of Mambango had been searched. The police were coming, it was said, but they were all employed in chasing ivory smugglers from Belgian territory and they would not get to Mambango until after Christmas. They sent the old man of Yussuf's acquaintance, and he turned up in Tamlin's office while he was clearing up the last details of pay for the labourers.

Tamlin told him to report to Chessing and said, "Don't

come back to me, old man. *Bwana* Chessing will deal with you." There was something of that C.I.D. look about the old man which he disliked. People who spied on other people developed a certain smooth falsity of manner, and this old man had it for Tamlin.

" Beat it," he said in English, and fawning, the old man left him. The Africans had the day off and were to dance for the Europeans that night. There were boisterous preparations afoot in all the villages, and painted Africans appeared on the paths gathering green leaves with which they would later decorate themselves.

At eleven o'clock, Tamlin went up to his house for coffee and found Maisie waiting with a budget of news :

" Guess who's come back ? " she said breathlessly. " Tammy, it's amazing." He knew at once. There was only one person who could come back.

" O'Riordan," he said.

" How did you know ? Someone told you." She was disappointed.

" My dear girl," he began, but sighed and did not finish what he was going to say. " How is he ? " he added. " Why has he come back ? Is he all right ? "

" He says he is, but he looks very ill to me. He's gone to his house. He stopped here for a moment and he gave me these lovely flowers he brought from Chugi. Wasn't that kind of him ? "

Yes, it was. Tamlin was only half hearing her. " He's come back to peg out here, that's what it is," he thought. " He's come back for Christmas, yes, but it's to peg out." It was O'Riordan's home, this steaming, malarial backwater. " Do you know how long O'Riordan has lived here, Maisie ? " he said. She shook her head. " A long time, I know," she said.

" Fourteen years," he said. She saw that there was a cloud

in his eyes, that he seemed downcast. " What is it, Tammy ?
You're worried."

" No," he told her. " I was just thinking of how nice it
was of O'Riordan to bring you those flowers." He was
thinking of how this place was more of home to O'Riordan
than to any of the others here ; he had been contented here,
had done his work well, had spent all his money on books
and on his house, which did not even belong to him. When
he died the Company would put someone else there. O'Riordan
would die in that house. That was why he had come back.
To Maisie, while he drank the coffee standing, he said, " I'm
going over to see O'Riordan. I'll be back soon."

" Tammy," she said, " what about lunch ? I've got to go
off now to make the last arrangements for to-night and
to-morrow."

" Back in an hour," he told her. She was relieved. She
had begun to enjoy the company of Mr. Plume, Major Mallows
and poor Mr. Mooning, who was bearing his sorrows so well.
That woman was still living in the house as though nothing
had happened, while poor Mr. Mooning was roughing it in
the Bachelors' Mess. The tide of Mambango opinion was
beginning to turn against Mooning and was supporting the
wife, who had been a brick to stand Mooning for so long,
but Mrs. Tamlin was behindhand in her view of the couple's
estrangement. She had not seen Mrs. Pryce for nearly a
fortnight, she had been so busy.

Now, with Tammy gone, she began to powder her face.
She had begun to use light cosmetics lately and as yet Tammy
had made no comment, unusual for him, though sometimes
he could be stubborn, manlike, and pretend not to notice
something which cried out for his opinion.

Mooning had said nothing to the Committee about his
struggle with his wife for the use of their cook, *my* cook, as
he stormed in a note to her. She had replied that she was

unwell and was not coming to the Christmas celebrations and she would need the cook herself. It drove him into a frenzy when he got a reply to another desperate appeal, telling him that *she* had trained the cook, had supervised his work for years, and he was *her* cook.

He had brought back the cured bacon, the hams and the legs of pork, the succulent chops, and they were now in the large Club frigidaire awaiting a cook. By midday, he was walking up and down the veranda, genuinely distraught, for he had put all his effort into these Christmas preparations. He wanted to go over to his house and corner her, but for many reasons he was afraid. What made it worse was that he had been mellowing, missing her, missing his home. The humiliating knowlege that he was talked about, misunderstood, laughed at as a man who had had to leave his home, even though he had implied in the mess that he had left of his own wish, was enough to bear. He had written a reasonable note to her reminding her that he would need the cook to do the Christmas cooking for the celebrations at the Club. In that note, over which he had worried for hours, and hesitated for days, he had infused a subtle note of forgiveness, of good will. She had not even noticed it. She had written a curt refusal ; there was even a hint of surprise at his request. The notes went back and forth, growing angrier, more unreasonable, more like the letters of married people estranged, with that keen-edged tone of accusation and that almost impalpable suggestion of malicious pleasure in the phrasing of refusal, one waiting for the other to open the way for insult and vilification. Her latest note had told him, " My cook is not the property of the company. He's mine and he's working here for *me*. Because you choose to make him public property is not my fault. I'm not coming to the Christmas dinner." Finally, and he could almost see her poised over it, thinking it out before penning it, there was this. " Since you decided to desert me I don't see why I should put myself out for your convenience. And the house is happier without you. I know *I* am."

He wanted someone to whom he could tell it all, to whom he could pour out the despair, the anxiety, the hate which all but engulfed him, and worse, the longing for her which turned into that hatred. There was no one. He prowled back and forth across the veranda, his fists clenched, and it was in this state that the voice of his assistant cook said :

" I am here, *Bwana*."

Mooning peered at him, for the man was standing in the full glare of the sun on the veranda steps. " Oh, *you're* here, are you ? " he said menacingly. " Well, I don't want you. I want the cook. Who sent you ? "

" Memsahib," said the African, subdued. " I am to cook the Klismas dinnel."

" Klismas dinnel ? " Mooning mimicked him through his clenched teeth. " Why, you bastard, you can't even boil a bloody egg. Out ! Get out ! Go on ! " The man began to retreat, and Mooning said, " No, don't go. Come back." If he sent him back he would give his wife reason to accuse him of " being difficult." He remembered her voice, soft and deliberately lilting when she would say " Are you going to be difficult now ? " As men in their blood hate each other, over money, position, women, he knew that there was a smouldering resentment between himself and his wife which could flare into the bitterest hatred of all, of a man and a woman who had plundered each other's spirits and stared at each other across the wreckage. He tried to draw back from that intuitive peep into the thing that was burning between them in their separation, each chewing the bitter cud of having given what was known in these situations as the best of themselves to the other. He tried to draw back but he thought of her lounging in the house, *his* house, smoking and smiling as she read his angry notes. The more he wrote that he needed his cook, the more she would oppose him and would goad him into losing his cool and reasonable attitude which he had, so far, he told himself, maintained. He was unable, though, to bear it when he looked at the assistant cook. He had no brain. He was just a walking piece of flesh who lived in the dark daze of a million years of forest. He was one of those servants who could not be got rid of. He kept coming back after each dismissal and would be found in the kitchen, surprised, dough in his hands, flour on his face, the dismissal and the curses forgotten by him, and pain and surprise in his small eyes when Mooning shouted " Back again, you bastard ? " and his wife would say, " Oh, leave him. He's harmless."

" So you've been sent to me, have you ? " His voice was sinister for the small squat African who nodded eagerly. The *Bwana* was looking at him in that strange way when he was going to start shouting, but the *Bwana* did not shout. He began to talk to himself.

" I'll have it out," he said aloud. " I'm going to have it out with the bitch. I can't stand any more." He thought of the richness of her body which she was now keeping to herself, owning it again, withheld altogether now, and he knew that she had never belonged to him. He had always felt inferior to her, in a way he could not define for himself. She had a kind of brutal courage, an arrogance which did not disturb men but which seemed only to be an accessory to her beauty and her confident, thrusting personality. He knew, that despite his secret condemnation of her past life, that he had been very lucky to get her and he had never understood why she had accepted him. But she had accepted two others as husbands, and yet, being the third, he had to tell himself at times that he was luckier than the others, for she had chosen him after much experience ; and he knew it was sad that he should thus. attempt to delude himself. It was the same as it had always been ; conflict was there even now that he was away from her. He wanted to see her now, thinking that he needed to fight with her, but he missed her and in his wish to see her was that deeper thing, pathetic, hopeful, jealous, a compulsion from the spring of his being which was still without bitterness.

" You come with me," he told the nervous assistant cook, who was watching him with slightly bent head, the lower whites of his apprehensive eyes like crescents of ivory. In his way he knew he was a bone between the Master and the Mistress.

Mooning composed himself as he went down the hill to his house. He must be cool, calm, reasonable. He must keep his dignity, for a few days away from her had taught him how much of this quality he had lost with her, and how much she respected this thing which she had all but destroyed in him. The sun and his nervous expectancy brought the sweat out on his body in a prickling wave, soaking him. He felt well and utterly in need of her, and hope rose fast in him as he quickened his pace. By the time he reached the house his temper had cooled and he was himself again, weak and ready to beg, and he felt very happy.

CHAPTER EIGHTEEN

" MADE your peace with God ? " said Tamlin, unable to conceal amazement. " You did that ? Honestly, chum, did you really do that ? " He looked at O'Riordan's thin face with its round Celtic dome, the fair lank hair thin, like strands of cornsilk across the high forehead. The greenish eyes still held that strange moving light, like a private amusement, but there was a thinness in the face that was not only the meagreness of flesh. It was a hollowness of a knowledge, of an inner acquaintance with doom, as if O'Riordan knew a continuous and devouring vision of the whole thing, the life which was mystery and the death in him which was annihilating, zero. But it could not be this. " Peace with God."

" That's right," O'Riordan told him, serious and quiet, but with a faint smile almost of apology, for he had been the great agnostic, the fearless one of Mambango, but mother had won, the mother of holy ruined Ireland. The family saying the rosary at night had triumphed. Father Hally and Father Kiernan, their dark jowls creased in smiles, had known, as it were, that this was how it would be, so long ago they had known, hearing the young man decry their superstition and their regard for the praying poor.

" This is amazing," said Tamlin, and then, cautiously, " R.C., of course."

" Yes, R.C.," said O'Riordan. " Once you've been that nothing else will do in the way of religion. I always knew and I always wondered if I would have the courage to deny it all when it was time to go."

" Was it lack of courage ? " Tamlin's eyes had softened, but they were wary. He could not understand. He thought, " So this is the power of the Roman Church." He could not forget O'Riordan's quietly-spoken blasphemies, and the amusement his dryness had caused over so many drinks. And now that was finished, like O'Riordan. Finished. Tamlin shivered, and, seeing it, O'Riordan gave him a knowing smile. He told Tamlin how it all came about. But he did not tell him about the confession. He sweated when he thought of that, raking the soil of nearly thirty years, being gently pressed to remember sin by the soft voice from the unseen face behind the small, high, wire screen.

" Pray, Father, give me your blessing for I have sinned. It is—it is—it is thirty years since my last confession, and I accuse myself of——" Thirty years ago it had been. " It is a fortnight since my last confession——" There was no surprise in the priest's voice when O'Riordan had paused after announcing his thirty years of silence. They had both waited and, halting, hoarse, with the strange peace that was suddenly familiar again, O'Riordan had begun the dreary catalogue of his sins. He told it like a story once the crust of private existence had crumbled and he felt the surge of what in boyhood had been for him innocence in surrender, feeling the peace of the nervous but comforting humility which had made him clear-eyed again in front of his mother when he had run home from confession, free again.

" It seems queer to hear that from you, you know," Tamlin told him. " You see, if anyone ever made me doubt, though only a little, you know, it was you, when you brought all your arguments out. I remember how you proved to me that all human life was pointless. That we came for no reason, and then went."

" I could still do it," O'Riordan said, ruminative, looking over Tamlin's shoulder, beyond the veranda on which they were sitting, to the hills which were like blurs of blue powdery smoke in the heat. " That's what's queer. I am still as I was and yet I want peace. I could still prove it's all pointless and yet I know there is a great mystery which we will never solve." It was right to have been humble and to have confessed. It was right to prepare for death in the way which was in his blood, which had been there for centuries, and even though he had associated his ancient religion with the degradation and suffering which the Irish people had endured, he felt now that it was their only strength, wherever they lived, Dublin, Sydney, Boston, Liverpool, never completely assimilated in the Anglo-Saxon calmness and politeness about God. It must

have been their strength or he would not have gone to confession. It could not have overcome his lifelong scepticism
otherwise. He preferred the Anglo-Saxon coolness about
God, envied them their essential unconcern, for he even now
despised the huge superstition and fear of the Irish, Spanish,
Italian Catholic poor, which he had seen and recognised, but
which had something in it of humble man's true condition.

They did not talk of the coming death. Tamlin wanted to
know when O'Riordan would die so that he could help to
make it as peaceful as possible, but he could not completely
believe in it. True, O'Riordan was pale, thin, but lying back
in that chair, he seemed confident, even normal, though much
quieter than ever before in Tamlin's remembrance of him.

" I think it is a wonderful thing, O'Riordan," he said
truthfully. " I'm glad you've gone back to your church.
You've done the right thing——" O'Riordan stopped
listening. He was thinking, " It's not the right thing. I've
been a coward. I fear death. I should have stayed as I was.
If there is a God and he thinks my life has been a bad one,
then let him burn me." For in his mind, the mind which had
never quite recovered from Father Furniss's Works, the
damned would burn in living flames. The conception of hell
was of fire, the hell of suffering and torment in fire. His early
childish aboriginal self had never ceased to believe in it,
though the man was now thinking, " It's fear that did it.
I should never have surrendered," and then the knowledge
that he was soon to die shook him again, tearing his courage
of opinion to shreds.

" I could still prove that it's all nonsense," O'Riordan told
him again. " I could do that even now. And that's what I
don't understand."

" You've no real faith, that's why. You have to have
faith." Tamlin knew he could die happily the next moment,
and he knew O'Riordan could not. What a fearful thing that

was. It was faith that made a man happy. Nothing else could
do it. He talked on, about his own faith, of what it meant
to him. When he had finished O'Riordan said, " I've never
had faith and I have none now. I only feel certain that there
is a plan in this universe that defeats all my reading and
thinking and all that. I can't get beyond that. Even though
I am afraid to die I know I will think these things at the very
end." So it was out. Death. He had said it. The dark,
sombre, lean word of ending, but for Tamlin, beginning.
" I envy *you*," said O'Riordan, " I do truly."

" Envy me ? " Tamlin laughed. " There's not much to
envy. An uneducated man with a good wife." But was that
what O'Riordan had meant ? Did he envy the man, Tamlin,
the man of faith, or did he envy Tamlin who was going to live
on in glorious uncertainty while O'Riordan died ? This thought
ended Tamlin's laughter and O'Riordan said :

" It's death that made me give in. For that was what I
did. I gave in. I am afraid of death." He offered Tamlin a
cigarette and they lit them, Tamlin making up his mind. He
sat back and caught O'Riordan's wise eyes, holding them
while he spoke in the direct manner which O'Riordan
remembered.

" O'Riordan," he said, " tell me something. How long
have you got ? "

O'Riordan blew smoke slowly from his nostrils, watching
it, his eyes squinting down his nose. His small neat body
was tensing as he looked up at Tamlin and said, " That's my
business." He smiled again. " I'm keeping that to myself."

" You wouldn't——" Tamlin's face was severe. " You
wouldn't——"

" I might. But that's my business too." They had gone
into the dark caverns, into the terrifying private labyrinth
wherein people do not know what they mean, what they are,
what they will become, the place where men struggle to keep

other men fast to the dream of the world. Tamlin spoke as though he was in a church.

"You mustn't, O'Riordan. You mustn't, after making your peace. You mustn't——"

"What are we talking about?" O'Riordan asked, puckish, shutting Tamlin up, embarrassing him, for Tamlin had to pretend he had been in the wrong while afraid that he was not. "I only thought—I only wanted to ask you to have courage." He wondered if Maisie could help O'Riordan. What could a woman do for him?

"Courage?" O'Riordan all but snarled the word. "I've got plenty, but not enough to defeat my own mind. Can you understand that?" How could Tamlin really understand that, he thought, when he was going to go on living, in happy uncertainty. O'Riordan had to fight hard against the wish to dramatise himself, the posturing which had always given him relief when he talked with others, but accusing himself always, speaking to the doubting one who lived behind the posture of his confident public self.

"You're not afraid?" said Tamlin quietly, and feeling his concern O'Riordan shook his head. "No," he said, "I'm not afraid." Tamlin put his big powerful hand on O'Riordan's knee. "Good," he said emotionally, surprising O'Riordan, who was watching him with shrewd, nervous eyes. "That's all I wanted to know. I'd feel it a lot if I knew you were afraid." O'Riordan was tempted to ask why, to explore that sentence which came so oddly from Tamlin's thin lips, but he was weary. He let Tamlin talk and did not answer until the other noticed and got up. They shook hands, Tamlin wondering if O'Riordan might not take his own life and if it was not the last time he might see him. What Tamlin had wanted to discuss was still untouched. He wanted to know if O'Riordan would live beyond Christmas. If not there would be no celebrations, at least not in the Club. It seemed so stupid to think of it, looking at O'Riordan, who appeared good for years of life, but inside him was death, feeding on his hours. Tamlin was pale and as he left O'Riordan he felt sad, but glad to leave the dying man, and sorry for feeling this gladness. On the other hand, it might be all a mistake. O'Riordan might live for another twenty years, but he knew that this was not true. In a way O'Riordan was already dead. There was only left the trouble, the awkwardness, the small chaos of his laying-out, the burial and the gradual forgetting in the great sun-glare of the dried-up, panting plains and hills. Tamlin regretted that, but he had seen so many go quietly, cause a day's trouble with their funerals, and then swiftly become the memory of an incident, something torn from the calendar and flung away. It was a cruel, heartless world, Tamlin never forgot. What it would be without faith in God, he could not imagine.

O'Riordan lay back in the long cane chair. He wanted to read but he could not begin. He wanted to go on with his studies of the universe, which his mind could only half comprehend as yet, but which he knew would dawn for him. And yet, why bother now? He knew more now than all the men who had written the books which waited on his shelf, but he could not marshal it into words, or even thoughts, for he was afraid of it, trying to hold on to the fast fading contentment which the approach to God had given him. He did not believe in God; he had tried hard. He was aware of the overpowering mystery, now more than ever, but it was not the God of boyhood to which he had tried to return. He lived now in two worlds, of doubt and of will to believe, and now both sought to give him relief and could not calm him.

"You have a dry soul," the priest had told him in a low voice. This desert of the soul burned before his inward stare and he felt lost and utterly ruined by books, he thought, all innocence gone.

He turned on the radio, flooding the bungalow with jazz. A woman, one of the new visionaries of the ether, was whining about her baby, not the baby of the body's fruiting, but that other baby, shaven, sprayed with lotion, tuxedoed, handsome in his love which he denied the singing woman. When the whining was done an Amercian asked O'Riordan, " Do you feel old before your time ? Do you feel you've no pep, no will to win ? You do ? Well, that's too bad."

He switched off. It was' too late for Krispo, the all-giving food, now. All that mania would go on after he was dead. It was a world from which a man should wish to go, but from which he would never finally be driven, only loaned to death for a while.

He began saying the rosary to himself, trying not to do it mechanically, as something to be got through, like a race. Deliberately he said it haltingly, trying to feel the trueness of Mary whom he hailed, of the Mother of God who would pray for him, sinner, now and at the hour of his death. He sweated as he sought to believe, going back to a trick of his childhood when he had sought to visualise the pain each sin, each wicked thought, each lie, each selfishness, had inflicted on Him. He tried to bring up the body of Christ to his inner eye, nailed, sagging in the final bloody love of man. It came, disquieting, but not with that truth of innocent childhood ; never again, he knew, could it be like that. To have faith he would have to endure, the voice in the confessional had said. There had been a professional ease, almost a glibness in the priest's voice, and he had ignored it, striving for humility, for compassion, for he had a thought for the corroding voices of the thousands of sinners which had lapped like a wave for years upon the priest's ears. The bitter sickening wave of man's animal longing flooding to the foot of the crucifix. He wavered in what he thought was his selfish agnostic courage

which had never truly sustained him, which had never won
over the childhood and the centuries of prayer. Could it be
that there really was God and the Kingdom of Heaven? He
hoped yes, but that sneering voice of the world's suffering
told him no. He switched on the radio again.

CHAPTER NINETEEN

THE search of the plantations had been an adventure for
the inhabitants of Mambango. After a day of it, pointless
tramping in the rocky hills, half embarrassed probings in
African huts, the Europeans and their helpers, the " off-
whites," had split up near the Club into their two spheres,
each half sure that without the other they would have had
better luck. It was Chessing who first grew angry, with
Mallows, with Burkington-Jones and others who grumbled,
" Waste of bloody time, that's all." Burkington-Jones was
surprised when Chessing snapped at him, " For Christ's sake
shut up about it then. You need not have come anyway."
There was gloom and bad temper after that as they went into
the Club. Only Pryce, his somehow walrus face solemn and
loose-lipped, cheered them up, for his heart, that legend, had
prevented him from taking part, and now they joked with
him, enjoying his concern with " the situation " and their
failure.

The next day, while Tamlin sat with O'Riordan and Mooning made his way to his house, they had what Mallows called
a " post-mortem " on the trouble at Mambango. After a day
or two the killing of one nig by another did not seem so
important after all. The freshness and excitement of what it
might mean had evaporated, and now there was an irritation

with Chessing, who continued to seek their interest and co-operation. He saw that they no longer cared about it.

" Why bother ? " said the usually quiet Glebb, coming out of his morose memories of gold, or failure, Chessing thought. " The wogs are working. Why interfere ? There's a police spy here among them doing his best. Why risk upsetting the wogs ? Leave it, I say." Several agreed with him.

" It's not as though they'd gone for one of *us*, is it ? " said Pryce, who before had regarded the search as a crusade against unrest among the nigs.

" So you think leave it ? " said Chessing. There was a nodding of heads, while those already at the bar did not even bother to answer.

" If one wog does another in, why worry ? " said Burkington-Jones.

" That's right," Chessing told him in an acidulous voice. " What's a wog after all ? "

" Let's all have a drink and forget it," said Mallows. He was thinking that Mooning would find Plume with Mrs. Mooning. He had seen Mooning entering his house and he knew that Plume was there. Plume was due to appear for the last Committee meeting with Mrs. Tamlin, Mooning and himself, in about half an hour. He had an uneasy feeling that everything was about to go wrong. He trusted that Mooning would not catch Plume in the act, as it were. He could not control his uneasiness, and Chessing saw him fretting and said :

" What's up, Major ?   Missing Plume ?   Where is he to-day ? "

" He's coming," Mallows answered, too readily, thought Chessing, especially when the older man's face reddened and he fiddled with the glass and the ash-tray on his cane table. By Chessing's eyes, Mallows saw that he had only deepened the other's interest, so he got up and walked to the bar.

"Must get some cigarettes," he mumbled. "They've had a row," thought Chessing. "Queer. It's the heat, I expect."

Mrs. Tamlin came in and went to the large corner table where the Committee usually met. Major Mallows, in relief, joined her, but saw that she was distressed about something. As soon as he sat down she said, "Major Mallows, there's a terrible quarrel going on in the Moonings' bungalow. I heard it as I passed just now. It sounds terrible. Mr. Mooning and another man. I could hear their voices, and Mrs. Mooning laughing as if she's gone out of her mind."

"Good heavens," said Mallows, the words strange in his mouth, for it was one of the expressions he saved to express interested surprise to a woman. "Do you think I ought to go and do something about it?" He wanted very much to go. He was worrying about Plume. Plume had gone after his greens, he was certain. The fool, the bloody stupid fool, when he could have had a nice cut off the local joint, and no trouble.

Mrs. Tamlin would not commit herself but she knew that he wanted to go, and she saw quickly that he was worrying about leaving her alone at the table ; a real gentleman, the Major. "Don't worry about me, Major Mallows," she told him, he thought rather gallantly. "I'll wait for you here if you think you should go. They *might* become violent, you know." She wanted him to go. He would get the news, for now she was curious. This was a man's job.

Though he knocked several times on the door leading off the Mooning's veranda, Mallows could not make them hear him. He could hear Plume's voice raised in rage over that of Mrs. Mooning's, which was trying to reason with him. He stood in uncertainty, not wanting to eavesdrop, but absorbed, quiet, drawn into the scene which he could not observe. They were both shouting now, but the woman's voice trailed away into silence. By Christ, he had never dreamed that Plume

could treat a woman like this ; that iron voice, not shouting
now, but quiet and threatening, almost silken.

"You knew all right, you bitch," he was telling her, perhaps
leaning over her, trembling with temper. "It's a bloody
trick. You knew he was coming. You want a divorce, don't
you ? You tried to fix it all up and he'd come to find me, in
flagrante virginum, or whatever the hell they call it." Then he
shouted at her, into her face maybe, "You bloody cheat."
Mallows heard the woman burst into tears. He squirmed and
opened the door. "What about the Committee ? " he said
loudly, glibly, bringing Mrs. Mooning to her feet.

"You silly little man," she cried, forgetting her tears.
"Who cares about your damned committee ? " Then to
Plume she cried hysterically, satirically, "The Committee."

Mallows was put out. Then he saw Mooning lying on a
couch holding something to his eyes, still, hardly present, it
seemed.

"Is that meat he's holding to his eye ? " said Mallows,
absorbed in the sight. Mrs. Mooning turned her eyes up and
said "God ! What a man ! " and Plume said, "Yes, meat.
It's meat. It's meat. Did you think he was watching an
eclipse, you silly bugger ? "

"Sorry," said Mallows, conscious of the gap, the anti-
climax he had caused, but Mrs. Mooning had forgotten him
for she was raving at Plume again. "You're a liar to have
accused me of that. You know why you came here. No one
invited you. You came for one thing." There was an unmis-
takable significance for Mallows in the way she had said "one
thing," and he knew she was right. "Whatever I may be,
I'm not a cheat," she told Plume bitterly. "I didn't know
this thing was coming." She pointed to her prostrate husband.
Mallows felt ashamed to witness this, this degradation of
Mooning, obviously injured by one of them, listening to their
quarrel.

" Who hit him ? " Mallows's voice carried an authority which appealed to Plume, and he answered, " I did, the little swine."

" What about the Committee ? "

" To hell with the Committee. You and Mrs. Tamlin do it." Plume turned again to Mrs. Mooning, who was lighting a cigarette. He was grinning, distractedly.

" But it's Christmas Eve. What about the dinner to-morrow ? Come on, now," Mallows coaxed them both, but the woman glared at him and he noticed that she was naked under the black dressing-gown, and it gave him a strange excitement he had not known for years. He felt an affection for her, wanted to help her. Those breasts. No wonder Plume —— But he fought down this mean, this dirty thought. He was sorry for them both. Mooning had interrupted them, and Mallows's masculine mind, hardened by years of absence from his own womenkind, felt loyalty and sympathy for Plume, his friend, thwarted of that gorgeous body unhidden under the silk. Mooning was only a bloody nuisance really. Poor Plume.

" I'll go," he said. " What about him ? " He nodded at Mooning. " Take him to the mess," said Plume. Without a word, Mooning got up, breathing hard through his nose, holding a large strip of meat across his eyes. He stood, waiting to be taken away, and Mallows was sorry for him.

" Can't take him like that."

" Take the car then," Mrs. Mooning's voice was casual. She had turned away. " Hard as bloody nails," said Mallows in an undertone to Plume, but she heard him. " Yes," she said, " I know enough about men to make me hard. You're all the same ; monkeys, bloody monkeys. Now take him away, please, and give him your sympathy." Mallows led Mooning away, and as he reached the veranda steps he heard them start again, passion and longing in their cries. " Plume should just fling her down now and get it over," he thought, chuckling. They were both head over heels in lust, it was obvious. Mooning seemed to be sobbing, in pain or grief, the older man could not decide. He let in the clutch and drove slowly out of the banana-leaf covered garage. A short, fat African started to get into the back of the car, and when Mallows said, "What do *you* want, you sod?" Mooning said thickly, "The cook. The cook. Let him come."

They drove slowly up the hill. When they were near the mess, Mooning spoke, in a voice which caused Mallows to fumble the gears.

"Don't let anyone see me," he said, faltering, his voice low. "If anyone sees me I'll do myself in. I just want to lie down in my own room."

"Of course," Mallows replied, sensing at last something of what this meant to Mooning. He had lost his woman and had been beaten into the bargain. He felt pity and contempt, and greater than these, a worry lest he be drawn farther into the other's tragedy. "I'll see you to your room, of course, Mooning."

"Plume hit me," whispered Mooning. "I didn't mean any harm. He hit me."

"I'll look at your eyes in a minute," Mallows sought for the right tone, but Mooning shook his head. "No," he said, "just leave me in my room." The defeat in Mooning's voice, his slumped head and shoulders, touched the Major.

"*I* know. I'll take you to O'Riordan's place. He's a good sort, O'Riordan, and he'll see you're all right. He won't say a word."

"He doesn't like me."

"Bull," said Mallows. "He likes everybody and he needs a bit of company."

O'Riordan did as Mallows had foreseen. He twisted his mouth and nodded while Mallows explained, forgetting his state as a man not long to live. " Bring the poor sod in," he said. " Got hit hard, did he ? By Plume, eh ? I thought he was a quiet chap." He sniggered softly.

" And here's his cook." Mallows pointed to the African in the back of the car, and seeing the African in that solemn comfort which Africans often achieved when others were in crisis, he cried, " Well, come on, you fat sod. Get out of there and help your bloody master."

O'Riordan shook with the silent laughter Mallows had not seen for weeks. " Look after Mooning," said Mallows, trying not to smile. " He's had a raw deal and he's hurt badly."

" I'll look after him," said O'Riordan calmly.

In bed in the silent hothouse of her room, Mrs. Mooning stroked Plume's head. He was asleep, silenced, his turmoil gone, spent in the brief upheaval she had created skilfully for him. She was wondering how to awaken him and get him out of the house, but in an hour or two it would be dark. Should she keep him for the night, or should she get rid of him ? It was Christmas Eve and he would be missed from the party. She could not decide. She lay down beside him and in a few minutes felt sleepy. She thought she would keep him. Later he would be cool and determined.

She had won in the matter of the cook. Mooning had been allowed to take that idiot assistant, but the cook, the only cook, was still in her kitchen. Damn him. She was glad Plume had hit him. She fell asleep smiling. Damn them all. She felt Plume's sleepy hand on her thigh, dreaming its way across her hot, perspiring flesh. Yes, he would stay.

CHAPTER TWENTY

THE drums were throbbing while the sun fell below the mountains. They set up a slow rhythmic thunder which grew slowly louder as darkness came over the plain. The Europeans in their bungalows or drinking on their verandas felt the disturbing sensation, the peculiar nervous pleasure of ear and heart as the simple rhythm increased in complication and volume. Soon it had climbed to a faster tempo, catching the listener's breath, not innocent or simple now, but demoniac and then frightening as the rumbling pattern moved across and above the deeper voice of the heavy drums beaten by slow, cunning, knowing hands. Fires glowed on the great compound between the two main villages. It was not time to dance yet, only time for the hundred drums to join each other in a voice which at last seemed to give Mambango back to the Africa that had once been there and which Tamlin had all but beaten. These drums which now made the air pulse and quiver were its real voice, the voice of the forest which the tractors had only driven underground.

"God, it's wonderful," said Mrs. Pryce. She was pale and nervous, her eyes glittering as she spoke to her husband. Pryce was lying on a long cane chair, eyeing her curiously. "Savage, isn't it, ducks?" he said playfully.

"Yes," she whispered, hardly hearing him, the deep drum voices like hands in her belly, breaking down her European guard, that cold withdrawn planning of the correct thing, the respectable word and deed. She wanted to run about, spin, shake, laughing in release as the thunder shook her. Pryce sensed something of this, resisting the drums, though feeling their probe in his fat, in his careful blood.

"First time you've really 'eard it, isn't it?" he said.

"Yes." She was swaying softly, her hands clutching the veranda rail, staring down at the winking fires.

"Well, after dinner you can watch 'ow the nigs dance to it when they get worked up." He felt a sense of ownership of this Africa which his wife was enjoying now before his eyes. "If only I was fit," he brooded, "I'd give 'er what for, all right." He sensed her weariness of him, a woman still young, very attractive, awakened by the nigger drums. How long would it be before she started looking around? Yet he could not believe she would ever leave him. They had a son at school in South Africa. He was twelve now, memory of a time when things had been all right, when he was fitter, younger, harder, hunter of the dream.

"Come 'ere, ducks," he said. She gave him her hand and he saw how the pupils of her eyes had enlarged. "I'm sorry I'm such a useless bloke to you," he said, and his sad, yearning eyes caught her mood, softening her to him.

"Freddy, it's all right," she said. She felt her abandon, her disquiet dampened, driven away by her will and by her loyalty to him. He was a good husband, a pig in many ways, untidy, even dirty in his habits, but kind and thoughtful. His worry about his heart had killed the warmth which their marriage had retained for a few years, had created a deep fear in both of them. Now she was sorry for him, holding his hand, the drums only a noise, their magic shed. "It's all right, Freddy," she told him. "You're good to me and that's the thing that really counts for a woman." She knew he believed these things; he was comforted by them. Only in her mirror at times did she feel a sense of waste, the mirror, friend and becalmer of the bitter lonely hour. She would have liked him to enjoy her. There were years of this lack ahead of her, but she had found a comfort in the knowledge of his selfish, fleshly suffering. He, grateful and desiring what he feared to have, kissed her arm, mumbling and whispering to himself, awakening the deep roots of her pity. She told him that she had planned a " nice dinner " for him. He ate deeply, voraciously, like a beast, and it was a joy to her to feed him.

The drums were a deep throb only half heard by Plume and Mrs. Mooning. He was kissing her throat, thoughtfully, staring at it each time he withdrew his lips, thinking of her words and of her moaning cries of lust in the dark under his deliberate and determined will, crushing her down into the surrender which only the dream-Jack had known so long ago. Now she was dazed, slack and slumbrous-eyed, like a cat before a fire ; feeling his mouth on her throat as though through a fog of calm warm flesh, his voice vibrating in her jaw like a purr. She felt rather than heard the deep throbbing of the drums, feeling their sound through her body as though it were a hall of peace and calm.

" We *should* go to the dance," he said into her throat. " We *should*. People will talk." He was caught between the new wonder of the conquered woman, beautiful in his hands, and that of the urgency of people, the world, opinions.

" *You* go," she said, her voice barely audible in the dark, quiet room. He could hear the clock ticking beside the bed, like a needle point against the boom of the drums. Her two words chilled him again for a moment. " *You* go," he said them to himself.

" Don't you care at all ? " he nagged. " Do you *want* me to go ? "

" You do whatever you want, Plumey," she told him, her voice coming to her own ears from far down in this daze into which he had crushed her. " If you want to go, go."

She struggled against his insistence, which was seeking to break the peace he had given her, the peace which only Jack had weaved until Plumey had discovered the gift of his own re-sharpened hunger. He could come or go as he liked, but he did not want this. He wanted her to want him always, to press him to stay, or to take her with him, not to be able to do without him. She baffled him. He did not know that she had known that anguish with another man, that torture which only the other's presence could soothe, eating her, like the fangs of the heart's ache, and that no man could ever have it from her like that again. He suspected something in his bafflement but could not find it, his jealous desire urging him to give her pain by some words which would awaken her from that private daze from which she whispered her uncaring words. He thought she had fallen asleep but her eyes were open now. She had sensed his change of feeling, and she resented him for destroying the almost stupefied dream she had lain in.

" Plumey," she said, her voice awake now. He grunted, drawing the tiny sharp thorns of his beard against her neck. Jack used to do that, but deliberately.

" Is it true that you've been in gaol ? " She almost laughed aloud as he released her from his arms. He sat up and she could hear his breathing quicken, almost feel him experiencing the shock she had given him. He sat still. She watched his profile against the faint luminescence of the warm night sky. In his powerful, almost thick-set way, he was good-looking. Now, subdued, as though sullen, he began to dress, and she could feel the tension growing in this silence between them, while the drums made a low pounding background to his wonder and shock, to her sincere and malicious interest.

" Have I hurt you, Plumey ? " she said, cooing but keen. " I didn't mean to. I really didn't." She began to believe herself and genuine sorrow for hurting him followed quickly after the vocal conviction of her lie. She knelt up in the bed, and he looked at her and felt the weakness of desire again but evaded it and he said :

" Who told you ? " There was a faint break in his voice, and she knew that the question had pierced him more deeply than she had hoped. She was frightened by what she had done and she strove to mollify him, wondering why she was frightened. There was one sure way. To get him down again into the embrace which broke all violence in a man, but he was cold and in a quiet way, fiercely so.

" Everybody knows," she said. " But nobody minds. They don't dislike you or hold it against you. At Mambango everyone has a skeleton in the cupboard. And we all know each other's secrets."

" Really ? " he said. " And what's yours ? What's *your* skeleton ? "

" This," she told him. She was icy now, willing to hurt him and pretend to hurt herself. " Everyone knows I'm a tart, that I can't do without a man. They like to say I'm a nympho, but it's much simpler than that. I did love a man once, properly, and I lost him through a mistake, and after that I never cared again. I knew that——"

" What mistake ? " he spat the two words at her.

" I never felt the same again about anything," she continued, evading his vehement eyes. " Men never meant anything again after I lost *him*. It was——"

" What mistake ? " he said again. " What mistake caused you to lose him ? " He knew what the mistake was and he wanted her to admit it, to tell him in pain. " I'll tell you the mistake," he said. " You simply slept with another man and this true love couldn't stand for it. That's the mistake, isn't it ? " He gripped her wrist, watching her eyes blacken to a largeness in which they seemed to swim with the dark lustrous threat of tears. " You did, didn't you ? " He shook

her arm and, sensing his force and his cruel urgency, she
said, " Yes, I did. That's what I did. You hate me, don't
you ? "

" No," he told her. " I don't mind a bit. I don't mind
what you did. I only object to your play-acting, your making
a lovely picture out of what was just a romp on a bed. It's
you that hate what you did, not I."

" Don't you think I'm bad then ? " she said in a low voice,
fishing, the words not becoming her as he had known her,
and he laughed, genuinely amused. She joined him, weaken-
ing, she knew, falling into the possessed state, he the possessor,
her freedom gone, loving him because he knew her and did
not hate her, and hating him too for winning her weakness.
She felt at once a great happiness and a sense of being trapped,
open to hurt and jealousy, for he knew her and she must
keep him.

" I'm going," he said. " I must make an appearance."

" Don't go," she said. It was what he had longed for her
to say, but now it irritated him. " I *must* go," he said, reason-
ing, unreasonable.

" Don't go, Plumey. Stay with me. Stay for always."

" For always ? " he cried. " What the devil do you mean ? "
But he did not wait for a reply. He must not weaken. He
stood up and put on his shirt, and she sought for something
to distract him, a mixture of despair and apprehension of
loneliness, causing her to feel a frantic anxiety to make him
tender to her, to soften this quality of dominance he was
assuming without yet realising its presence.

" Am I the first woman you've loved, Plumey ? " she asked,
her voice almost husky, her eyes sincere.

" Who said I love you ? " he replied. " Do *you* love me ? "

Freedom was gone from her, she knew. She would have
to say what she felt. She would enter that sphere of suffering
in which she would not possess but be possessed.

"Yes," she said, "I love you. I love you. I do, truly I do."

He smiled at her, cruelly, she knew with a leap of her heart, his hands stilled at the collar of his shirt. "Always," she thought, "when he is dressing we have these scenes. He is always going away and I never minded and now it's hell." There was still drama for her in her life, but her camera gaze was fading.

"You have no right to love me," he said, playful, now feeling his position, savouring it, remembering what he had gone through for all those weeks of dumb hunger for her. "You don't belong to me. You belong to Mooning." If he had not said that she would have run to him, embraced him, humbled herself for some tenderness from him. Now she knelt still, her arms folded across her breasts, watching him, and he saw her and without effort she had won, she thought, for he sat beside her and stroked her shoulders.

"You're a good sort, Amy," he told her. "If you love me, I hope it makes you happy. I need time to think. I don't know what I feel. I don't know what is going on in me, that's all." A good sort. Time to think, to——

She knew, though. He was worming out of it in the way men always worm out when they have cooled, and a woman, desperate, seeks assurance. She felt the pain, the cold freezing pain of it sink right down into her, like ice falling slowly through the water of the deep, dark well of herself. She began to cry and he got up and went on with his dressing. Of them both, she saw, he was the harder, especially when she had satisfied him. All men were cruel at heart, seeking freedom when the magic was gone from their eyes.

When he was ready he turned from the door and began to say those half apologetic things men say when they are going out to their own life beyond the bedroom, the flat, the hired bed. "I'll be in again. Don't cry. It's only a dance I'm going to. I *must* go." A pause. "Be reasonable."

She shook her head, silent. The door closed with a long click, his hand careful with it, shutting her off as gently as he could. She heard his steps quick on the veranda and she knelt on, cold, raging, despairing, thinking, "How can it happen? Why can't we just ignore these feelings? Why do I allow myself?"

From the beginning she had loved him, she thought, but she had been free, testing her barbs on him. When does it begin, the enslavement to the other's moods, when a look is a knife, a cold word an icicle in the heart? She could not remember. She needed him. Why? She did not know. What should she do? There was no one any more to say. Yesterday was gone, like a leaf on a heartless wind.

There was a sinister threatening note in the drums which had moved to the pit of her consciousness, like fear, like lostness.

CHAPTER TWENTY-ONE

SAMUEL, Paul and Luka said farewell to each other in thick forest on the ridge overlooking Mambango. In the darkness below they could see the fires, blazing brightly in the compound between the plantations. The flood of thunder from the drums came up to them in a steady wave of staccato and deeper pulsing sound. They could see the harsh bright pools of light from petrol lamps where the Europeans sat to watch the dancers.

"You see them? They dance gladly for the white men," said Paul. "It will not always be so."

"They are happy perhaps," said Samuel, feeling for courage. The burning hate of the other two had all but finished his zeal, yet he tried to show he was not their disciple.

"Happy?" Paul gave a dry, hoarse laugh. "Fool," he said. "You are one of them in your heart."

"I am not." Samuel knew he was standing in two worlds which were tearing him slowly and agonisingly into two nothings. "I, too, love my people, and yet I do not hate as I thought I hated. I would not kill a man for words."

"Like I did." Luka's grin was almost evil in its confidence. "You are a slave as they are, Samuel. Why do you not take a blade and work as a slave with them in the plantations? But "—there was menace now in his voice—" if you open your mouth about me or about what you may think you know, we will come for you and we will cut your head off." That was a true saying, Samuel knew. His throat seemed to close. He had to make a physical effort to speak.

"I shall be silent," he said. "I do not want trouble."

"Good." Paul and Luka smiled at each other. "It will never be the same down there again," Paul told them, older than them now, more knowing, more certain of what black men did and thought without their knowing really why. "They will think differently and there will be those among them who will listen in the future when the time comes. We have no organisation, no plans. There are only these religious fools, like you, Samuel, who seek to make a new religion. But one day we will have a voice. We will not need your kind. You are only one of those disappointed ones who wish you could be a slave again, eating and doing as you are told." They laughed again at Samuel, saying good-bye and warning him to remember silence was like the wise buffalo which never went to drink at sunset but awaited the hot midday when the lion might be asleep.

Samuel sucked up a few tears of gratitude from his lips

when they had gone. He wanted to go and surrender himself to the white men, telling them all, knowing he was a coward, ashamed, but telling himself that this was what God would want after the evil which had been done down there and of which he had been a part. God was a tyrant, like a terrible chief who might wipe out all who displeased him. The dark swirling jumble of tribal custom and European legend shook his heart. He sat down on a rock, tired, and grateful for freedom from the company of Paul and Luka. Paul was a new kind of man for Samuel. He was like a black white man, with that same quiet confidence of the white man, even the expressions of his face when he spoke or listened, had reminded Samuel of a white man. That suggestion of certainty, of knowing what he was about and yet not discussing it, had, to the sharp, fearful eyes of Samuel, a hint of knowing something beyond men and their days, like a secret of whose nature he could not guess but only fear; like a ghost. No one knew where Paul came from nor where he was going, or of what tribe he had been born into. Yes, on his face was that white-man look, a repose, as though Paul had read all books and known all things. Paul had been altogether ominous for Samuel, but not for Luka, who had no understanding, no real fear of this thing in a man that cannot be seen but only felt, like a breeze in darkness.

Samuel made his way down in the darkness towards the fires, intending to stay the night in a disused hut. When he reached the track which led to the first village he did not hear this man following him, for the drums were close now, filling the world, it seemed, with their deep rolling and thudding sound. Two hands gripped his arms and a voice said, " Do not struggle, pig. It is I, Yussuf. You are caught."

Samuel threw back his head, the moon silvering his glisten-ing face, his opened mouth working. " It was not I," he cried in fear. " It was not I. I have done nothing. I am a man of God."

" Come, pig," Yussuf said. He pushed him roughly before him. " I have you and I keep you. I knew you would come and you have come." He laughed, his voice like iron in Samuel's ears. " All men meet their masters," he said, his mouth close to Samuel's ear, who whimpered again and again. " It was not I. It was not I."

Two hundred men and women, the young, had for an hour been slowly shaking themselves in a pattern of whirling, stamping, panting circles, each circle revolving as though driven by the drums which surrounded them. Thin flashing needles of sweat rained out from them as they jerked to some message thrown to them by the smaller drums, which altered their beat every few moments from the maddening deeper rhythm which, even now, after an hour, had not reached that pitch when the women would begin to moan and yell for some release from their itching, convulsed enchantment. The hundreds of naked feet stamping the earth had long left care behind, that early care when the feet measured the hands of the drummers, before the ecstasy began. Now the feet rose and fell as one, striking the earth with a flat thud, causing it to tremble, of flesh beyond pain or timidity ; the eyes of the dancers were wide, distended, the mouths open, revealing the teeth, wild yet generous in an unusual happiness, each dancer panting to the rhythm which had annihilated their world of the day-time. They struck the earth with their feet, doubling and trebling the beat, an engine of black glistening flesh, gone back into that world of trees, of man's brotherhood with sap and root which the Europeans, watching them, sought patiently to destroy, the thing which would never fit into the great suburbia which was eating the world. The rhythm seemed to have entered the leaves and the grass, electrifying the visible and invisible, shattering the peace of certainty.

Mrs. Pryce and Mrs. Tamlin were pale, afraid, thrilled into a wonder, seeing men and women swaying on the edge of enormity, as it were, but they looked upon this almost devilish splendour, with a sense of coming release as though they, too, might cast off their thoughtful poise, and rush in among that happy, swaying flesh. They sat together in armchairs brought from the mess, the men ranged in camp-chairs and easy-chairs on each side of them, Europe seeing the thing they worked to obliterate, the savage, the non-world man who had danced and died on the edges of civilisation for thousands of years. It was something they had never seen, it was man before the rules enveloped the mind which made them. It stirred demons which had all but died under centuries of the Christian habit, and Mrs. Pryce said in a shaking voice to Mrs. Tamlin, " It's weird, isn't it ? Weird." Mrs. Tamlin, her face peaked with concentration, unable to take her eyes from the dancing men and women, nodded as though in a trance : at any moment, she thought in panic, these men and women might forget themselves, seize each other, God knows what. Like most Europeans who had lived in Africa as though it were an uncomfortable and, as yet, half prepared England, she had thought that Africans only danced what were called " war dances." This, this rehearsal for orgy, was not what she had expected. She wondered if the menfolk realised what might happen at any moment, for like Mrs. Pryce, though with a very different reaction, she could definitely feel sex in the air. She thought it was time to go, and turning to Mrs. Pryce she said so, her kindly face a little drawn, a hint of worry in her eyes. " Time to go ? " Mrs. Pryce saw what she meant, but was unwilling to acknowledge it.

" It's hardly a sight for us now, dear, is it ? " Mrs. Tamlin's mouth all but smiled, but her lips were weak, quivering, down-drawn across her small false teeth. " Just look at that man." They looked. A young man had seized a girl, and had forgotten the *Bwanas* and *Memsahibs* of whom the head-man had said, " They do not like their women to see seed moving in men and women, so dance with care until they have gone." The young man had taken a girl by her hot waist and had begun to rise and fall in a series of quiverings, his head thrown back, simulating the passion which had caused him, the girl shaking, laughing, as he gripped her slender waist in his hands, dancing his father's dream of seed and soil; for the flesh was like land; it burned, was ploughed, was sown, was deserted when a death wind came.

The Portuguese, the French, the Italians, thought Chessing as he put his pipe stem into his smile, would have stayed, but from the moment when Mrs. Tamlin remarked on the young man and woman whom the drums had captured, it became a very English scene, confused, uncertain, but with one object, to get the ladies away from it all. No one knew how to start, but in the manner of these things it staggered in embarrassment to its conclusion, and Tamlin and Pryce, with their wives, moved away from the compound, followed uncertainly by some who were conscious of their boss's sense of the unfitness of things, for his wife's sake, and of her anxiety not to spoil the men's fun. So they wavered, each waiting for help, until Tamlin called :

" We'll be in the Mess. You fellows stay on until you've had enough." When did a chap have enough ? If it was not good enough for the ladies, to stay was disagreement with that moral view, no, it was worse, it implied that men liked this kind of suggestive cavorting by savages.

" *I'm* staying," said Mallows to Chessing, but addressing them all. Slowly, after waiting until Tamlin and Pryce and their wives had gone, the men sat down again, Burkington-Jones saying, " Now they can really get down to it, eh ? "

Then, "Bring on the dancing girls, chum," he called out to the swaying black bodies. "Let's see the whole thing."

When they saw that the white women had gone, the drummers changed their rhythm. It became faster, intoxicating in its intricate pattern which the leaping hands of the drummers changed continually as though by some supernatural instruction, until underneath was a swishing, surging thunder, like the beating of a great heart beneath the rhythms which the now demented drummers hammered from the polished hides and membranes between their knees. Dust swirled into a silver haze in the bright light of the lamps, and in the dust the young men took the women and sang to them with their bodies, the arena becoming like a dried lake in which black glistening fish mingled as though in moonlight in the throes of a force not their own. Stunned by this animal happiness, this scene of men and women caught up in joy, the Europeans sat quite still, but electrified, gazing into what man had once been, the uncaring child, tormented by gods and devils, but free in this envelope of flesh which the drummers had lit with fire, with a demoniacal energy which cancelled bone and muscle. It cut down through the layers of toil which their world had put on them, where lay the germ restless under the curb of reason, but crying in their blood which the drums had awakened, making them forget their place, their worth-while tyranny of will, but not completely.

"African drums are queer," said Mallows to Burkington-Jones. "They make you feel queer in the head if you listen long enough."

"I'd give a lot to be one of those chaps with the girls for a short time," the younger man replied, meaning it, the good school, the aunts, the vicar and the fear of sin forgotten. "I envy the bastards in a way. Funny, isn't it?"

"Bloody funny," said Chessing. "Funnier than you think. I'm off. What about you blokes?"

"Can't we wait for the consummation?" Burkington-Jones was flippant, but he wanted to stay. Could it be that this was all, this promise of African abandon?

"Listen," Chessing told him, "if they were white people who'd gone that far out there," he pointed to the dancers with his pipe, "you'd see your consummation. But the old nig has definite ideas about what is what and that's all you'll see. This isn't for them what it would be for you—or me," he added thoughtfully. "It looks hot stuff to you, but you'll learn if you are interested."

"Quite right. Quite right," said Mallows, sententious, even a little pompous, seeing for the first time, with Chessing's eyes, what he had never quite seen for himself. "He's right, you know, son." Burkington-Jones was piqued. "Come on, then," he said. They left, and soon the others followed. At the other side of the circle sat the " off-whites." They, too, had brought chairs, and now they sat on, glad that their superiors were going, for in the presence of Englishmen it was best to be subdued.

There were drinks and sandwiches in the Mess. It was obvious that Christmas had been ruined. Mooning had sent a chit to Mrs. Tamlin and Mallows saying that his wife could not spare the cook after all. Everyone knew what that meant. Someone else's cook would have to take it on. Mooning was ill, would not be coming. He was very sorry about it all.

The only thing to do, suggested Mrs. Tamlin, was to use two or three cooks, and she would supervise them. No, said some others. The best thing was just to get the food cooked and have a kind of buffet dinner at the Club. It was too late now to make new plans. It was Christmas Eve. Nonsense, it was easy to make a decent Christmas dinner, even now. Mooning's cook was not the only cook in Mambango, even if he was so wonderful. No, Mooning had after all been in charge. He had made all the plans and now he had backed out, well, not backed out, sick if you like. They all quarrelled aimlessly in the Club when they returned from watching the dancing. Some of the men said to hell with it all, anyway, just fry a few chops or roast a few legs of pork and leave them around the Club. There was plenty of booze and that didn't need a cook, anyway. No, Mrs. Tamlin thought, aloud, " It was not right to treat Christmas Day like that." Finally they agreed to her suggestion. She would supervise the cooks and there would be a Christmas dinner in the Club the next day as had been promised. Everyone was relieved when the subject was dropped. Few of the men had ever really believed in it. The main thing was to get a bit of pork; that *was* something to look forward to. But all this howd'yerdo about dinners and tables and cooks was just so much damned nonsense really. They were drinking fairly hard now. It was Christmas Eve and the bar was crowded.

" D'you notice Plume didn't turn up at the dancing, Major," said Burkington-Jones to Mallows. Mallows had been standing alone at the bar, quiet, almost morose.

" What about it ? " The Major was quick and his eyes hostile. He was sick of this bloody puppy hanging about, jawing, like an old woman.

" No offence, Major," said the young man, airily, affecting surprise. " I only said he didn't come to the dance, that's all." But the Major had lost his temper altogether. " Well, don't," he said angrily. " Don't, that's all."

" But what's wrong ? "

Snared, not sure if Burkington-Jones knew where Plume had spent the evening, and furious for being drawn, the older man slammed down his glass and, putting his red face close to that of Burkington-Jones, he shouted :

" Nothing's wrong. *Nothing.* D'you hear ? Now leave it alone." The noise had brought a hush over those who had been standing nearby, or sitting in groups at the tables. Anxious

to keep his dignity, though very annoyed, but guilty, Burkington-Jones began to address the room while looking at the
contorted angry face of the old man in front of him.

" I didn't mean anything wrong," he said, raising his
voice higher with each word. " I only asked a civil question
about Plume and you start shouting as if you've gone out of
your mind. It isn't as if we've had much to drink——"

" Shut up, you cheeky little bastard," Mallows was trembling and appeared as if to strike the younger man. " Plume's
affairs are none of your damned business. Take him away,
somebody, before I punch his jaw."

" You've no right to call me a bastard. You've no right
to threaten me. Who d'you think you are ? " His voice was
shrill.

" Burkington-Jones," called Chessing from the end of the
bar, his voice carrying an order, " come here and stop yatter-
ing. Come on," and gladly Burkington-Jones withdrew, his
eyes on the Major. Then everyone began talking at once.
They knew what had caused that scene. People had been
dropping hints to each other all afternoon about Plume. He
was with Mrs. Mooning. Now the women, Mrs. Tamlin and
Mrs. Pryce, who sat with their husbands at the same table,
united by their retreat from savage lust, began looking at
each other significantly, Mrs. Tamlin afraid to start the subject
before her husband. Mrs. Pryce came to the rescue, saying,
" Of course it's true. They've been carrying on for months."
Tamlin got up and said to his wife, " Must just see Chessing
about something important." His wife felt she should follow
him, afraid to gossip, Tammy hated gossip so much. But she
could not control her curiosity and she stayed, Mrs. Pryce
enlightening her as to " that terrible woman's " character,
her past, the shame of it all.

" You see the way old Major Mallows went for that lad
just now. *He* knows. That's why he was angry."

" Oh, so that's what he meant about Mr. Plume and everything just now."

" Of course," said Mrs. Pryce, scornfully, Mrs. Tamlin's stupid innocence provoking her. " There's a lot goes on here you don't know about, isn't there, Freddy." She turned to her husband, who had assumed his most grave expression. " There is that, by Jove," he said, his voice heavy with hint of volumes to come should he choose to tell. " There is that, 'orrible things."

Mrs. Tamlin was thrilled but guarded. It was amazing how much could go on, right under your eyes, and you never suspected. They sat on, Mrs. Pryce detailing all she knew about the goings on in Mrs. Mooning's house.

The drinking went on, the voices louder, and soon singing began, reaching that point of Albionic abandon when the men began to sing in loud, roaring voices " Two Lovely Black Eyes." Even Mallows was drunk, and Burkington-Jones, flushed, carried away by whisky and the sentimental nausea of the songs, seized the Major's hand and said, " I'm bloody sorry for saying the wrong thing. Bloody sorry." Taken off guard, and jealous of Mrs. Mooning, who had drawn Plume away from him into her bed, Mallows said with a grin, " Greens, that's all it is. Let him enjoy his greens." There was a roar of laughter from everyone at the bar, some calling out, " Well said, Major. Why deny a chap his oats," and " Lucky man, I say, the best bit of stuff in the place." " Serves. Mooning right. He's like a bloody undertaker. Can't blame his wife." Then began those conversations in which men discuss the deeper problems of their fleshly life, of the great hunt which never ended, Burkington-Jones, the youngest, intent on the words of the older men, hearing that there was even more in the mystery than he had dreamed, initiated further into the queernesses of older men who had been to the well so often. Chessing, sardonic with drink, told of the strange customs of tribes he had known, but delicately, seeking to keep the subject general, for one or two of his listeners were in danger of personal reminiscence, and Mambango was small, after all.

Later Chessing and Mallows agreed to go and call on O'Riordan. It was late, but it was Christmas Eve.

CHAPTER TWENTY-TWO

O'RIORDAN had sat quietly for over two hours, listening to Mooning tell his story, reading the weak and the good in him, the rotten core of envious love, the generous will to take back, but never to cherish again. " We're all ruined children. No more," O'Riordan told himself.

" I'll never forgive her," said Mooning, staring with one bloodshot eye at his host, the other closed, purple ; " like a large ripe fig," O'Riordan was thinking.

" You will," said O'Riordan, but Mooning was not listening.

" I'll never get over what she's done, and Plume of all people. I knew something was going on but she denied it. She was always lying to me, but I tried to tell myself she was not." He fell into reverie. " I wanted to do something with my life, something big, but I was dragged down into the mud." He believed it. It solaced him. " She ruined me. I tried to give her a decent life, to show her what marriage could be, but she dragged me down with her. My eyes are open now. I've seen it all. I hate her. But I still love her. I wonder why."

" Hate her ? " If the pain had not begun, O'Riordan would have laughed, but now his eyes were wary, as though listening while he awaited the onslaught of the hot claws in his belly. The pain was far off yet, lurking, feeling its way below the mist of whisky, for O'Riordan was nearly drunk. He felt a new kind of faintness, like a warning of greater agony to come.

"Hate. Yes, hate," said Mooning. "If I were a real man I'd kill her. If I had a pistol I'd kill her, kill her. She's ruined me."

"I'll lend you a pistol if you want to kill her," O'Riordan told him, serious, mocking. "Cruel, cruel," he told himself. "Will I never change? Will I never finally admit compassion?" "But shooting's no good, you know."

"D'you know what she did once?" Mooning almost cried the words. "Know what she did to me once?" O'Riordan knew in his intuitive skin that the revelation of some private, secret hurt was coming. He did not want to hear it, but he could not resist the temptation, the mean, human longing. "What did she do?" he said. Mooning, without knowing it, was watching the shining beads of sweat which had formed on O'Riordan's face. He saw the intent eyes and the thin, straight nose, the stubble gleaming like a sprinkling of golden salt on the pointed chin, and he had a vision of O'Riordan's life, a life spent watching and listening like this. But it did not deter him. O'Riordan's life was suddenly open to him in his face, for he, too, was drunk and could see with that sharpened eye, that awareness which at moments is like the wisdom of childhood. He went on with his tale, his cry of complaint, for he was afraid O'Riordan might change the subject, might begin thinking of another thing, might fall asleep. "It's not so much losing her to Plume," he said. "It's the humiliation of it, here, in a place like this. In a big place, a city, it would be private, but here it's everybody's business and I know they think I'm a bloody failure." He cried the last words, the whisky having eased

away, with its warm sodaed feelers, his last defences. " A
bloody failure." Then he looked with wide-open eyes at
O'Riordan. " I suppose you think that, too, but you wouldn't
say. You've sat there and got me to talk but you've said
nothing. You've just sat there and said nothing. You think
I'm a failure, don't you ? "

O'Riordan said nothing for some seconds but his mouth
tightened and he pushed it out a little, cogitating, watching
Mooning with shrewd, cruel eyes, feeling his own pain
jumping in low, slow movements, the claws reaching for the
branches of his body's tree.

" Yes," he said in a low voice. " You're a failure. What
more d'you want ? Jam on it ? "

" What d'you mean ? " Mooning was anxious for O'Riordan
appeared to have wisdom in his face.

" How the hell do I know what I mean ? How the hell
can anyone tell you what they think ? I've only heard *you*.
You've lost your woman. That's terrible. But you lost her
because no one is meant to have her. She'll never belong to
anyone, not properly. She doesn't need anybody, yet. I never
needed anybody, never in my life. But I do now, and it's too
late. See ? But it's no good my telling you about it. You
want to suck your own bloody wound. You're lucky to have
a wound."

" I don't know what you're talking about," said Mooning.
" Do you mean you wish you had a wife ? "

" No. Forget it all. What d'you want to do ? " He was
cruel again. " D'you want to kill her ? Kill him ? Kill
yourself ? "

" No, I don't want to kill anybody." O'Riordan had
knocked the spirit from him. He felt spent. O'Riordan did
not care. O'Riordan was hard.

" What about grub ? You said an hour ago your cook was

doing some pork. What about it?" O'Riordan spoke
sharply and urgently.

"Are you hungry?" Mooning was leaning forward, his
elbows on his knees, his lean body slumped. He wanted to
go on talking about his wife, his loss, his wound. "You want
to go on talking, don't you?" said O'Riordan, smiling with
his lips, his teeth bared, sweat pouring from his face on to
the neck of his shirt. He could feel its warmth rising about
his jaws like steam. He wanted to scream, with fear, with
agony, with the despair with which the pain of the world
filled him. When he died would he be holding its pain in his
face, shaking it, shouting, "See! See! That's all it is, really.
Pain and dirt and degradation relieved by illusion." He twisted
in the chair, gripping its arms, trying to appear merely uncomfortable. "I'm not hungry," he said, almost panting. "Not
hungry."

"He's as tight as a coot," Mooning was thinking. "I'm
ill with grief and he's tight." He tapped O'Riordan on the
knee, saying, "Hear me out and we'll have the pork. Only
hear me out. *You* understand. No one else does. You told
me I was a failure. I am. I am. But I'm not beaten yet. Why
should I give in because my wife has fallen in love with
Plume? Why?"

"Fallen in love? You poor bastard," said O'Riordan.
"You're lucky. She'll come back and you'll be glad. You
must take her back. It's too late for you to pretend you can
manage alone. You're meant to have a woman always.
You're like that. You're happy with a woman. You're weak
and you're lucky because of it. I'm not. I've got nothing."

"You've got God, though," the voice in the cloud of fear
was telling him. "You've got pain and you've got God.
Not like him. He's got life. That's all." He was laughing,
only realising it when Mooning said, "What are you laughing
at?" He did not tell him, could not say, did not know. He

felt alone, Mooning's presence widening this loneliness. He
had not the support of God, of a single human being, nothing.
He was alone. Would kneeling down and saying the rosary
help? How could it? How could he? He wanted to cry
out, to yell in Mooning's face. "Clear off," he wanted to
cry. "You selfish swine. Clear off. Leave me alone."

"What's up?" said Mooning. "Are you sick?"

"Drunk," said O'Riordan. "And hungry." He knew he
was pale, soaked, thin, part of the reduction which had begun
of his warm, confident self when the doctor's solemn, searching
eyes had looked into his. The voice from the eyes had said,
"You're done for. Finished." The doctor had said, "You're
very ill indeed." Then he had told him, had opened the huge
silent doors of the world, and he had stared through into the
cold darkness of eternity.

"Grub?" said Mooning. "All right. I'll go and see."
There was plenty of time. He had a lot to say. The whisky
had drowned the tick of time and it was Christmas Eve.
"Listen to the drums," he said. O'Riordan nodded. "I've
been listening all the time," he said. "They always make me
jumpy. They're exciting, aren't they?"

"Not for me," said Mooning. "Nothing can excite me
any more." He was going to go on, but O'Riordan said,
"Grub." "Clear out, for Christ's sake," he was crying in
his mind. "I want to be alone for five minutes, that's all."
When Mooning had gone, he took the bottle of whisky and
drank deeply from it, until the burning spirit enveloped the
pain of the claws. He fell back, his shirt sodden, sticking to
his body. "Done for," he murmured aloud. He knew he
was drunk for he had begun to fight the desire of his mind
and body to turn slowly upside down, the mind spinning like
a wheel of brightness, making him laugh with the sensation
of falling from the precipice of his struggle. He knew he
was going to die, vaguely he knew it now, half ready, knowing

that when the pain broke through the spirit mist this time it would rend him to exhaustion and death.

Plume came in before O'Riordan heard him. He saw him, great with life against the slowly swaying wall, smiling. He heard his voice far off, but rushing up alongside his effort to survive the drunken drag downwards of his mind. " Hallo," he said, almost shouting lest he not be heard. " Hallo. You know Mooning's here. He's getting the grub ready."

" Here ? " Plume recovered. " Do you think I ought to go ? "

" I think you ought to get out of here quickly. Mooning's tight. Do you want to see him ? "

" No. I came to see *you*. How are you, old chap ? " " Old chap." Plume had never called him that before.

" I'm going to die any minute," O'Riordan said. " Any minute now."

Afraid that he had upset O'Riordan by asking after his health, Plume was quick to assure him. " Sorry," he said. " I only meant to ask if you were well." He began to flounder, knowing he was speaking of the death which he had sought to avoid mentioning. His eyes brightening, O'Riordan said, " But I am. I am dying, I assure you." That was more like the O'Riordan of the Club evenings, the quick voice adding to some outrageous saying, some grotesque statement, so that those listening could not be sure what was meant, what was true, what was the joke.

" All right, you're dying, you're dying," said Plume in kindly mockery. " What about him—Mooning ? Is he in a state ? "

" A state ? " O'Riordan jerked his head, his lips sardonic. His voice was slurred. " He's got a load of that Scotch on board," thought Plume, goodwill and humour showing on his face, his curving lips, that affectionate pity for one who is happily drunk and does not realise. " A state, by Christ.

I should think he is. He's got an eye like a black pudding and you've taken his wife. Do you think he should be happy ? "

Now Plume was thoughtful, not sure of what O'Riordan thought of him, not certain that he was not on Mooning's side, for Plume now cared what was thought of him. He had been chewing Amy's words in his mind during the walk from her bungalow. He had sat on the wall of O'Riordan's garden, watching the fires and lulled by the drumming. " Have you been in gaol ? " Everybody knew, she had said. He wondered if O'Riordan knew, would add it to the story which Mooning had told him, the black eye, the brutality which he seemed to have carried with him into this room.

" You'd better go before Mooning comes back," O'Riordan closed his eyes as though weary, irritating Plume, but he saw the almost grey pallor of his face ; of course, he was really ill, you could see that, but these small wiry chaps were as tough as nails. He was tired, that was all, should have been in bed, not up boozing and listening to Mooning. He was doomed anyway. God !

" Did Mooning come here on his own ? " he asked, and without waiting to hear an answer, added, " Why ? "

" Mallows brought him."

" Mallows, eh ? "

" You'd better go." O'Riordan had opened his eyes. He sat up, brightness flowing back into his shrinking pupils. " Go on. Mooning's upset enough without seeing you here."

" It's not as bad as you think," Plume told him, his eyes asking for a word of understanding, for a kindness. It was no use. O'Riordan smiled again, that knowing, ironic smile. " Of course not," he said. " What's a wife ? What's a punch in the eye ? But it's not my job to moralise, to see the smalls wrung out in my bloody sitting-room. Mooning came to talk, to talk to Bishop O'Riordan about his soul. You've got his wife to listen to, so we're in the same boat, really, though yours is perhaps more pleasant. You'd better go."

"Cheerio," said Plume. "Keep well."

"Well? I told you I'm dying." They laughed, O'Riordan in mockery, making Plume uncomfortable again, but he went, and O'Riordan lifted his hands and watched them tremble. He seemed to see through the hard yellowish palms to the frail framework of bones, the actual seldom remembered contents of the body's envelope, dying a little more each day, but rushing now, the centre of his body having housed the pallid guest for an unknown silent, secret time. The guest was now in all the rooms where his strength had been, the strength of enjoyment of the daily life, for him, generally, through his eyes; the book, the horizon, the sunrise, the sunset, the stars, for he seldom went far from his house. The guest had come into possession quietly and was now tearing down his prison, millions of voracious cells mad with death, growing through him like a hungry creeper, but its root afire, burning now more fiercely in his belly. He drank some more whisky. "I won't do it," he said. There was the automatic pistol in the drawer, oiled, loaded with release, the silver shining pill which would send his spark soaring into the dark, the dark without measurement into which, soon, the ravening guest within would drag him. He stood up, his legs apart. "Jesus," he said, "Jesus, help me. Jesus, Mary and Joseph, help me." Not to open the drawer, they were to help him. Not to open the drawer. The rosary. He began to gabble to himself. Hailmaryfullergrace. Again and again, like a cracked record. "If this is all," he thought, sneaking behind the rosary, still gabbling, "then God is a devil. Why do I feel no relief, no forgiveness, no sight of God, no faith, nothing, just like when I knew that day in church years ago that I had no faith, never had had, felt nothing, never had felt. Why? Ugh! Ugh!" Two long forks of pain crashed through him like lightning, illuminating his swinging mind like the white glare of a furnace, and in its light he saw inside himself, the storm of death begun. He fell into an armchair, the two livid forks of fire shuddering like lightning in a dark sky, the pain screwing up his face, until, like flame sinking into a pool, the lightning fell to his drunkenness again. He moaned with relief, wanting a cigarette, dreaming of it, his hand waving in the air, awaiting its owner's struggle on to the narrow ledge again. Faintly he could hear the drums.

Mooning was standing in the doorway, humming to himself, watching O'Riordan waving his hand. O'Riordan saw him and recovered, went on waving his hand, changing it into a gesture. " Turn the radio on," he said, twisting his hand to and fro as though turning a knob. Mooning was unsteady on his legs. " Good idea," he said. He licked his lips slowly, like an ox, barely able to control his tongue's movements. He switched the radio on, the green glow of its face friendly, ready to release the million voices crying hate and beast-culture into the room.

" I got Hitler one night on mine," said Mooning. " Raved like a bloody maniac. Ever heard him ? " His mind was wandering, placid now with drink.

" Yes," whispered O'Riordan. " I can get him on mine when I want him. They put records on of his voice. Some day someone will take that sod by the throat and strangle him."

" He's done a lot for Germany, though. You can't deny that."

" He'll shag the world before he's done," said O'Riordan. " Shag it until it cries for mercy." Mooning burst into laughter. " It's not funny," O'Riordan added, forgetting the death walking about quietly now inside him. " He'll destroy the bloody world. Wait and see. The enemies of the world are the Germans, and they love Hitler, and Hitler is a sod."

" The Russians are worse."

" They're all the bloody same. They're going to end it all. All this. Everything. That's why I've been happy here in my room for years. Out of it all. And when I want to go back I can get it on the radio. Yapping and howling like dogs, they are, screaming about the bloody new world full of beaten-up Jews and capitalists and Communists and Nazis and Fascists and Christ only knows what. Me ? Give me Mambango."

Mooning remembered the world. " We've got to face up to it. We've got to face the fact that they're there." His eyes softened, sentimental with the world.

" Don't," O'Riordan shouted. " Don't. For God's sake, don't start that stuff. What about the pork ? "

" It's doing. That swine of a cook has gone somewhere, though."

" Gone for a pee, I expect. Maybe sneaked off to the dance."

" Maybe. Anyway, I'll give him hell when he gets back." Mooning began to think about the cook, imagining kicking him. He hated him again. She had his real cook. She had ruined his plans. Ruined Christmas. He started to talk about her again.

Swelling up out of the tunnel came the radio voice, tripping over static, the inane gibbering of the many voices shoving each other on the starting lines of the world's dementia, Italian edging in on German, both thrown back by thin piercing needles of jazz. Mooning switched it to and fro, the crying and bubbling and swift beheaded shouts, the liars and prompters of the world at his drunken hand's mercy, the illusion of the ability to choose. He found jazz that satisfied him, throbbing, idiot ejaculations of frenetic joy, the *castrato* in the hired dinner jacket, telling the great lie of the consummation to come one night.

O'Riordan was praying. Later, he would kneel down by

his bed, a child broken from a wondering man. He could hardly control the boozed ghost movement of his legs, the beginning of the upside down, the controls loose in the hands of his sodden will. If he let go he would sway upwards into final intoxication, but not yet ; only if the guest flung the forks of lightning up through him again. " He's out to kill me," he thought through the prayer. The claws had become a thing, an inner man, a killer from the dark now lost and uncertain in the whisky. Mooning had picked up a chair and was dancing with it, a wooden woman.

People walking along the veranda, talking loudly, laughing. O'Riordan was glad, glad. " Come in," he called, " come in." Chessing and Mallows came in, Mallows unusually gay, a little unsteady, Chessing saturnine, hiding his drink. " Look at this bloke," said Mallows, pointing to Mooning, whose dancing slowly came to a standstill. Mallows laughed, seeing Mooning's black eye, and Chessing looked solemn, winking at O'Riordan.

CHAPTER TWENTY-THREE

FOR over an hour Yussuf beat Samuel in the shed near the factory, his cries drowned in the slap and thump of the drums which echoed from the corrugated iron walls and roof. Sometimes Samuel screamed, sometimes he prayed, mystifying the lean, sadistic, dutiful judge of men, who beat him. Pausing to listen to these implorations, Yussuf would say :

" What are you saying now, pig ? It is the English tongue you use." He recognised the name of Jesus, the false prophet, the name which white men cried when someone had cheated or annoyed them. So it was to Jesus that this yelling one was

now calling. He had taken Samuel's dark glasses and smashed
them before his eyes, grinding them under the heel of his
sandal.

" Do you see that, eater of bananas ? Do you see that your
two glass eyes of darkness are broken now ? Why have you
worn these things ? You are a black man, not a white man.
You have not the pale eyes of the white man which need eyes
of darkness to cover them from the sun. These things do not
make you a white man, pig. You are black, like me, but you
are a devil too. You have a voice in you that is like a snake
under a plate of food. Now I am going to make that clever
voice rise up like the voice of a woman in trouble. I am going
to make you scream like a hyrax in the night. What have
you to tell me of the evil you brought here ? The black
medicine and the teaching of disobedience and the killing of
a man who spoke of Luka ? And where is Luka ? "

He began to flog Samuel, who screamed, as Yussuf had
promised him, like a woman in trouble, no, like a hyrax seeing
its shadow. For hours, while not far away the stamping feet
of hundreds, and the drums, throbbed through the eve of
Klistian Klismas, Yussuf questioned him, beat him, without
mercy, for it is not only for wages that a man must stamp on
evil. It is for honour, too, and duty and the abstract thing of
" they," the white men and the world they were building on
savagery, the world which had trained him, taught him to
drill and kill, fed him and then turned him loose with papers
and a sharpened, iron mind. For that world he was willing
to die when the order came.

Foam on his lips, passed beyond precision and the numbered
mercy, Yussuf flogged Samuel until he howled, and jumped
about like a scalded frog. Cruel, only half tamed by drill
and the casual kindness of officers anxious to shoot elephant,
Yussuf saw in Samuel that horrible, revolting thing, the
Klistian with book-learning who wanted to undo the world.

He could not bear the Klistian banana-eater of the soft slave people of this land, so different from those others with whom he had soldiered and who were satisfied with the world of rations, blankets and curious duties earning pay. " Pig," he cried again and again. " Talk, pig, and all will be well."

Sobbing, slavering, trembling, Samuel raised his head, and the panting devil with the whip stood back, his teeth bared, spittle drooling from his mouth, his chest heaving. " Enough, pig ? " he gasped. He had not beaten a man as he had beaten this one since that time when one of the slaves had stolen *Bwana* Plume's tin of cigarettes and had denied it. But moaning after the whip, he had admitted all. Now this one whimpered, " Yes, yes, yes, yes," like a man who is mad.

" Are you ready to come to *Bwana* Tamlin and tell all ? " he whispered. He cut the whip through the air in a single hiss of reminder, and Samuel struggled, uttering a gurgling scream. " Yes, yes, yes, yes, yes."

" It is good, pig. Come." He seized Samuel's shirt collar and dragged him to his feet. " You can tell all to the *Bwana* and you will then be able to atone for all your evil." He tore off the wet, heavy sack which he had wrapped round Samuel's loins for the beating.

" Put on your white man's trousers again, pig," he told him. Samuel took a long time to dress, falling about as though drunk, half unconscious from pain, breathing in short moans, broken, terrified of tarrying. In his blindness and desperation to please, his body aflame from the flogging, he felt a gratitude to Yussuf, a gladness that he had been beaten into submission, into agreement to tell all, and he knew now the zones of suffering which broke men who had been terrified to tell. Had Yussuf told him to kneel down and pray to him he would have done so, for he knew now that Yussuf was pitiless, an appalling quality he had never met before in a man, for not even God was without pity. And it was this which had snapped him, looming across his terror of Paul and Luka, his will broken by the knowledge that Yussuf was willing to kill him, would go on with the six-foot rhinoceros-hide whip until he died.

" *Bwana* Tamlin," he babbled, imbecile with pain and shock. " Want *Bwana* Tamlin. Tell all. Want to tell all." Yussuf's black leather face cracked into a smile, wolfish with the goodwill of one who had withheld death. " Come," he said. " We will go to the *Bwana*."

Mrs. Tamlin, staring down from the veranda, saw the two figures in the light streaming from the open door of the living-room. One of the figures was rolling about on his feet at the end of the other's arm. " What is it ? " she called. Yussuf saw she was afraid. She was a woman, childless, a woman who had done nothing in her life, but the *Bwana*'s wife. He was impatient with her fear, but he was careful in his words.

" It is I, Yussuf. I have the man who caused the trouble here. I seek the *Bwana*."

Relieved, Mrs. Tamlin said, " He is in *Bwana* O'Riordan's house. There are several *Bwanas* there. Go to him." She sensed that Yussuf's prisoner was hurt. She could hear his strange moanings, not loud or urgent, but like that of a sorrowful dog.

" What has hurt him ? " she cried. Yussuf thought she was seeking to bring out her medicine box. He knew her softness, had sneered to himself when he had seen her dress the sores of one of the laziest, one of the most useless of the labourers.

" He fell down a hill," he told her. " But he is not hurt. He pretends."

" Take him to the *Bwana* quickly." As Yussuf led his stumbling prisoner away she thought, " What has happened to Mambango. Terrible things, one after another. And at Christmas too ! " It was almost like a curse on the place. One day the black people whom she had seen in their savagery to-night at the dancing, might turn and attack them all. She should take Tammy away from here, go somewhere quiet, for she felt she had glimpsed the bared teeth of an Africa she had not known, beneath the hot eventless silence which had for so long been the background of the Mambango she had lived in. Fearful, she went back to her knitting and the novel about a she-devil who had at last found a master in the person of a sheik. Tammy had gone across to see if O'Riordan was in need of anything, and had sent a note to her saying there was a party at O'Riordan's and they had pressed him to stay. She could go to bed if she wished. But she could not sleep now. She would wait for him. She would cut some sandwiches in case he was peckish when he returned. She wished the awful drums would stop. Would they never get tired ? Did they never feel that enough was enough ? No. They were like children, that was what many people said, just like children who did not know when to stop. Why could they not control their happiness like everyone else in the world ?

When Tamlin came out on to the veranda of O'Riordan's house, Samuel fell on to his knees and then on to his face, weeping, jabbering, crying for mercy, saying he was not a bad man but he would tell all, all. Chessing and Mallows came out and stood beside Tamlin. They were silent watching the disgusting spectacle of the man on his face, rolling his head to and fro in the dust, slobbering and whining for clemency. Behind him Yussuf stood like a statue, waving his straight whip slowly to and fro over the man's body.

The others, silent, awed, by the sight of this broken human being, saw Tamlin's eyes turn into two dull, cold stones which moved slowly from the sobbing man to Yussuf.

" Come up here, Yussuf," said Tamlin, his voice flat, toneless almost.

When Yussuf stood before him at the top of the steps Tamlin said to him, " You beat him ? "

" I beat him until he agreed to confess, *Effendi*."

" Who told you to do that ? " Tamlin's question was conversational, no hint of the feelings in it which Chessing and Mallows could see in his pale face, his still eyes.

" Give me your whip." When Yussuf handed it to him, puzzled, Tamlin threw it to the floor and then drove his right fist into Yussuf's face, knocking him down the steps. He rolled slowly on to his back, a sound between a groan and a mewing coming from his gaping mouth. Like a man carrying an enormous load, he climbed slowly and laboriously to his feet, turning his astonished eyes upwards to O'Riordan. No one had ever hurt him before in his life. Anonymous men had fired at him from behind rocks, heat-maddened soldiers had threatened him, an officer had called him a stupid pig, but no one had ever hurt him. He thought he might go out of his mind. He stood uncertainly on his feet and through his broken lips he cried in a stammering, blood thickened voice.

" Why ? Why did you hit me ? "

" To see if you felt pain," Tamlin shouted at him, and then Yussuf saw that the *Bwana* was mad with fury and it cowed him, despite the incredible insult, the blazing swelling pain of his face, and the desire to kill which now receded before the white man's threatening stare. He appeared as if he was going to come down the steps and attack him again. Yussuf understood that he had done something wrong. It was because he had beaten this pig without permission that the white man had struck him.

" Get out," Tamlin cried. " Go on. Get out or I'll kill you, you bastard."

Yussuf saluted and reeled away, leaving Samuel still whimpering on his face. They heard him talking to himself in the darkness, his sandals dragging on the dusty road.

" You shook him up a bit, I'd say," said Mallows. Chessing said nothing, only holding his pipe in his mouth, his eyes on Samuel lying at the foot of the steps. " Look after this chap and keep him somewhere till the morning," said Tamlin, curt, walking down the steps. " Good night. Oh, say good night to O'Riordan and Mooning for me."

Chessing took his pipe out of his mouth and said, " Merry Christmas." Tamlin looked at his wrist-watch and then turned round. " So it is. Christmas anyway. Merry ? All right. Merry Christmas." He waved his hand to them and then walked on.

" D'you think he did right ? " said Mallows. Chessing shook his head. " No," he said without taking his pipe from his mouth. " No. Yussuf's his own creation. Why complain if the creation does his job ? "

" I don't agree. Yussuf was here before Tamlin, you know. He's always done the official beating. Tamlin never taught him to smash a man up like that poor bastard down there. Look at him. Whining like a bloody puppy. Don't you think that's too much to do to a man."

" I do," said Chessing. " But what d'you expect when Yussuf gets his chance. He's spoiled. He thought he was free to beat anyone up who offended against what he thought was the code. But that's the result of a swollen head and Tamlin's wrong to blame his tools. He just lost his temper, that's all, but he's to blame for that poor bastard down there."

" Whether we agree or not, one thing's certain," said Chessing. " Yussuf'll never be the same again. That's finished him. Types like Yussuf don't understand what Tamlin meant. It's all or nothing with him."

" I suppose you're right." Mallows's head was aching, his
new soberness forced on him by what he had seen. " I'll take
this bloke and lock him in my kitchen. I'm worn out. By
the way, I don't much like the look of O'Riordan to-night.
He's bloody drunk, too. D'you think he's all right ? "

" Yes," said Chessing. They both knew that O'Riordan was
not all right, but what was a chap to do, say, think ? " Are
you staying on ? "

" Yes." Chessing added that O'Riordan had asked him to
stay for a time. He wanted to talk.

" If you need me send a nig, won't you ? "

Chessing knew what he meant. " D'you think he's that
ill ? " he asked, and Mallows nodded, his eyes sombre. " I
think he'll go fast and sudden when he goes. I've never seen
him drunk before and I've known him for years. He looks
like death warmed up."

" Ah."

" Merry Christmas," said Mallows.

" We'll see," Chessing replied. He watched Mallows take
Samuel's arm and lift him to his feet. Then they lurched
away into the darkness, Samuel's moanings less heart-rending
now that they had become part of his breathing.

CHAPTER TWENTY-FOUR

CHESSING went back into the living-room, which was
loud with jazz. O'Riordan was sitting upright, staring,
almost glaring in front of him, grey-faced, but he heard
Chessing and seemed to come out of a reverie, yet against his
will, seeking to give normality to what was, for him, some
ordeal of his own. Outside, at the back of the house, there

was the sound of quarrelling, and Mooning's voice was rising and falling, English curses mixed with those in the local dialect.

O'Riordan said, " Mooning's in the kitchen. He's having trouble with his cook. It's nothing."

" He's tight, isn't he ? "

" Chessing, I'm going to die," said O'Riordan, his voice calm, but his face working as if he had a bad taste in his mouth, a mask of distaste, disgust, contorting over the frame of fine bones now more prominent, the nose peaked, the thin jaws tremulous with clenching muscle.

" I know," said Chessing. " What can I do for you ? " For the first time O'Riordan saw the other Chessing who lived behind the cool, saturnine figure who looked well dressed even when soaked in sweat on the hottest day. There were the eyes, usually clear and ironically understanding, now full of a concern as they studied the other's sunken eyes which had begun to dart about, belying O'Riordan's tranquil voice.

" It's beginning to hurt now," O'Riordan explained. " I'm drunk and yet I know everything. The pain has been coming and going more frequently the last two days. It's coming again, and I know this time it's going to crease me." His voice began to rise. " I know it's going to be hell. I can't stand any more of it. I'm afraid. I'm afraid."

" Haven't you got any drugs to keep it down ? Didn't they give you anything ? "

" I left them there at the hospital. I cleared off. I came away of my own free will. Hospitals terrify me. It's through being poor. My family was poor and hospitals were places where they killed you. You were a nuisance. So I couldn't stand it. I wanted to die here." Having said so much, O'Riordan had come beyond his defences, turning to Chessing for help, for words were help even if he did not listen. " If it gets too bad, I don't think I can bear it. It's like tearing you inside."

Chessing said, " I'll just go and stop that row."

In the kitchen which was a small separate hut, he found Mooning standing over his cook, who was kneeling before him. They were both drunk. The cook was holding a leg of pork in his hands from which he had just bitten a large lump. He was chewing it mournfully, his eyes sleepy, apparently unconscious of the white men. Mooning was grinning down at him, unsteady, a kind of affectionate contempt on his thick mouth.

" It's his Christmas dinner I'm giving him, see ? " he told Chessing. " He's drunk as a lord and that's the pork supposed to be cooked for us. But it's raw. It's half cooked. It's bitched up like everything else the swine touches with his filthy hands. Go on, eat it." He bent down and spoke into the shining black ear of the cook. " Eat it all up. If it's good enough for the bloody *Bwana*, it's good enough for you."

They appeared to be happy. Mooning sat down on an empty wooden box and drowsily watched the cook taking another bite from the leg of pork.

" Did it to him before once with a dozen jam tarts he bitched up on my wife's birthday. Burnt them, didn't you ? Well I made him gobble up every little bit and he was sick. Now we'll make him eat the pork. He's ruined my Christmas. All ruined my Christmas, your Christmas, my Christmas, everyone's Christmas ruined by wog cooks and the wife. I'm sick of the bloody country and the bloody wog cooks with their muck and getting stinking boozed up while I'm going through hell because the wife has let me down. Only O'Riordan knows what I've gone through. *He* knows." He put his foot under the pork and lifted it to the cook's mouth. " Eat up," he shouted. " Eat it all up." Now he grew despondent, remembering the ruined Christmas, the wife, the voices who would discuss his failure to give them the happy Christmas after all the plans, the journey to bring the pork, the promises. He put his fingers tenderly to his eye where Plume had struck him. He began to cry.

" I'm going away," he said as if to the munching, drunken cook whose mastication of the pork continued as though he ate in the peace of his own hut.

" Where'll you go ? " said Chessing, amused by this sight, of Mooning sitting before his cook, muttering, " Won't be able to show my face on the place."

" Don't know. But I love my wife and Plume stole her. I love her but she likes to hurt people. I hope she hurts Plume, but he's not in love with her and you can't get hurt then. Can't get hurt. Invulnerable."

" Go home to her now. Go on."

" Home ? " Mooning was amazed. He got slowly to his feet.

" You forget that it's your home as well as hers. Why don't you just go home and go to sleep ? "

" *He'll* be there." Mooning appeared to be in despair ; as if he might cry again, might surrender to his own pity. But he clutched at that straw, knew he would go.

" He's not there. He's with Mallows. They're still drinking, all of them. Why don't you go home ? " Chessing watched him hesitating, knowing he was afraid of further disgrace, saw that always he would be Mrs. Mooning's clay.

" Listen, Mooning," he went on. " I want you to listen to this. O'Riordan's very ill. He's dying." Mooning's brows furrowed and he lifted his dull eyes to question Chessing. " Dying ? But he's been the life and soul. Been boozing and joking all evening."

" He's dying."

" God. Already. But I thought he was good for a long

time. I didn't really believe he was that ill. God! Dying.
Poor bastard. D'you mean he's dying now?"

"I don't know," said Chessing irritably. "But be sensible
now and bugger off home out of it. I want to look after
O'Riordan. Now come on, go home."

"I'm in the way everywhere. No one wants me around,"
Mooning grumbled. "He's going to eat all that pork and not
get sick. Look at him. He'll do it to spite me." Chessing
took Mooning's arm and pulled him from the kitchen. "Go
and make it up with your wife."

"Never," said Mooning grandly, his solemnity returning.
Chessing saw him put it on like a cloak. "Never. I'll go to
my own room in my own house. I've got pride. I know when
I'm not wanted. I'm not wanted here. I know that. I know
what it is to suffer, believe me. Grovelling for love. Grovelling."

"Shut up, you silly bastard." Chessing shook him. He
imagined Mrs. Mooning hearing her husband enter the house.
She was the kind who might call him to her bed as though
nothing had happened and Mooning would go. "Get off
home now. Beg your wife for forgiveness and she'll forgive
you."

"I have to forgive her, not the other way round. I've done
nothing. I've been a good husband to her, put up with
everything and never said a word."

"It's all your fault. If only you'll believe that and ask for
forgiveness she'll take you back. Pretend it's your fault.
But go home."

Mooning considered it while Chessing led him to the gate
of O'Riordan's garden. He knew he was going to do it but
he was afraid, knowing that the time had come for him to
enlist the help of others, so that his degradation might be
complete.

"Come in with me and talk to her," he pleaded. "Please,

Chessing. Come with me. You don't know her. She's hard. She's hard." He tugged Chessing's sleeve, agitated, now wanting to go home, his ache for her greater than his day's experience, his long months with her in that bungalow.

"Damn you," said Chessing. "You're a bloody nuisance. Come on." He took his arm and began to walk him quickly down the dusty road. The moon was out and the plain was like a lake of silver mist. The fires in the compound sent a red quivering radiance into the sky on their left. The drums still kept up their rhythm and it had become a part of the night which would die without them. It was warm but the breeze was clean and cool on their faces, Chessing breathing it, glad of it, Mooning walking unsteadily, obsessed again with going home, his face drunkenly intense, unheedful of the moon or the cooling breeze.

"If she'll only forgive me and take me back," he said suddenly, fiercely. "If she'll only take me back, I'll make her happy." Then shrewdly he said, "If you've never loved a woman properly you don't know what you can go through, like I'm going through it now. Ever gone through it yourself?" He laughed.

"No." For a moment it seemed to Chessing to be a virtue to suffer so for a woman, not a weakness. No, it was both. But he could only imagine Mooning's suffering. He could not compare it with his own for he had never known it. Women occasionally got in Chessing's way and were taken to bed or brushed aside. He had not known this experience which humbled a man, made him a liar, a cheat, a supplicant, a contemptible nuisance to those who must bear with him in his delirium of the soul, or, thought Chessing idly, "the glands."

"No, I've never had it like that," he told Mooning, feeling a new sympathy for him, understanding a new experience. "You're the father type, I suppose. You definitely need the

wife and children and a home. Why have you no children ? "
" Don't tell anybody if I tell you. Promise." Mooning
stood still and his face had changed in the moonlight being
in some way proud and like the face of another Mooning. Only
the hard stare of his eyes reminded Chessing that he was
drunk.

" You'd better not tell me," Chessing said. " You're drunk.
Come on." Mooning resisted his tugging hand. " I'm not
drunk," he said sharply. " I'm not that drunk. I know what
I'm saying. But nobody knows about it. Nobody under-
stands. I trust you. I know you think I'm a bloody coward
and a worm. They all do because I put up with her. But I
understand her better than anyone and I can't convince her of
it. I'll tell you why we can't have any kids. It's the cause of
all the trouble."

" Please," said Chessing. " You'll regret it to-morrow.
I don't want to know anyway, I don't want to hear about it."
He did not wish to be drawn in, to be caught up in that secret
world within another's bedroom, the unmapped territories of
pity, enormity, where the ape chattered anxiously, or a man
and woman, like machines, went through the gestures of the
world's scabrous dream. " Come on," he urged. " Home."

" She had herself fixed up," said Mooning doggedly. " For
a year I didn't know. ' Fixed up,' she called it. ' I'm invulnerable,' she told me, and I didn't know what she meant.
She laughed." Remembering it, Mooning bent his head
slightly to one side as though listening, his voice falling to a
low evocative huskiness, summoning the atmosphere of that
night for Chessing without knowing it. " ' Fixed up ? ' I
said to her. ' How ? ' Then she told me she'd been sterilised
when she married the first time. Didn't want to lose her
figure, she said. It made me turn cold. I'd only heard of it
vaguely, never come across it. It smashed me, like being hit
to-day by Plume. So we can't have kids. If she had a kid

she'd be different. Different. I know she'd be different. Don't
you think she would ? " Pity for him moved Chessing to nod
vigorously. It was as though he had been in that bedroom,
watching Mooning live those moments, that meeting with
the truly cold of blood who had severed the body's tree,
freezing its promise in a sort of clinical amber.

" It's hard lines, Mooning," he said, his eyes giving the
words meaning.

" She's restless, you see. That's the trouble. One man to
another, like a cat on heat." Seeing Chessing's expression, he
added, " Oh yes. Like a cat on heat. I'm not letting her
down when I say that. It's true. It's heart-breaking. She's a
good woman. She's clever. She's got brains. But she never
rests. Sometimes she walks up and down her room at night.
I hear her. She never says what's she's feeling. She likes to
hurt me. Now she'll hurt Plume and he'll deserve it. She
knows I'll never leave her. Never."

" Come on." Chessing forced him to walk.

" If she kicks up a row try and understand. Tell her I'm
sick. Tell her I need looking after. That I'm ill, hurt."

" You're frightened of her, aren't you ? " said Chessing
softly, sympathetic and interested against his will, drawn in
after all, seeing into this furnished den in which they both
had lived together, the shining scalpel between them.

" Yes, I am," Mooning replied. " There's something cold
in her. Something dead. Like stone. It's frightening. She
loves nothing, only uses things." He could not tell the rest.
How it was to be used, to be put aside. How it felt to know
that he could never reach inside that bright, vivacious, clever,
crystal person who would take a plate of cakes to bed and
eat them slowly, thoughtfully, her eyes still, like those of some
strange bird.

The house was dark save for one softly lit window.

" She's in there," Mooning whispered. In a pain to which

Chessing sensed he was accustomed, Mooning added, " I wonder if she's alone."

" She's alone. Come on." They walked along the veranda, stopped. They heard her voice call out, " Who's that ? "

Mooning gave a breathless little laugh and Chessing saw his innocence, an innocence all but ruined by Africa, which meant nothing to him, which was only a place in which to earn, in which to plan the vagaries of his marriage. He was like so many, Chessing reflected, watching him, so many who would not adapt themselves to the pity and the dumb request for love which Africa asked ; they fought its unarmed, simple power which finally demanded the very dregs of their patience. They built suburbs in this Africa in which to prepare for the final battle. They fretted about the days to come when Africa became a man, not wanting them, yet fond of them when simple like children, but afraid of the days to come. That innocence which Africa had corroded in Mooning answered now.

" It's only me, Amy," he called.

" It's Chessing, I've brought your husband home. He's ill." Chessing thought for a second and went on, " Please hurry and let him in. I've got to go back quickly."

" Don't rush off," she called. " Bring him in. There's some supper in the frig if he wants it." " He's got a frig," thought Chessing, the bachelor of years in Africa, " a frig and he leaves home."

" She's playing up because you're here. The hell will start when you've gone," Mooning whispered. " You don't know her."

" One of these days one of them will poison the other," thought Chessing. His police experience clung to him like a skin as he heard Mrs. Mooning's voice, gay now, calling, " It's about time he came back. Running off like that, like a silly child." He had seen them, the good, the silver-haired, who had wiped out a family. The beautiful and gentle who had slipped the tablets into the soup. Evil was goodness's spectacles through which goodness peered at the world.

Mooning said in his ear, " Thanks, Chessing. You've done me a good turn." Had he ? He was not sure. He had brought him back into that zone where he might fail altogether one of these days. He was a creature marked down by those vague but sinister forces which enmesh, strangle, annihilate, while the sun shines and the normal covers the dark waiting thing. Mooning was anxious now to get into his house, to be endured, to make her happy. Chessing was certain that deep in Mooning was a patience which would endure all because it loved. Why ? He was anxious to go now, but Mooning pleaded with him to come in for a few minutes. Mrs. Mooning opened the door. She was smoking a cigarette in a long holder. Chessing knew she had lit it specially to hold in that cool poise when she faced them, and he knew at once that she knew he knew, and this attracted him, against his will. There was force in her.

" Come and have a drink, Mr. Chessing," she said. She smiled at her husband, her eyes resting on his swollen eyes. " I'll put a piece of ice on that eye for you," she said.

" Oh, Amy," he told her, striving not to abase himself, to say the detached yet proper thing for a husband coming home, " it's so good to see you again."

" Poor bastard," Chessing was thinking. They followed her into the living-room.

CHAPTER TWENTY-FIVE

YAMANGA had been O'Riordan's servant for nearly ten years. He had made beds, laid tables, ironed laundry, cooked, scrubbed, poured drinks, wound gramophones, made bread, told people that the *Bwana* was not in, nursed him through illness, wound the clock; had matured slowly in his service. Now, as Klismas Eve faded and became Klismas, in darkness, he sat down on the veranda steps and wept, his eyes open, staring ahead into the darkness, hearing the drums of his tribe, knowing that the *Bwana* was to die. There was a fire in the *Bwana's* belly that no drink could extinguish, no food placate, no medicine cure. The *Bwana* had said this after *Bwana* Chessing had taken *Bwana* Mooning home.

Yamanga had kept out of the way when he saw Mooning was drunk. He did not like drunken strangers, for once one of them had hit him and had made trouble for him. When Chessing and Mooning had gone Yamanga went to the kitchen, where Mooning's cook was sitting with the leg of pork, regarding it as though it might speak. " Go," Yamanga had told him, and the cook had gone, for Yamanga, though slender and gentle, was known to anger quickly with those who upset him. Then he went in to see O'Riordan and found him lying on the floor, a high wheezing sound coming from him, a horrible sound he had never made before. His hands were on his belly, the fingers dug deep as though to seize something. He knew, too, that this day the *Bwana* had drunk as never before, and yet his brain was not destroyed.

" Carry me to the bed, Yamanga," O'Riordan implored

him. His eyes seemed to roll back into his head, and when Yamanga lifted him up by the shoulders he emitted a long shuddering cry and fainted. As Yamanga dragged him to the bedroom he groaned and tried to tear the servant's fingers away from his shoulder. When Yamanga got him on to the bed he turned over on to his face and began to curl up, straighten out, tremble, like a man poisoned. " What is it, *Bwana* ? " Yamanga begged frantically. " *Bwana*, tell me what to do. Tell me what to do." O'Riordan gasped again and again until Yamanga understood that this was now how the *Bwana* must breathe, in pain and terror of the pain. O'Riordan could hear nothing, understand nothing, as the pain overcame him, hanging on to himself with his hands, his mind like a fast wheel of light and darkness spinning, forcing its way out of its skull as though to speed into the space in which he was impaled by pain. His mouth had filled with spittle as he pressed his forehead with all his strength into the hard bed, whining to himself, yet seeing flashes of his thought, pinned for seconds, before the eye of his failing spirit. " Yamanga," he cried again and again, and frantic, Yamanga answered but his master did not hear him, only continuing to cry his name like an incantation as he writhed and contorted, his shirt now transparent with sweat.

Suddenly, and it was like a small dark breeze blowing through him, Yamanga knew that O'Riordan was going to die. There had been a time years ago when he would have thought of his pay, the problems of his future, of what might have come to him of the white man's clothes, but that time was gone. This dying one had become like his brother, had taught him to read, to remember, to know a good white man from a bad, to think about the strange meanings of things like the stars, the forest and the rain, the meaning of a lie and that other lie, the truth, sometimes which made his head ache, sometimes lightening his heart like a leaf on the wind. Now he wept, his long black hands clasped, seeing the ruin of the small quiet world of this house in which he had been at peace, feeling the coldness of the great death which took all as the old men in the villages had always said. For to Yamanga, who had not tasted Christianity, or Islam, who had not denied the god of his tribe, Twurut, who thundered and flashed in the rain, death was the end of all things, a void into which a man passed, his name useless. Only the creature of a man's seed stayed until he, too, was taken into the dark, for it was like a bird for whom none cared, which rested on a branch before the eye, then flew away, and that bird was not seen again by that eye, and that eye did not regret. But this dying one was the world. Not white now, not brown or black, but one who had become all, and this strange hurt, love, deep affection, was strong like a dagger in his centre, a hurt which he had not known before; for kindness, as this dying one had shown him, was not like anything he had known.

He struggled to turn O'Riordan over on to his back lest he strangle because of the depth to which he had pressed his face into the bed, but O'Riordan could not be moved. He could feel the muscles in the lean body like saplings under his straining hands, fighting against him. Weeping, he stood up and ran from the room, forgetting his life here, his ordered world of contentment, and while his shoulders moved with this new emotion, grief, he sat down on the dark veranda, half wondering what to do, half paralysed by the experience of this anguish.

O'Riordan found himself swinging slowly, like a long pendulum of dream in his own sky of darkness, knowing he was there, in brief relief from the burning storm in which he had been lost, as though God was watching him, thoughtfully, smiling, cruel. He watched himself swing, hearing his voice vibrate in his flesh, there, yet not there, going but still delayed, the dream of the wrung body. First, let us consider sin. At that time O'Riordan spoke unto the multitude, quelling them with fun. *Veronica Mundi?* One of the County Mundis surely? Very well, the small voice always whispered, you'll pay for that. Not a woman. Never, not really. Every Irishman was a spoiled priest. Ask mother. Silver threads—— My heart's scalded in me, Mother told the sons, the brood watching, satirical, silent, for blasphemy was in all words which denied. He swung upside down. The drink. The drink. Magic words of ruin, for the drink had ruined your Da. Then again the vision of the crab crouched within him, was huge in his single watching eye, his envelope limp, awaiting the rush, the bite and the million needles of fire raining from his flesh. Ah, it was never so bloody bad as the priest made out. Next, the hell of Father Furniss, the spoiled writer with the mind of a demon. Children clamped down in vats of bubbling fire. Women who had danced to hell, dancing still, their poor feet leaping up and down on the red-hot floor. Others, worse, caged in bondages of burning cells, yelling for just one drop, just one drop of the drink. The ruling passion strong in death. And all consumed with the doom of for ever in this blazing underworld. " Bull," he screamed. " Bull." But it was not bull, he said, spinning gently across the infinite cool opacity of this other night, stars burning beside his ears, a whole moon like a lamp in his eye.

Yamanga listened to those two screamed words, numbed, cold tears in his eyes. " Die now," he said, the writhing body painted on his eyes. " Die, *Bwana*," for death would loosen that fearful knot of flesh which had become the master.

Next the Sacred Heart, greater than Jesus crucified, than God, that huge white stone towering in the stopped mind of childhood. The Sacred Heart was there, great with thorns and a blade of flame through it, the sins of men. " Each time you do that you stab Him," the Heart. Night after night in the attic, poring over *The Messenger*, all other books locked away by Mother. "If only I could win you for God, my child," she had said again, and again he heard her voice whispering in that other night in which he carelessly swung, to and fro, seeing her black hair, her large sorrowing eyes. Old before the right time, old with the repeated agony of a million Irish Christs, sanctuary lamps soft with reddish glow before the nailed Man, wall after wall, room after room, Mother there, waiting for a priest in the house. Twelve o'clock. Night. One day he would go. Went. A wilderness of years away the lurid childhood of the fanatic days, of a world full of the dying son of man. And it was right, swinging in the waiting-room of this other night, it was right. A good confession. Could not dig far enough down to the original root of evil, the arrogant intelligence which laughed, thin mouthed, bitter-sharp, deeper than the small voice which urged him to bow in humility before the great arctic night of eternity. "Think," said the priest. "Think, my child." Bigger than *Bwana* Freud was the animal padding up and down in that unexplored crack below the racing blood. The animal with no shape which waited to cry in terror, which made a savage meal of reason when the keeper was losing the war with mystery.

Next, an explosion, a rain of clods, a mouthful of cordite smoke, the bouquet of the shattered century. If all those men on the wire, dried with old death now, were planned, then how could He—how could He sort of—— Into that forest of explosions, red eyes winking in it, he advanced, bayonet first, dry mouthed, weak with the fever called up out of the forgotten brute of the tribe. Chlorine in the water, in the bread, in the soil, in the nails and skin and teeth.

He shouted for water, righting himself in the blackness, crouching for the spring of the claws. "He'll do for you this time," he cried, seeing Yamanga's eyes enormous near his own, like the eyes of a crab.

" *Bwana, Bwana,*" Yamanga said. " *Bwana,*" for his master was whining, his mouth wide, " Die, *Bwana.* Die." He poured water into the open mouth and it gurgled, spilled out of it, some swallowed. The *Bwana* was like a beast, dying, lost from his servant who urged him to die.

" Go and call Mrs. Tamlin," said Chessing in Yamanga's ear. He pushed Yamanga angrily. It was always the bloody same. When there was a crisis they were paralysed, shocked to a standstill. He heard Yamanga's bare feet running down the path. Looking at the dying man on the bed, maskless, his quickness torn from him, he felt sick with the awareness of the waiting death. O'Riordan was slavering, moaning, gibbering; God, this was the way it finished for the lively, clever man who had hypnotised so many evenings with talk. Never a dull moment, and now this, a struggling, groaning husk on a bed grey with sweat. Chessing sat beside him and, soaking his handkerchief in the glass of water, he sponged O'Riordan's face.

It was the third hour of Christmas Day, dark, warm, scented with frangipani. He thought of the others in their bungalows, asleep, or still talking, arguing, boozed up, not knowing of this dying man who had amused them. The whole thing was a lot of bloody pointlessness whichever way he looked at it, but greater was sorrow, shrinking his acceptance of the world.

" O'Riordan," he called. " O'Riordan. It's Chessing."

The body groaned and muttered. It began to mumble a prayer, must be a prayer. He bent and listened. Yes, it was a prayer. How damn' queer to hear that from that mouth, its curious attractive sneer gone, gone for ever. It sounded like R.C. stuff, peasant stuff. And that library in the other room, filled with the razor edges, the broken idols, the flashing brightness of a thousand intellects which put the mind at courageous ease. O'Riordan was gabbling now, anxious, and then he began to scream, his hands like talons on his belly.

On the shelf in Chessing's bathroom was a small bottle of stuff for poisoning jackals, quick, stiffening in its impact. He thought of it and shook his head, ashamed, yet torn by this frightful thing on the bed which was begging to be extinguished. It was the pain with which Chessing was concerned, yet he felt a superstitious shame for thinking of that bottle. "It's what I'd want," he said to himself. "Not this, Christ, not this." He wanted to turn away, so as not to see this horrible reminder of man's estate. He had no religion, only a reverence for the life which from time to time made him silent in praise, when he saw its swimming, coloured mantle, after dawn, its abandoned lovely evenings, in this Africa, or when the herds of game streamed in dust clouds across the plains, or the eye of an antelope watching him before he shot it, that eye soft with innocence, like disdain. Always, after killing, he stood a moment, aware of a feeling he could not name, like awe, but quickly dismissed.

O'Riordan was dead before Mrs. Tamlin arrived. He died slowly, for there were many stages, the last being like a weariness, a moaning weariness, as though someone inside the body was saying, "Don't go yet, keep awake. Don't go yet," and O'Riordan sighing, "Please, please," yet faltering. He gripped Chessing's hand and then saw him, Chessing knew, for into the eyes came a light of humanity, fluttering for a second or two, then they were covered with a light haze, like dust. That was the end. He murmured, clearly, and thoughtfully, it seemed, "The dinner. The dinner. The roast pork ——" Sleepily he turned his head, and Chessing saw the nose grow thin, the mouth pinched, the indefinable shades and planes which had made O'Riordan's face, fading out as he died. He made sure he was dead and then found himself sprawled in an armchair, exhausted as after a race, his heart beating in his ears. Vague, obsessed with the remembrance of O'Riordan's struggles and cries, he saw Yamanga kneeling by the body, his head resting on the bed, crying softly. " Christ," he thought, " they actually do feel. They feel. They cry. They love. Christ." After years of seeing the callousness of tribesmen and watching his own grow like a shell about his pity, he was amazed, but feeling his always hidden pity now justified. He watched Yamanga, sad for him, and thinking, " It might be love they want, love even when they snarl at it, for this one has felt it and will not quite recover from it." Maybe it was love. If he told the others, some would be silent, allowing another to say, " Bloody nonsense. He put on a show for you. They feel *nothing*, you know that. *Nothing*. They laugh when they see another in pain." They did, too. They laughed uproariously, children of catastrophe, and yet here was one who wept from his strange unknown heart.

CHAPTER TWENTY-SIX

CHRISTMAS was spoiled. " There's a reason for all this," Tamlin told his wife as they moodily ate their breakfast. Mrs. Tamlin had " laid O'Riordan out," efficiently, alone, while Yamanga had sat dazed and greyish faced on the veranda. She was tired now, facing her husband, whose gloomy eyes watched her.

" What do you mean, Tammy ? What reason ? "

" I don't know," he said. " All of it. The witchcraft. That poor labourer killed. Yussuf. I hit him. The Moonings and all that and the way she refused to let her cook do the Christmas dinner. And now O'Riordan dying on Christmas Day. Why does it all happen like that at once when it's always so quiet here ? " He did not expect an answer. She was thinking how unusual it was to hear him express himself without certainty of this and that. He had liked O'Riordan, she knew.

" It only seems quiet here," she told him. " A lot goes on that we don't know about. A lot."

" Oh ? " he said. " How do you know that ? "

" It must," she replied. " Look at the people we've got here. We don't really know them. Look at the Africans, the half-castes, look at our own Europeans. Of course a lot goes on, but we don't know about it."

He looked dour, a little grim, and then amused. " You're right," he said, and laughed when he saw how he had pleased her. " You're right. A lot does go on; feuds and quarrels, but so much boiled up here lately that poor O'Riordan going like that has quite knocked me up. Chessing said he had a terrible end, didn't want to die."

" Clever men usually die like that, Tammy," she told him, confident, for she knew all about men dying. " Especially if they have energy like Mr. O'Riordan." She had surprised him.

" Will I have a difficult death ? " he asked her, pretending to joke but anxious she knew. " Don't talk like that," she said, watching his eyes. " Eat your toast before it's cold." He knew she was feeling the death of O'Riordan, and he was annoyed with himself for not seeing more clearly into her. How much there was in her that he could not know. On that he got up, irritated. It was time to take the special short service for the Africans; Christmas Day service, but now darkened by a white man's death. He did not feel that usual exaltation of Sunday mornings when he went over in his mind what he would say about God and man's mission on earth. This morning God had put his hand in amongst them and plucked one of their number into his silence, a reminder that Christmas was not a closed season for the one that came like a thief in the night. Tamlin shivered, though the sun burned already with the sweltering promise of midday. One forgot how quickly death could come in this country; a chill, a hasty fever, a bite, and you were rushed into the ground as O'Riordan would be by afternoon. After the service, Tamlin, Plume, Mallows, Chessing and Burkington-Jones were going into the small town where the Catholic Mission slumbered through the long burning days, one priest and his small flock whom he taught to lay bricks and to deserve their bounty through sweat, for he made them labour.

For over two hours they jolted in the lorry until they saw the tin roofs shimmering and throbbing, trying to dissolve into mirage, the grey, scorched scenery flat, sucked out, the trees like designs in dust against the sky. They had wrapped O'Riordan in a sheet of canvas and had placed him in the coffin nailed together by one of the carpenters in the factory. The priest, a small withered man past his sixtieth year, and his twentieth in this sun-conquered wilderness, was patient with them. Yes, yes, he would bury him at once. Tamlin took him aside and described O'Riordan's "return to the fold," his awful death.

"Poor boy," the priest said, blowing his nose into a big red and yellow handkerchief. "Drink, of course."

"No," said Tamlin. He described the illness, its severity, its speed.

"Drink helped," the priest assured him. "Drink kills you all in the end in this place." He saw Tamlin's frown and smiled. "You must not mind me," he said. "We are all a little astray here." His gentle, lifeless eyes flickered.

"He's drunk himself," Burkington-Jones whispered.

"Cut that out," Tamlin was short with him. "Right out."

The priest was not drunk but he had taken drink; he had a large sore on his foot where a jigger had laid its eggs and it would not heal. It kept him awake, and threatened to devour his foot. He took small nips of rum when he could no longer bear the torture, and, weary of his weakness, he prayed for strength when he lay awake at night, and he listened while Tamlin talked about O'Riordan.

For twenty years he had laboured and prayed, prayed mainly for strength to believe that his work was not wasted, for he had been a proud man and this was his punishment. He had not been one of those strongly-built powerful men whose celibate priesthood amazed the uninitiated, whose physical strength and joy knew no doubt. He had, he sometimes thought, been born for disappointment, with an eye that traced the sharp grinning outlines of the skull beneath all promise, and he had fought this with prayer, with work, with study. He had almost learned too much about the tribal people among whom he worked, for their simple, cruel life all but seemed the right one for their background, and that fear, too, required prayer. In his heart he had had to struggle against hatred of them, knowing it for pride, for they were cunning and patient but could never outwit him. He knew, too, that they saw his cunning as he saw theirs, appalled by it, but not one of them, he was sure, knew he took little drinks when he felt he could bear no more of it. Because he was small and grey and thin, they called him "the cinder," for there was heat there, too, if one blew hard enough.

He blew his nose into the red and ·yellow handkerchief which Father da Santarem had sent him from Portuguese territory. How different a man's death was in this land of heartless heat. No candles, no flowers, no requiem, no tenderness of eyes gazing at the final journey, faces solemn with renewed awareness of the transitory life on earth. He looked at the box containing O'Riordan. It was only a box, a rough wooden box, so that there was not even the dark polished shape of coffin to call on their solemnity. And these men who had brought this box ; obviously not Catholics. Men who did not know the atmosphere of the spirit which the dead man had absorbed in youth and which nothing could ever wipe out again. H'm. He questioned Tamlin now about O'Riordan. Tamlin told him of O'Riordan's illness, his return to the religion of his—to the—well, back to the R.C. Church, and the priest smiled faintly at his confusion. So there it was, a return to the fold. He nodded, deep in some curious reverie of his own, a longing for a drink like a whisper below his thoughts. Tamlin was uncomfortable. Dealing with R.C.s was like dealing with foreigners. There was a sense of conspiracy, a plan to outwit the open clean, frank casualness of the British religion ; the R.C. Church was not a religion really, it was a nationality with borders, aspirations, secret agents. All his biblical boyhood was revolted by the satisfied nodding of the priest's head, but he thought of O'Riordan, felt more kindly, and then found himself thinking, " Poor misguided fellow," but after all he had acknowledged the Great Scorer, the Master of them all.

The burial was quickly over. Burkington-Jones experienced a sort of boyish awe and fear of the strange rites, the prayers, the sense of doom which the little priest seemed to call down with that glare, on to the dried grey soil and among the numbed little group of Europeans who watched him.

They gave a donation to the priest. He knew they did not care very much if all his work here ended in failure. He knew they felt more comfortable having paid him for his work. He knew, too, that they had no inkling of what he suffered in his weakness, of what deserts sometimes stretched between his soul's eyes. When they had gone he stood in the shade of a mimosa considering as to whether he should have a nip of rum now or not. It was a problem that he could never truthfully solve.

" There's something queer about the R.C. religion," said Burkington-Jones as they climbed into the lorry.

" About all religion," Mallows added.

" Not *all* religion," Tamlin warned him.

" That's your opinion," Mallows told him as the gears meshed noisily, Tamlin's eyes cold on his.

" You're wrong to say all religion is queer, Mallows," Tamlin told him as though speaking to a small boy. Mallows was silent, but Tamlin was irritated, thinking of how they must all secretly think him a fool for holding those Sunday morning services. He wanted help before he quarrelled with Mallows, and he asked Chessing for an opinion about religion.

" I never think about religion," Chessing answered in a voice which threatened hardness, warning of privacy, of a fellow's right to his own thoughts about religion and politics, the two subjects which the British said " never argue " about. It only made life uncomfortable to discuss it, Mallows thought bitterly.

Nobody spoke for a couple of miles, and then Tamlin said, " Do you mean to say, Mallows, and you, Chessing, that religion means nothing to you ? "

Chessing would not reply but began to fill his pipe, his mouth tight with annoyance. The bloody funeral had upset Tamlin's peasant soul and he wanted to thrash it all out. Mallows answered in a deliberate and almost insulting tone, causing Burkington-Jones to stare at him, hopefully, scenting a real row.

" If you really want to know what I think, Tamlin, I'll tell you, but you won't like it. So I warn you to think before you ask for my opinion. In my experience religious people, after asking for an irreligious person's opinion, get bloody annoyed when they hear the answer. D'you see what I mean ? "

Chessing watched Tamlin's neck grow red and his hands tighten on the steering wheel.

"I see what you mean, Mallows," he answered with assumed pleasantness.

Chessing said, "Could you slow down a minute while I light my pipe?"

"No. We've got to hurry. It's past lunch-time, and you can light up when we get there. All right? Only another ten miles." Tamlin was definite.

"I want to smoke, now," said Chessing. They all felt uncomfortable, tensed, wary of each other's burden of irritation. Tamlin slowed down, braked, sat still without turning his head. They could feel his emotions like thunder far off. Mallows's eyes were beady, watching Chessing light his pipe, and Burkington-Jones was still and quiet with eyes like a child hearing a short story. There was something about Tamlin which had always awed him, and now it was going because Chessing, so quiet and sure, wanted to light his pipe, and Mallows had shown that his opinions were his own. Though he did not know it, Burkington-Jones, still comparatively fresh in the company of men, had grown up a good deal in the past two weeks. He knew now, watching Tamlin start the engine again, that one man could make another respect his wishes without shouting, if he was like Chessing, of course. He began to study Chessing, envying him his cool knowledge of what was what.

Tamlin was searching for something to say, though knowing, despite his rage, that he had been mistaken in refusing to stop. He knew that nothing would ever polish away the raw edges of his character, nothing would compensate him for his fierce struggle in the world which he had had to face without education. That struggle had left him wondering secretly what it was that made people like Chessing victorious in situations, big and small. It could not be merely education. There was a certain insolence which dwarfed rage, and people like Chessing and Mallows had it. It was a lack of warmth which saved them from disaster, in argument, in the daily exchange of opinion's currency with others. It was something which baffled Tamlin's simplicity for he thought that a man was a man for all that, and these others didn't. That was it, by Christ. Yes, that was it. He stopped the lorry, and, turning to Chessing, he said :

" Just for curiosity's sake, Chessing, why couldn't you wait for your smoke ? " Chessing puffed smoke through the corner of his lips and his eyes, narrowed in the sun-gilded smoke, studied Tamlin's hard bronzed face with its blue, glittering gaze and its simple power.

" Because I wanted to smoke, that's all, I assure you. To light a pipe takes about half a minute." He puffed thoughtfully and then said, " It's just as important to me to know why you refused to stop. It surprised me."

Tamlin knew he had been mistaken to ask the question. He saw Burkington-Jones watching him with concentration and wonder and he felt alone, shut out of this suave, knowing certainty which stamped " the others," the ones who had had it soft, to some of whom work was a disaster, a bitter necessity, not a birthright. They were always planning to escape from it, to arrive at a desk with short hours, or a directorship and leisure. He tried not to hate them for it, telling himself again that he was worth a hundred of them, but their certainty always made him doubt miserably.

" I don't know," he snapped at Chessing. " I just wanted to get us all home quickly, that's all." He nearly added, " No offence ? " but caught himself in time. He saw now that of them all at Mambango, Chessing was the most formidable, might even manage the place one day, and do it well. Life and the engine he had built into it, crumbled to a kind of tawdry dust.

" That's all right," Chessing told him. " Forgiving me, by Christ. Forgiving me," Tamlin thought in rising temper.

He nodded and smiled, " Just a small difference of outlook, shall we say ? "

" Yes, if you like." Chessing laughed good-naturedly, helping him, despising him, yet liking him too, seeing the rawness under Tamlin's honesty.

" D'you know something ? " Mallows asked them all, drawing them to him out of their yawning traps. " This is the queerest bloody Christmas I've ever spent. Strikes, black magic, death, and now a bloody quarrel over Chessing's pipe." Relieved, Tamlin burst out laughing, his laughter taking him back again into the territory which he knew was now diminished, but they all laughed with him, for him, assuring him of their support. " What we need," Mallows went on, " is a bloody good tankard of cold beer, eh ? " They agreed, all their voices exaggerating, save Chessing's.

Tamlin let in the clutch and pressed hard on the accelerator, wondering if it was all worth it, this struggle to be boss, to win, to be respected, when he lacked that thing so vital, the insolence which drew poise from certainty of social position, even in poverty. That was the most baffling and infuriating thing of all. The intensity of these thoughts had driven his foot down until the lorry was speeding in a swirl of greyish dust and only Chessing knew and sympathised with his thoughts.

CHAPTER TWENTY-SEVEN

" THERE'S one thing I want to make clear right here and now," Mrs. Mooning told her husband. They sat facing each other across the living-room. He saw how the lamplight varnished her black shining hair with gold. The

hangover had all but paralysed him ; only his eyes moved.
His will and nerves were separated from his body, which felt
as though he had ceased to own it or command it. A slow
hammer beat up and down in his skull, and he watched her
in a haze of pity, for himself and her. Sentimentally, he
remembered how, in the past, she had urged him to greater
efforts in his work. " Why should you slave here ? " she had
often asked him. " Why shouldn't you have a job in the city
where we can live properly ? " He longed for her love so
much that he saw her hardness, her coldness, as of his making.
He had ruined her life. He had dragged her to this back-
water and left her to rot slowly away.

" You're not listening to me," she cried. " Listen to what
I'm saying."

" I am, Amy, I am," he told her, his eyes pleading, seeing
her contempt for him.

" What did I just say ? " she asked. When he did not reply
she snarled, " You bloody drunken fool. Listen. There's one
thing I want you to understand right now. It's important."

" Yes ? " he said.

" It's this." She watched him lean forward, giving her all
his attention, so pathetically, she was moved for a second, but
her contempt could not be overborne. " From now on there
is to be no physical relationship between us. You can go with
whom you like, and I too. We live together if you want to
but that's all. But you can find any woman you like as long
as you do it quietly. As for me, I can do the same."

She saw a dark curtain of some powerful feeling move
down over his face from his furrowing forehead. A bright
small glow came into his uninjured eye, waking it to a largeness she had not seen before. She saw this eye moving over
her face, like the eye of a man seeing something strange
for the first time, something which fascinated yet frightened
him.

"Why?" he whispered. "Why, Amy? I don't want anyone else. I never have." He paused, working his mouth strangely. "You know that," he added. "You know that." She saw she would have to make him want the new arrangement for her sake. She smiled sadly, looking away, suffering, as it were, God knows what things, drawing him after her into her new mood, the mood of mystery which always threw him into a confusion and made him clay for her careful hands. But now he knew what she was doing, vaguely, yet he hoped, he longed. He knew she was going to be clever and yet he desired it. He had to, but he did not know why.

"When you left me it killed something deep down in me," she told him. She began to believe it. He saw her eyes tragic with a new darkness, her trembling lip. How beautiful she was when she was sad. She was watching him while she lived this new scene, part of many lived dreaming on her back in the hot afternoon dusks of her curtained room. "Something died when you walked out on me and left me here alone. You were brutal, you know. Brutal."

He was trying to imagine the new life she had drawn for him, the new barren life between them, and now he sought the fragments of that day when he had left her, but it was confused with the explosion of pain and shame when Plume had struck him on that other day.

"I want a drink," he said suddenly, nervously. "I want a drink."

"Not now," she said sharply, disturbed in her cocoon of cinematic dream. She saw his teeth showing. "I want a bloody drink," he roared like an animal, bringing her to her feet. She gave him a sly meaning look out of the corners of her eyes. "It's in there," she told him. She pointed to a cabinet. "Where it always was."

"Won't you have one too?" he begged her. "Won't you pour one out for me?"

" No." She lit a cigarette. " Pour it yourself."

He looked at the floor and she was sorry for him, amazed at the depths of weakness in him, loathing him too. How far was it possible to go with this man ? Was there no point where violence began ? Once he had struck her, but never again. Something was broken in him and, like an animal, she had sensed it and was finished with him.

" You won't pour me a drink, even ? " he said in a dull voice, still looking at the floor. She did not answer. A nervous flickering had begun in her cheek. She was afraid, but apparently without reason. He got up and poured his own drink. His face was worn, resigned, hollow, like that of a monk after penance, alone in his cell, yet called by the world so near him.

" You're cruel," he said to the wall, holding the drink in his hand. " You're cruel. Why ? " He faced her. " Tell me why you're cruel, Amy ? Just tell me."

He had moved her. He saw it in her throat, her eyes, in the way she slowly pulled the lapels of her dressing-gown together. A glassiness came into her eyes. He thought he had reached deep and touched her, but she said : " You killed something in me." He knew it was a lie but he could not say so. If he did not play to her lies, he knew, he could take her in his hands and slowly kill her, silently and gladly. He could feel this instinct in his hands now as he watched her acting. He could feel all the wounds she had given him opening at once, drenching him with their ache. Lost in her private drama so long rehearsed, she did not know his sensation of hate in struggle with his crushed, muddied love. He flung the drink in her face. Gasping, she looked at him, at his one glittering eye, at the other peering like a splinter of oily glass from between its dark puffy slit.

" What did I kill in you ? " he asked her. He spoke through his teeth and her sinuous intuition told her she had gone too far, had hurt him too much. Strange how she could have won all her points by pouring him a drink. Men were queer creatures. Their pride was broken by the small things in private rooms, marking them in ways which the world could not guess. He did not give her time to shout. He threw her a handkerchief and cried in a voice she had not heard before. "What did I *kill* in you? What did I *kill* in you?" In a moment he would spring at her perhaps.

"Love," she said. It was the first thing that came into her head, from a script she had forgotten she had used, far back, before Jack, before the body had become an instrument of rare hunger.

He was wondering if he should not fling her down and take her, fiercely. Somewhere far off, in the compounded legend of Hollywood and women's magazines, he had read, heard, that women respected men who did that, but his spirit, hedged and pruned by generations of good form and playing the game, was not with that legend. But he considered it, yet knew he did not own enough of her for it to impress. Her body was a map of other men's memories. His was a shell of weakness. He laughed, thinking of himself as a cave-man of the magazine legend. Then he said to her :

"How could I kill love in you? Do you mean you loved me?"

She had to think before replying, "Haven't you loved other women?" she asked him. "It's different," he told her, his eyes far away suddenly. "It's different for a man. A man doesn't remember the women he's loved. They fade away, most of them, that is. A couple remain, but they don't mean the same thing as men do for a woman."

"How do you know?" she asked, sneering into laughter, seeing him with another woman. "Why do you ask anyway?" he countered.

"Because you must know what it is like when love dies

in you. When someone kills it." She began to believe it again. It warmed her tragic eyes.

"Amy," he said. "You're not telling the truth. You're lying to me. You're acting again." He put out his hand. "Say it's all over, the past. Let's have a real try at fixing it all up."

Now she did not know whether to storm at him or take him down one of those heartaching byways again ; the byways, which for her became real and charged with life's qualities once she was lost in them.

"I can't," she answered. She clung to the idea of holding Plume, of keeping it like this with Mooning in the house, perhaps involved quietly with another woman, while she held Plume near, but far enough away to keep it whole and safe, so that he could never have too much of her. But she was not sure as to the best way of breaking Mooning to fit this new and, to her, logically arranged scenery. She had come up against a hard substance in Mooning's clay—and she had to test it, to feel its quality before she could know the future. She did not hate him. She despised him. Yet she must not be too hasty with the new Mooning who looked at her now. He still had powers which he could use. He earned the money. She had none. It was his home, his furniture. He owned everything, but he did not own her. She knew he had not thought of it in that way, yet, and she did not want him to.

"I'll go," she said. "I'll leave you. That's the only solution to this mess." She ran the antennae of her mind along his heart.

"No," he said. "No, Amy." Her ear, tuned to his voice, heard the semi-tone of panic, of loss, of desolation. She thought, despite her soaring heart, of how strange this man was who could sink so low.

"Amy," he was telling her, "although you don't know

what it is, although you don't know what the word means, I love you. You think love is something that happens in bed. You've always thought so. But it isn't. It's something you don't know about." His voice trembled in her body.

She sat down in a quick weakness, thinking of his words. She had not known this certainty in his voice before, like religion, quiet, like faith, stupid and childish, but moving her strangely, and, she now saw, unbreakable. It was like a cage round her. It puzzled her. She knew she could never shake him off and this she could not understand, for he absorbed all her malice and went on and went on with his abject love. She saw that this capacity of his to survive all her barbs had defeated her.

" You'll never get me to love you," she said, more to herself than to him, feeling comfort in this. " You go your way and I'll go mine."

" What went on between you and Plume ? " he said. " You'd better tell me." Sitting down, thinking for an answer to that question, she felt instinctively at a disadvantage, and without knowing she rose to her feet. She wanted to deny that anything had " gone on " and she wanted to hurt him, telling him that Plume had overcome her, but not what hurt it had given her. Both answers were on her tongue. He saw her hesitation and he crossed to where she was standing, and put his arm round her shoulder. " Tell me, Amy," he coaxed her tenderly. This action caused her to tremble, deepening his fluxing compassion and pity.

" Don't you understand *anything* ? " she said, easing herself out of his arm, but dominated by his powers of forgiveness, his stupidity, his weakness which was a terrible strength she could not fathom. " Don't you understand that there are some things I can't tell you ? "

" You gave him the lot," he said. His breathing had deepened. She looked up and saw his face twisted as if a

bright light had appeared near his eyes. He was trying to
take this knife of Plume's fortune into his compassion for her
for, voiced, it rang in the room around them. " You did,
didn't you ? "

" Yes, I did," she told him again. " And I will again."

" Why can you not love me ? " he cried into her ear,
seizing her, letting her struggle free again. " Is it because
you can't understand why I take your bloody meannesses,
why I put up with your ways, your whims, your cheapness ?
Is that why ? Do you think I'm a coward because I don't
beat hell out of you now ? " The silence was enormous with
his grief ; she could feel it on her body like a weight. Then
he said, " Because this minute I could kill you, but you don't
understand what holds me back. It's because I love you.
It's because I think you're cracked inside. You're not bad,
you're just nothing at all. You're only a body and only I
understand it." He wondered where these words were
coming from in him, for only now as he spoke did he see her
as he described her. " Just a body for a man to climb on to,"
he went on, whipping himself, revolted but chained to her.
He continued until he made her cry, telling her that she was
only a body with no mind and only he understood it and
went on understanding her. " All the rest have had you and
spat on you," he said. " Sometimes I have wanted to kill
you but I don't know why, I keep on loving you until I am
sick of myself." He poured himself another drink. " Give
me one too," she pleaded, her voice small and unsteady.

" Pour it yourself," he said.

" Please," she showed him her wet eyes and he ferreted
into them, seeking the actress but she was not there. He felt
he had done enough for her, yet that weakness won and he
poured her a large drink. " Drink it all down, right down,"
he said. He poured another for her. Then he began to tell
her things she had not known. He told her of how, when he

was a boy, he had wanted to be a soldier but had failed in every exam. Then he had run away to sea for a year and had whored his way through the ports of South and Central America. " But I never in all my life felt anything for a woman as I felt it for you," he told her. " Yes, there were women, brief and nothing. But I loved you and you hurt me. Your greatest gift is to hurt. Something went in me and went out to you when you told me you had been sterilised because your bloody figure must be saved. If we could have had a kid everything would be all right. But we can't. And when you lie down for Plume I don't blame him, only you, because you're a whore but you have no heart. Most whores have hearts. Why can't you have a heart ? " He tossed down his drink. " Finish it," he said. " I'll make you another." Meek but wary, she gave him her glass, and when he turned his back she stared at it, trying to read him, trying to find out what she had missed in him. She wished she were dead, and wondered if she was acting, if she really wished to die.

" Why don't you answer ? " he asked, not turning round, the glasses clinking under his hands. When she did not reply he turned and saw that she had bent her head and was shaking it.

" There's such a lot you don't know," she whispered.

" I don't want to know it," he shouted at her immediately, fearing she would tell him. " There's a lot we could all tell but yours would be special, I know. Yours would be a case history, mucked up, twisted, rotten. I know that. So keep it. But what about us ? What about us ? Bugger everything else. What about us ? Do you still think we're going to live our lives, as you call it, our own lives whoring from the same house ? " He gave her her drink and waited.

" I'm not going to have any more to do with you physically," she told him. Then as an afterthought, straying down one of

her by-ways, she said, " I'm not fit to. You deserve better.
I'm a whore, that's all."

" Shut up," he yelled. " Shut up that bloody acting or I'll
kill you. I'll kill you right now." She shuddered and the drink
dropped from her hand. She covered her face with her spread
fingers. " Yes," she said, " I'm acting. But we're finished
physically."

" Wouldn't you even go on with it out of pity for me ? "
he asked, sardonic, but, and he hated himself, hopeful. Anything would do. Anything. She shook her head. He was
beaten. He walked up and down the room slowly, worn out,
quailing before the ruins of their life. He had nothing now.
She had herself, secure in it, walled in by that body he so
desired and which would not quicken to him. He lay down
on a couch. She heard him sigh like a dying man and her
strength began to flow back to her.

" I'm sorry," she said. " I'm sorry. I am, really."

" I don't understand anything any more," he replied.
" What's to be done ? Do we go on like this ? Or do we
separate ? "

" Go on like this," she told him. Then he heard that
familiar voice again, confident, hard, the voice of the woman
who had always moved ahead of him. " After all," it said,
" what's the harm in it. It's a good home. It's ours. Because
I can't love you, it's not my fault. I'll do anything else
for you. I like you but I can't love you." She went on
and on until he shouted, " Shut up, for Christ's sake, shut
up."

" All right," she said, " I'll shut up." They were back
where they started. She was secure in her sense of grievance
now. She got up, saying, " It's three o'clock. I'm going to
get some sleep."

" Amy," he almost wheedled her, " let me sleep with you.
Please ? "

" No," she said, her heart rising. " It's no good. It won't work."

He covered his eyes with his hands as she left the room. She heard him sobbing, It reminded her of a dog whimpering in its dream. She banged the door of her room and went to her mirror. She sat there staring into it, hypnotised by her eyes reflected in its black and silver pool. She rested her head on her hands, murmuring " Why won't he give up ? Why won't he give up ? " She sat there for some time, in a numbed vision of all she had gone through, but thinking, " Only a body with no mind. Only a body." It was true. But it was a beautiful body, wasted. She began to dream again, but she remembered the time. It was time to pack. Wearily she got up and went to the large cupboards Mooning had given her for her last birthday. He had had them made by the best Indian carpenter in the country. They meant nothing to her, never had. They were for hanging clothes in. She took two large suitcases and started folding dresses, breathing the camphor fumes from them. Far away a few drums were still beating. She hummed, " O, come all ye faithful. " It was Christmas Day, four o'clock on the morning of Christmas Day. She should have told him straight out instead of trying to lead up to it. If only he had accepted the idea of no more physical relations she could have told him the rest. She put her dressing-case on top of the folded clothes. She took a bottle of heavy oily Indian perfume and sniffed it idly, seeing brown, smooth Indian women in their secret lives, they, too, caught up in the plans of men. All women everywhere were caught in the snares of a man's world, fighting to keep on top of other women who waited to steal. Not Mooning, though. Why could he not find a woman of his own kind, a slave, someone like that dank dreary Mrs. Tamlin ? No, he wanted to spoil everything for her in his selfishness. Because he was her slave he expected her to reply to this slavery. She took the glass stopper from the scent bottle and brushed the nipple of each breast with it, her eyes shining, her teeth partly bared, like a young girl in her first thrilling danger. The scent tingled on her nipples. She drew a circle of scent on her belly. How dreary to be a woman, beautiful, knowing it would not last, the bloom fading year by year until there was only a dry woman and a chilled moon. A body with no heart. Somewhere her life had gone wrong. She was glad she was sterilised. All modern women should be sterilised and then one day it would all stop. Why could Mooning not be glad she was sterile ? Most men were glad. It was such a relief not to have to make the bedroom into a laboratory. But he hated it. It seemed to have broken his heart. Why could he not find a dull woman and have a dozen children ?

She closed the suitcase and began to pack the other one. Men liked good underwear on a woman, frills, lace, so she packed the thin gauzy black ones Jack had given her years ago when he came back from Europe. Mooning had no eye for such things. He was direct, rather pitiful, like someone in urgent need.

She did not know whether to wear the light golden silk dress which fitted her like a sheath and showed off her long white legs, or that bluey-grey misty thing with the low neck. It was over a hundred miles to Chugi and she wanted to look nice because they would stop on the way at that ridiculous little pub run by the Italian. Cold beer and sandwiches, and if you wanted it and didn't care about your figure, delicious *gnocchi* or *agnelotte piemontese.* Oh, it was going to be wonderful. If only Mooning would clear out, into the background, accept things as they were. She cursed him quietly, feeling a curious sorrow for all his pointless self-inflicted woes.

There was a knock at the door and, though she was already in a state of great nervous agitation, she jumped, dropping the hairbrush on to the bed. She remembered to record the

number of brush strokes in her memory. She always brushed
it one hundred times, thinking, her arms aching. She had
reached seventy-three when the knock came. " Who is it ? "
she called, her nerves screwing slowly to unbearable tension.
It was not yet half past five. Who could it be ? Mooning ?
Yes. " It's me," called Mooning. His voice did not sound
as though he suspected anything. He might only want to
make another attempt, another try for the male drug. " Wait,"
she called, but he had already opened the door. " I couldn't
sleep——" he began, and then he saw and understood it all.
He looked at the suitcases for a long time and then he looked
at her. She was wearing the bluey-grey thing. He saw the
soft blooming cleft of her bosom in a foam of white lace,
her reddened mouth glistening, her eyes, hopeless but defiant.
She picked up the silver-backed hairbrush and went on brush-
ing her long thick hair, which rose and fell and shone under
the white bristles of the brush. Under his gaze her arm
moved slower and slower until it stopped altogether.

" Going away ? " he said, closing the door carefully with
his back. She sought menace in that movement and was not
sure what she found. His good eye was clear and without
violence or threat in its scrutiny of her. She felt hopeless and
sat down on the bed. " Yes," she said, " I'm going away
for a bit."

" Who's going with you ? " She would not answer and he
spoke loudly now, a crack in his voice which distracted her
from the various lies she was considering. " Who's going
with you ? Plume, isn't it ? Isn't it ? It is, isn't it ? " She
nodded like a doll, on and on, her eyes dull. She was wishing
he would die. This nausea she felt, this gathering hatred of
him, she considered, was what women felt when they decided
to poison their husbands. A big arsenic sandwich, a bowl of
hot, rich cyanide soup, like in the English Sunday papers
which Pryce left about in the Mess. " Woman carried

struggling from dock. Fly-papers hidden in chandelier."
She understood the longing which had made them do it.

"I hate you," she cried. "Why can't you let me be? Why
do you torment me?"

"When did you know you were going? You had it all
planned, didn't you? You knew you were going last night
but you kept quiet. You bloody cheat. You two-faced bitch."
His voice was calm, as though he had no more anger, as
though at last it was all spent on her. "You're going with
Plume, aren't you?" He nagged her until she said "Yes,"
in a hoarse undertone, and then as if loth to admit it wrong,
she said, "And what about it?"

"What about it?" he said, raising his eyebrows. "You're
not going, that's what about it." He saw her consider that
for a second or two and noted the dark, almost ox-like
expression that came into her face, the sullenness of a draught
animal which has seen the load. "I'm going," she said.
"I'm going in half an hour."

"To Chugi? Has he booked the rooms in the hotel? Has
he been given leave? Has he arranged it all properly?" It
surely must mean that people considered his marriage finished.
"Is he taking you away for good?"

"No," she said, "only for a few days." She heard the
cold-blooded suggestion in her answer, amazed with its
meaning now it was voiced.

"And then you come back here again?" He was even
calmer now.

"Yes," she answered. "That's what I meant last night."

He started to laugh, his eyes closed. It was like the noise
of one of those birds in the forest, mirthless, like a wooden
clapper.

"You think I love you that much?" he said, breathless.
"You think I despise myself that much?" He laughed again.

"Are you out of your mind?" she said indignantly and that

made him laugh harder. " You can't stop me going," she shouted. " I've got to have *some* life. I'm entitled to *some* pleasure, surely. I've been cooped up here for months on end."

" Yes," he was sympathetic, " you've had a hellish time of it. But you're not going. You're staying here. If Plume tries anything I'll swing for him. I'll kill him."

She laughed. " You kill Plume ? " she said. She laughed again, throwing her head back, showing him her long full throat. He studied her, how much he had lost. Was it her beauty which had brought him to this, or was it because something in her, something sad, had made him her warder, her spineless, forgiving doctor ?

She went to the dressing-table and took a large blue paper box of liqueur bon-bons from it. When she sat on the bed again she put one in her mouth and cracked its soft, sticky case, flooding her tongue with sweet burning syrup. " Benedictine, I think," she said to herself.

" Who gave you those ? "

" Who do you think ? " she said. " Some men think about a woman and do little things for her. It's not much but it means a lot to a woman. But you wouldn't understand that, would you ? "

" Stop that," he told her. " Stop acting. I can't stand it any more."

" Then let me go!' she countered, chewing another bonbon, Curaçao this time, she was certain.

" I told you," he said, " that if Plume makes a move near you again I'll kill him." This time she believed him. She lay down on her back, the box of bon-bons on her chest. He could hear her soft, slow, sensual chewing. She did not know what to say or do, but she had plenty of bon-bons in the box. When they were finished, if she could eat them all, she would do something, say something. Then they heard someone in

shoes, a European, walking along the veranda. She knew
who it was. He guessed. Then Plume called her. " Amy,
you ready ? Come on. I've got the car on the road."
" Cool about it, isn't he ? " Mooning hissed. She ignored
him and got up, clutching the bon-bons. He saw now her
face seemed flushed and fuller than usual. Her whole body
seemed filled with a rosy, heavy bloom, making him desire
her, the promise of her which could never blossom. " Come
in, Plumey," she called. " I'm ready but I need a hand with
the bags."

" Oh, hallo," said Plume pleasantly when he opened the
door and walked in. " Has she told you ? "

" He said he's going to kill you," she said to Plume. " He
said I can't go with you."

" Kill me ? "

" You brazen bitch," Mooning told her. He did not look
at Plume. He kept his eyes on his wife, but she had changed
since Plume's arrival. She was no longer cowed, and her
eyes sparkled.

" We don't want to make a thing out of this, do we, Mooning ? " Plume asked him reasonably. " She doesn't love you.
She loves me. It can't be helped. What's all this about killing
me ? Chaps don't kill each other over a woman. Come now.
Admit it's the best thing to let Amy go free."

" What you mean, Plume, is that chaps don't kill each other
for a woman like this one. That's it, Amy, you know, he's
got you weighed up. You're good for a few more nights
and then it's over."

" I wouldn't take that attitude if I were you," Plume warned
him, his eyes kindled to a greenish light. He knew Mooning
was right, knew it in a sickening thought of the bedroom on
the day it would end, Amy snarling, weeping maybe. But he
wanted her, now, urgently. In a few hours they would be in
bed in a Chugi hotel, a magnum of champagne on the ice for

the coming to. Plume's whole life was full of light and pleasure for the first time in years. He was surprised at the cool, clever way he was handling things. Mooning would eat out of anyone's hand.

"Listen, Plume." Mooning moved close to him. "You get back to your bungalow now, quick. If you try to take Amy out of here I'll shoot you. Think it over. I mean it, I promise you. I'll put a bullet through you." They inspected each other's faces and Plume felt a warning in his flesh, assuring him, as did Mooning's calm brown eye, that he would certainly die if he took this man's wife.

" Be sensible." He played for time, trying to think, wanting Amy to admire him, yet wanting to live, to finish with it now. But how.

" Think it over," Mooning said in the same polite voice, " but make your mind up."

Plume thought he saw his way out. He edged along it, anxious not to meet the woman's eyes. He could sense her understanding of his retreat and his face coloured as he began to speak.

" But I thought, I honestly thought you were finished with her," he said. He could not keep his eyes still. He could feel them shifting under Mooning's stare. " That was the whole idea, that Amy would be happier with me. You don't love her any more, do you, surely ? I thought it was all over."

" She's *my* wife," said Mooning. " She's mad. She's a whore. She's a lot of things, but she's not yours. So clear off and leave us alone."

" Plumey," she sobbed with fury and alarm, seeing his treachery in his eyes, " Plumey, you coward. You can't let me down now. You can't sneak out of it now. Can't you see he's bluffing. He's bluffing, he's bluffing. He couldn't kill a fly." She burst into a storm of tears. They flowed over

her face and on to her bared teeth. She was deranged, and
Plume watched her, hypnotised. He knew that Mooning was
not bluffing, and he was afraid. She watched him squirming
out of her life and her shoulders shook. " You're like all
men," she screeched. " You're a coward." Plume made as
though to take her in his arms, but Mooning pushed his
hands away and said " Get out now. Clear off." He knew
that Plume had had her, otherwise he would have fought for
her, his combativeness made careless by desire. There was
nothing like fulfilment to change a gallantry, a bravado, yet
he himself could have nothing. It was senseless.

" It's no good, Amy." Plume was contemptible, and
knowing it he grew shifty. " I'm sorry about all this, Mooning.
I'll go."

" Get out, you rotten pansy." Mrs. Mooning had begun
to scream hysterically. She threw herself to the floor, her
arms under her face, and let herself be carried into a dementia,
a biting, screaming, clawing paroxysm. Plume left quietly,
white-faced and relieved, knowing that this was the right
ending. He felt a gratitude to Mooning and a grudging
respect.

Mooning sat down on the bed and ate a bon-bon. He
knew the servants must have arrived and could hear this
hysterical screaming of his wife. In the early days he had felt
ashamed when they heard her tears, her cries, her curses. But
nowadays he just said, " Memsahib is sick again." They
thought she was not right in the head and respected her for it
as they had been taught to feel towards the insane in their
villages.

It was morning. The sunlight streamed in on to his quivering wife. She was whimpering now and uttering long,
tremulous sighs. He knelt beside her and stroked her hair.
She did not evade him ; he hoped it was a good sign. " Never
mind, Amy," he said. " It's over now. Never mind. Go

to bed and I'll send you some strong tea and a good breakfast. What would you like? Boiled eggs or scrambled?"
She sobbed again. "Scrambled," she said. "Scrambled."
He patted her hair. "All right," he said. "Bed. Go on."
He had vanquished Plume and his life had changed in some
way. The fight would go on with her, always. He knew she
was waste. He knew she had burdened his life, but he was
old enough to know now that he could not hope to change
her much. She had changed him and he no longer cared.
Why did he keep her? He could not think. He went away
to tell Gesuka about the scrambled eggs. The woman was
happy now, for a while, enjoying the tender pain of her
wounds. There was always a certain happiness for her in
seeing the cowardice of men, which she had experienced
early, translated before her eyes, even when it broke a dream
of flesh. She opened her stained lips and popped a bon-bon
into her mouth.

CHAPTER TWENTY-EIGHT

THE evening after O'Riordan's funeral the men drank
heavily in the bar, and Tamlin broke down and cried
for a minute or two, and without meaning to, drew heavily
on the affection of Mallows and Glebb, the older men who sat
with him. "He's a kind of symbol to me," Tamlin explained,
stronger and more impressive with his eyes damp with tears.
"I was thinking to-day, Christmas Day, how we all work
our guts out and then die—in a place like this."

"For nothing," Mallows interrupted from some boozed
reverie of his own. He knew it was for nothing. Mellow
with Scotch, he had always known.

" Not for nothing," Tamlin explained hastily. " It all has a purpose."

" You mean God is watching us all," said Mallows seriously. He frowned.

" There's a reason for all the trouble we've just had here. I've had to ask myself if it's because I've been too soft with the Africans. All the trouble has come at once. Why? Look at the Moonings. Look at the way she's gone hysterical to-day. Mooning came across for my wife in a hell of a state. His wife's smashed half the furniture in their house. I think the bloody magic used on the labour the other day has affected us all. There's something evil in the air."

The way he said that, the effect of the evening's drinking, the quickly extinguished tears of Tamlin, which the other two had witnessed, all had an effect. Mallows actually felt the evil and was annoyed with Tamlin for it. Glebb had sat woodenly all evening. Now he put his hand on Tamlin's shoulder and said, " We all miss O'Riordan. But he was your special friend, wasn't he? "

" Not special, so much, just a good friend." He could not forget the funeral, the shrivelled priest, and beyond that, the torture O'Riordan had suffered which Chessing had described to him. O'Riordan's servant had disappeared. No one knew where he had gone. Thinking of him, Tamlin grew maudlin again.

" They say an African doesn't feel affection. What about O'Riordan's boy? He wept like a child. But I've been soft with the labour, I know." When nobody contradicted him he asked for an opinion. " Do you think I've been soft with them, Mallows? " Mallows wished to warn him, to remind him that he was drunk, but he threw the wish away. What was the bloody use? When a chap was tight, he was tight, and that was all about it. So he said, " You'll have to watch them a bit more now. They're changing."

" A great pity." Tamlin shook his head and had another drink. " Remember the old days when they used to come up in skins and covered with paint, simple-hearted and innocent. Christ, they were good days, weren't they ? Only a couple of years ago too."

" They're still like that in a lot of places, you know," said Mallows, for he, too, was sentimental about the primitive, happy men who were bewildered by a mirror, fascinated by the invisible killing bullet and the lamp that switched on and off. Gone now, that weird joy of the laughing savages.

" Yes, they were good days," they told each other.

" Why did Mrs. Mooning smash the furniture ? " Glebb wanted to know, disturbing the sentimental memories of the other two.

" Are you drunk, Glebb ? " Tamlin asked him.

" Drunk as a bloody coot," said Glebb with his familiar seriousness. " We're all drunk."

" That's right. I've just had a little cry, haven't I ? " Mallows laughed with him. " I couldn't help it. O'Riordan's death shook me up a bit. Let's have some more Scotch." He wanted to forget his lapse, but something had got into him.

" Why did she smash the furniture ? Why ? " Glebb persisted. " She's a fine-looking woman," he added in the disappearing, respectful way of the past, " a fine-looking woman."

" Her husband's soft with her," Mallows explained. " She gets hysterical if he won't let her set fire to the house or tear his clothes up." They laughed for a long time after that. They would not tell Glebb about Plume and Mrs. Mooning.

In Mooning's house Mrs. Tamlin sat beside Amy Mooning and bathed her forehead. The woman had high fever, perhaps an old malaria come out for a romp, Mooning had suggested. Mrs. Tamlin's heart went out, as she told her husband later, to poor Mr. Mooning after she had listened to his wife's feverish ravings. The woman was a demon, a terrible, bad woman. She had learned things of which she had never even dreamed. Strange, dark feelings expressed in frantic monologues, or in conversations with strangers, as the sick woman's mind floated through those zones of fever where the hidden lifetime walks again. Mrs. Tamlin listened to long talks with a man called Jack, obviously not Mr. Mooning, and this Jack must have been a real devil by the sound of him. The wickedness of Mrs. Mooning's mind upset her and allied her with Mooning. When the woman grew quiet she went into the living-room, where Mooning was reading an old *Times*. He looked run down and tired.

"Would you like some tea, Mr. Mooning?" she said.

"No, thank you, I've given you enough trouble already."

"Oh, no," she assured him. "It's my job, you know. I'm a nurse, don't forget. If it weren't for that my husband wouldn't be alive to-day."

"He was badly wounded, wasn't he?"

"Very badly. Do you think there's going to be another war, Mr. Mooning?"

"Bound to be," he said. "There always will be until the end of the world."

"Oh, dear," she thought he must be depressed. Men were easily depressed. It might be his liver that was out of order. With a wife like that he was bound to be depressed.

When the tea was ready they sat together and he slowly understood that her presence had made him happy. He had forgotten what it was like to have tea with a woman who was not afraid of serving a man and being loved for it. Her quick understanding, her desire that he enjoy his tea, the jam, the scones, the sandwiches, made him happy and desolate as well, for he saw in her what he could not have. How lucky Tamlin was. This woman was not smart, not beautiful, but she was something men were fools to ignore. They went after the high-breasted, the red-lipped, the clever, and when it was bedded and done they had tea with Mrs. Tamlin. They became good friends. " Do you remember the wonderful Christmas we planned on the Committee, Mrs. Tamlin ? " he reminded her.

" Yes," she said, " and look how it's turned out. A terrible Christmas."

" It's turned out well," he said. " This is the best tea I've had for years."

" That's lovely," she said, " have some more." Men were like boys, all of them, just boys. Her happiness was something that Mooning could share, and he thought that this tea would stay in his memory for a long time.

He forgot the broken mirrors, the splintered chairs, the berserk ravings of his wife. One half of his heart was sorry he had prevented Plume from taking her. The other half, where his surviving shreds of pride fluttered, was glad he had defied their passion and won. But that was all he had, for now. But there was this tea and this kind, peaceful woman. Then he understood it in a flash. She was like Mother. It was a revelation, taking him back years, wringing him for a minute.

CHAPTER TWENTY-NINE

FOUR days after Christmas the labour struck work. There was no magic this time. They wanted more money, more food, more rights. One section attacked De Gaugin, Bakkar and Pryce, who tried to reason with them, as it was described later. Bakkar was badly injured and, as Chessing told Mallows,

" Ruined their case, you see ? When they use violence that's the end of it all. They deserve more money, of course, but they won't get much now." Tamlin was very worked up and very severe. He was afraid of being soft. When they set fire to the petrol store he locked the ration store and, save for some lorry patrols through the plantations, all work ceased. He almost lost his head and apologised to Yussuf for striking him that night on O'Riordan's veranda. But he thought better of it and merely let Yussuf know that the iron hand was after all the sensible way. He knew, though, that he was wrong, and that he should have forced the Company to pay better wages long ago. But what was not done was not worth thinking about now, he said in the Mess, yet he knew a guilt was being hidden by each condemnation he made of what was becoming the problem of the labour. Some of the Africans who respected him for his fairness were surprised to see his hard mouth snap at them, but they knew that a great evil had been done. They told him that Bwana Bakkar, the huge one, had punched three men in the face when they told him what the strike was about, but Tamlin waved them away. He feared that he had been too soft with the African who had struck De Gaugin on the first occasion. He was worried, too, by the fact that the Africans had found that the world did not end when they struck a white man. Mrs. Pryce had created a scene in the Mess after her husband was carried home with what appeared to be a heart attack.

" What are you going to do ? " she had demanded shrilly of Tamlin before the others in the Mess. He had tried to calm her but he knew she wanted what was called " action." He rounded up suspected men of the section which had been involved in the affair and Yussuf flogged them. Afterwards there was not that light-hearted laughing drifting away of the Africans. They stayed there, sullen, iron-faced, looking with dull eyes at the white people, and Tamlin saw all his work slowly coming to pieces. Perhaps Mambango was going to beat him ; not the soil, but those who belonged to it. He could not eat. He brooded. He snapped at his wife and she did not try to prevent his drinking which seemed to be increasing. Why should they not just give up and go away, she wanted to urge him, but she said nothing.

Samuel, who had been working as a servant for Mallows, while he recovered from the beating Yussuf had given him, was suspected of all kinds of things. Mallows protested, but he soon saw that he would have to hand Samuel over to the police when they came. He told Samuel, who burst into tears and implored Mallows not to give him up. " I want to go back to the Mission, *Bwana*," he said. " I have been a fool, I know." But Mallows shook his head. " You'll have to take your medicine," he told Samuel dejectedly. Truly the old Africa was on the way out. On the afternoon of the strike a labourer threw a clod of earth at Mallows and was shocked when Mallows chased him and caught him. He got ten on the behind. And then Tamlin panicked. " No more *kiboko*," he said, " no more flogging. Don't forget I've sent for the police and we don't want any nonsense with them," for flogging was illegal, if discovered.

" The police," people said in the Club. " H'm."

A police officer and half a dozen constables with rifles came in a truck at tea-time. They would arrive at tea-time, of course. The officer was expert on labour problems. He knew that the wogs were going bad all over the country. He knew that the old days of the African back-water were going. Crime was increasing. Crime was part of civilisation. The first case of a wog forging a currency note in his district had occurred three months ago. It was quite fantastic but true. It was no use getting excited. People had to keep cool. The police knew what was at the bottom of it all. It was a dark hint he threw out but they knew what he meant.

The officer had tea with Tamlin, Chessing and Mallows on Tamlin's veranda.

" We're looking for a bloke called Paul," he informed them.

" Paul," Tamlin said. " Who the hell is Paul ? "

Paul was a wog aged about thirty-four, lived for six years in England, where he had been spoiled of course. He had been taken up there by one of these crackpot anti-Imperialist societies, and, mind you, had spent a year in Russia studying. Studying what ? Ah, that was what everyone would like to know. When they got their hands on Paul this time they were going to arrange a quiet life in a far-away place where he'd be under the eye of the District Commissioner. In England he's probably played about with white women. Nothing was the same after that.

" But Russia ? " said Mallows. " Do you mean to say one of the wogs has actually been to Russia ? " The pompous air of the middle-aged police officer had irritated him and he went on, " Lucky chap. I wish I could go to Russia, but a wog gets there first. That's progress for you ? "

The policeman moved slow, dark eyes on to Mallows and measured him up. Height, age, weight, colouring. " Do you favour Russia ? " he said in what he thought was a neutral disarming way.

" I'd like to see it," Mallows told him. " After all, it's a big subject to-day, isn't it ? "

" It is," the policeman brought all his official weight into his voice. He looked from one to the other. " It is," he said again. " It's the enemy of all we stand for. Look what they've done in Spain recently. Burning convents and killing priests. I hold no brief for the Romans, they get what they deserve —no R.C.s here, I hope—but you've got to draw the line somewhere."

He had been a very good policeman for a number of years, but had lately been put on to " labour problems " and it had

gone to his head. He saw himself as the defender of all that
was dear in the dull, grey, money-grubbing life which, for
him, was civilisation. Separated from the working class by
two generations, he hated them. They had to be kept in
their place. Look at the way the taxi-drivers talked to you
when you were on leave at home these days. And the porters
and the bus conductors. When he heard of " labour troubles "
among Africans for the first time he had said in the office,
" Mark my words, this is the beginning of the end." He saw
only the disturbance. If he had looked at its cause he would
not have understood it. In this was his official virtue. He
had no doubts, no qualms. He was a machine that thought
it was pure brain. He had taken a dislike to Mallows.

"Which side did you support in the Spanish war ? " he
asked Mallows airily. " It's a rotten business, isn't it ? The
bloodlust of those bloody Spaniards is something amazing,
eh ? Don't you think so ? "

" I'm for the Republicans," Mallows told him. " I hope
they win."

" Do you ? " He looked significantly at the others. Chessing
was smiling in a friendly way. " It's a Russian government,
you know."

" Let's cut politics out altogether," Tamlin suggested.
" They get us nowhere." But it was not possible to cut
politics out at all, they found, for the policeman told them
that their labour troubles were due to politics. " Moscow
gold, as usual, the same gold that financed the 1926 strike in
England."

They heard Mallows murmur " Christ, I didn't know,"
and saw him turn innocent eyes to the policeman, but Tamlin
had had enough of Mallows's clowning. Heavily, he said to
the policeman, " What do you want us to do ? "

" Have you any suspects ? Politically-minded chaps who've
been stirring the others up ? " They saw Tamlin's hesitation.

He wished to tell the policeman that it was all very simple, really. It was about time the labour was paid reasonable wages, given better rations, understood as men and not as wayward simple children. But it was too late now. A root had flowered and they would deal with the flower. He saw Mallows turn his head away and say, " You'd better tell him about that poor bastard, Samuel."

" Samuel, eh ? " The policeman was right in, sniffing. " That's a Mission boy, I'll bet." Tamlin told him that that was so. " I knew it," said the policeman. " The Mission boy is the curse of the country."

" Give them a little learning and before you know where you are——" said Chessing. His face was blank when the officer looked at him gratefully.

" That's right," he said. One day soon, the policeman was going to retire. He had a bit of land in the country, not far from Mambango, and though he did not realise it, his outlook had changed from the day he had bought it. He was going to live here as a civilian and unless something drastic was done to smash this new spirit among the wogs, where was it all going to end ?

" Communism is spreading among the natives," he told them. " That's my own opinion, of course, not official. It's got to be rooted out."

" Communism ? " said Tamlin. " I've got a few thousand head of labour here and I've never seen Communism among them and that's a fact." Perplexity was like a ring of light in each of his eyes. Could he have possibly missed such a thing ?

" You don't *see* Communism," the policeman explained. " You just feel it, like to-day. They work quietly."

" But Communism in Africa ? It seems crazy to me. I thought you said it was the Mission boys who were at the bottom of the trouble."

"They were," the policeman told him adroitly. "But Communism's bigger. Look at Spain."

"But Communism here? Why? The bloody country's a wilderness still. Where does it come from?"

"That's right," Chessing joined in. He was bored with the policeman. "How can they have Communism until they've tasted Capitalism? They're not dissatisfied enough yet. If they get Communism first they might want capitalism afterwards and that'll bitch all the Moscow plans. It just can't work." Mallows liked this and came in to assist. "And there's something else," he said. "How can Communism work in a hot country? It's a thing belonging to cold countries. And as Chessing says, if Communism has started here it's started too soon and that'll mess the whole Moscow plan up. It stands to reason. The wogs haven't had any capitalism yet. They're still in the trees, you see."

"Where is this chap, Samuel? What's he been doing?" The policeman was suspicious. "He's a religious maniac," said Mallows. "A harmless clod with a pair of dark glasses. But he got mixed up in some magic they laid on here——"

"Yes, we got a report about that," the policeman explained. "It's not quite as simple as it looks. So this Samuel was in it, eh?"

"That's right." Tamlin was restless. He wanted action. They had sat here too long. "We'll pass him over to you." He wished he could stand in front of the board of directors and have his say about wogs and wages. All his work was to be wasted, frittered away in bitterness with the Africans he had hoped were his friends. It was unfortunate for him that he saw their case. It inhibited him, driving him on to a more brutal view of their inexperience, their inflammable innocence. Still, better forget all that now.

Samuel, after long questioning, and in a mingled fear of the stern police officer and of Paul and Luka, at length told

his story. He had to explain that if Paul and Luka knew he
had informed on them they would kill him. This was a surprise to Tamlin, Chessing and Mallows, who listened. The
policeman, not able any longer to contain his arrogant
knowledge, turned to them and said, " D'you see what I
mean now ? " They had to nod in agreement. It was a shock
to Tamlin, but it relieved his mind in a way he knew was
false, but still it relieved him. There was an enemy then,
bigger than the original mistake of failing to offer justice
before the violent request came, bigger than the too little, too
late. That settled it. He said to Mallows, " Well, there's your
religious maniac for you, Mallows. There was more to it
than you thought, eh ? "

" Aye," said Mallows, " there was." He was depressed.
This was an Africa he had not discovered. From now on
it was the policeman's world, the soldier called in when the
fort was falling, the sentries having slept.

" Do not tell Paul I have spoken." Samuel leaned forward
on the table, trying to impress his fear on this fat, forbidding
man who appeared not to care about him.

" Take your hands off the table and keep quiet," he was
told. He obeyed, his eyes full of Paul's strange, still face, and
Luka's wolfish grin. One day they would find him, wherever
he hid, they would find him.

" You say it was Luka who killed the man ? " the policeman prodded him. He would go through the story again
now, jumping in from many angles, hunting for a lie, an
evasion, a crack in the structure of the tale.

" Yes, he killed the man. He killed him." Tragically,
Samuel said it, seeing the knife in Luka's hand turning to
him. He wept again, but nobody cared now. This man went
on, feeling the story with his merciless mind, trying to make
it into something else but not able to do so, for it was the truth
he was being told. He knew that the policeman despised him

for his fear and for his betrayal of Paul and Luka, while at the same time he had only done his duty in confessing it. Such were the strange ways of this cruel world of men.

Two constables took him away. He saw the policeman lighting a cigarette as they led him off and he cried, " You will not tell them I told, *Bwana*. You will not." But the officer did not move. He saw the broad, fat khaki back and it did not respond to him. He cried again and one of the constables said, " Are you with child that you go on like this ? Shut your mouth, woman." And that was the insult that burned the heart.

" So there we are," said Mallows. They were gloomy, sitting there under the tree.

" We've been fools, I suppose," Tamlin replied. " Living in a fool's paradise. You said it was religious fanaticism, didn't you, Chessing ? " He would like Chessing to share in that paradise, Chessing who was always quiet, always looking in as though not part of what he saw.

" Yes, I did. There are the religious sects I told you about, and Samuel is one of them. But Paul is a surprise."

" Samuel's just a decoy. There's not much of the fanatic about him." Tamlin was determined to have Chessing right in with him in the foolish past.

" Samuel got a fright and ratted," Chessing said. " The religious sects can easily be used if they don't get frightened."

" I don't understand that stuff. I understand this Paul thing, though. That's clear enough. It's queer to think we've had it so quiet here all these years and suddenly this crops up. It'll be different from now on."

" What's going to happen now ? Will the labour get more money ? They don't get much now, do they, when you look at it straight ? " When Chessing had finished, Tamlin said, " What do you mean by straight ? "

" Well, if we'd given them more before this started it would have saved a lot of trouble, wouldn't it ? "

" You forget something," Mallows reminded Chessing. " We're always afraid that if we give a wog something before he asks for it, and even when he asks for it, we'll spoil him. That's the trouble with the whole thing."

" That's true," Tamlin said, convinced, supported at last. He had not thought of it in that way. It was true, you were always afraid of spoiling the wogs. Give them a shirt and they'd want a dress suit. But he knew that that too was only an escape from the fact. He could not speak his mind. He had to support the company which waited for profits in London, for profits were important. The Mission to the wogs was discovered later.

" How does one know just how much one should give ? " Mallows wanted to know. " Is the fellow a man or is he a special kind of thing which has a long way to go before he becomes a man who can expect the rewards that white labourers should get ? That's what I'd like to know."

" That's what we'd all like to know," said Tamlin. He was upset again. Peace was gone. The quiet back-water was moving into the plans of unknown forces. Something was gone for ever.

" I'll tell you who knows the answer to that one," said Chessing.

" Who ? "

" Paul."

" That's what I'd call bad news," said Tamlin. " Paul wants the earth and he's not ready for it."

" So do we all." Chessing blew through his empty pipe. " But it'll be a long time yet before it comes to a head."

" I wonder," said Tamlin. " I wonder." He was bitter, cheated, and he had done it himself. Now he must find a new way of seeing the recently discovered territory where Paul lurked.

" Paul might be a myth," he suggested. " That police chap may be wrong, eh ? " The others shook their heads and regretfully Tamlin climbed back to his new scenery, the scenery of an Africa he was going to distrust and in which the Africans had grown blacker and the white men whiter, and he could not think why. Not yet, anyway.

THE END

Srinagar, 1953—*Barcelona,* 1954